THE SMUGGLER'S CHASE

Also by Cap Daniels

The Chase Fulton Novels Series
Book One: *The Opening Chase*
Book Two: *The Broken Chase*
Book Three: *The Stronger Chase*
Book Four: *The Unending Chase*
Book Five: *The Distant Chase*
Book Six: *The Entangled Chase*
Book Seven: *The Devil's Chase*
Book Eight: *The Angel's Chase*
Book Nine: *The Forgotten Chase*
Book Ten: *The Emerald Chase*
Book Eleven: *The Polar Chase*
Book Twelve: *The Burning Chase*
Book Thirteen: *The Poison Chase*
Book Fourteen: *The Bitter Chase*
Book Fifteen: *The Blind Chase*
Book Sixteen: *The Smuggler's Chase*
Book Seventeen: *The Hollow Chase* (Spring 2022)

The Avenging Angel – Seven Deadly Sins Series
Book One: *The Russian's Pride*
Book Two: *The Russian's Greed*
Book Three: *The Russian's Gluttony*
Book Four: *The Russian's Lust* (Summer 2022)

Stand-alone Novels
We Were Brave

Novellas
The Chase Is On
I Am Gypsy

THE
SMUGGLER'S CHASE

CHASE FULTON NOVEL #16

CAP DANIELS

ANCHOR WATCH
PUBLISHING

** USA **

The Smuggler's Chase
Chase Fulton Novel #16
Cap Daniels

This is a work of fiction. Names, characters, places, historical events, and incidents are the product of the author's imagination or have been used fictitiously. Although many locations such as marinas, airports, hotels, restaurants, etc. used in this work actually exist, they are used fictitiously and may have been relocated, exaggerated, or otherwise modified by creative license for the purpose of this work. Although many characters are based on personalities, physical attributes, skills, or intellect of actual individuals, all of the characters in this work are products of the author's imagination.

Published by:

ANCHOR WATCH
PUBLISHING
** USA **

13 Digit ISBN: 978-1-951021-30-6
Library of Congress Control Number: 2021953390

Cover Design: German Creative

Printed in the United States of America

The Smuggler's Chase

CAP DANIELS

Chapter 1
The Shots Unfired

Autumn 2004

Sometimes, the battles in which no shots are fired, no swords are drawn, and no punches are thrown are the most terrifying and destructive of all.

My name is Chase Daniel Fulton, and I had just stepped through the door of the jump plane from an altitude far too high for my lungs to glean enough oxygen from the atmosphere to sustain my life. I would pull the ripcord, or at least try, as I plummeted toward destiny—if I lived long enough to do so—but I had little faith in the parachute that should promise a gentle landing far below. Everything about my plunge left me feeling as if I should've never stepped out of the door while flying so high. The fall wouldn't kill me, but my imminent collision with the world below would be impossible to survive.

I was trained by some of the finest covert operatives on the planet to not only survive, but also fight and win inside the torrent of combat in which everything and everyone existed with singular purpose: to annihilate me and leave me as nothing more than a demolished, hollow shell of the warrior I had once been. On those conventional battlefields, I had few equals and likely no superiors.

My mind was honed to razor-sharp precision, and my body was hardened in the sinister forges of war and tempered in the oils of love for the only remaining bastion of freedom on Earth. But that bastion, America, the nation I treasured beyond life itself, had finally asked more of me than I was capable of sacrificing.

Duplicity often leaves a man dangling helplessly between two worlds. In my case, those two worlds were my responsibility to my country and my commitment to Penny Thomas Fulton, my wife who I loved more than words could capture.

Penny had dreamed of life as a screenwriter since her stage debut in fourth grade as tree number two in the play written by her elementary school music teacher. My beautiful North Texas wife had apparently made a terrible tree but fell in love with the idea of creating a story and having others bring it to life. That dream had finally come true some twenty years later when a Nashville talent agent sold Penny's first screenplay to a Hollywood producer. The producer hired a director, and the director hired a cast and crew. A year later, the unfinished screenplay Penny showed me the night we met aboard a sailboat in Charleston, South Carolina, had flourished and grown into a feature film, and its prescreening was scheduled for Saturday, October 9th, 2004, just three short days away. On more than one occasion, I'd committed by promise, vow, and oath that nothing could keep me from sitting beside my wife the first time her movie touched a silver screen. I had meant those words as solemnly as any man could. However, a telephone call no one could've ever foreseen or imagined possible changed my life, and potentially, my marriage . . . forever.

John Woodford, the United States ambassador to The Bahamas had pulled invisible strings to extricate me from a particularly hairy situation involving two dead bodies tied beneath *Aegis*, my 50-foot sailing catamaran, on Eleuthera only weeks before. Believing I'd never hear from him again, I pressed the telephone to my ear as I sat on the back gallery of Bonaventure Plantation, my ancestral home on the North River, in the quiet, peaceful, southern town of St. Marys, Georgia.

When I ended the call, the pain I saw in Penny's eyes was the most agonizing blow I'd ever endured. She stood from her chair, turned her back on me, and disappeared deep inside both herself and our home. Every fiber of my being cried out to pursue her and make her understand the gravity of the dire situation into which I'd been thrust.

Accepting the reality of the immeasurable failure such an endeavor would become, I turned, instead, to the only other mistress who'd ever quieted the screaming madness a world such as mine invariably emitted.

My hangar door slid open on its well-oiled tracks, allowing the midday sun to penetrate the cavernous space within. The glistening, elegant curve of *Penny's Secret*, my North American P-51D Mustang, revealed herself as I stood in awe of the warbird of a bygone era when men faced men and fought toe to toe. Those days are gone, replaced by the technology and unthinkable cruelty of battles beyond horizons in electronic worlds capable of destroying what humanity remained in our world.

I counted seven passes of the propeller blades before the twelve-cylinder Rolls-Royce Merlin engine belched fire and smoke as the dragon awoke from her slumber. The sound that engine produced carved terror into the hearts and minds of the Germans in 1944 and instilled pride and confidence beyond measure in the men who strapped themselves into the Mustangs over England, France, and Germany sixty years prior. No sound or feeling came close to those of the supercharged Merlin engine on the nose of the Mustang.

The wheels left the bitterness of Earth and found their way into the gear wells on the belly of the beast as both speed and altitude increased, leaving modernity and her trappings well astern.

Flying the Mustang required solitary focus, making it impossible for my mind to wander. Though obedient, she was far from placid, instantly executing the commands of my mind, hands, and feet. I pulled the nose through sixty degrees and let the massive blades of the gnawing prop bite into the cool afternoon air. She climbed like a homesick angel until gravity overcame horsepower, and the propeller, once again, faced the Earth. Instead of grass and trees and asphalt and homes, though, the planet was liquid, blue, and endless when it filled my windshield. The unforgiving North Atlantic stretched out beneath me to the limits of three horizons, freeing my tortured mind and heart from the prison of my own creation back on the ground.

Sixty minutes passed like fleeting seconds, and I surrendered myself and my beloved flying machine back to the asphalt and steel of Saint Marys Airport and the hangar that housed not only my magic flying carpets, but also, too often, my soul. I'd spent countless hours inside the steel walls of the hangar doing everything from absolutely nothing to complex mission planning that, sometimes, held limitless lives in the balance. I felt as whole and at home in that hangar as I felt anywhere else.

The burden of an irrefusable mission balanced against the thought of betraying my promise to Penny and left me torn and fraught with thoughts that would've been unthinkable before that day. I climbed the wooden stairs to the office overlooking the hangar floor, where I believed I could sit, pray, think, and reach decisions I never wanted to make.

My office, thirty feet above the deck of the hangar, was anything but plush, although the chair behind the ancient desk was more comfortable than any chair I'd ever filled. That's where I practiced the art in which I'd been trained at the University of Georgia a decade before. I made no effort to impart my craft onto others, but psychoanalyzing myself had become a full-time career.

I pulled open the bottom drawer and lifted a bottle of Gentleman Jack single-barrel Tennessee sipping whiskey. Three fingers of the honey-colored spirit in my favorite tumbler laid the groundwork for my psychological practice that afternoon. As I replaced the bottle and closed the drawer, the lap drawer slipped from its aged track and fell to the floor, sending pens, paperclips, batteries, and various detritus bouncing in every direction. Fighting off my desire to curse and stomp the debris, I patiently leaned down and collected the junk. Still resting inside what remained of the lap drawer was a miniature tape recorder containing a single microcassette I'd long forgotten.

I pressed the play button, only to discover depleted batteries. It took longer than it should have, but I finally gathered the two required batteries from the heap of otherwise worthless stuff and shoved them into the spring-loaded plastic case. The speaker the size of a quarter crackled until it produced the tinny sound of the voice of the president of the United States recorded during a telephone call a year earlier. When I remembered what waited on the opposite side of the tape, I yanked it from the player and flipped it over. It seemed to take an eternity for the tape to rewind, but when it finally clicked to a stop, my trembling fingers could barely manage to press the play button.

With the herculean task accomplished, the small speaker came to life with the unmistakable, heavily Russian-accented voice of Anya Burinkova.

"My Chasechka . . . I believe day will come and you will find—I do not know English word for device—is *rekorder* in Russian. Maybe is same for English. I will be gone from your life when this finding happens, but is for you only to listen."

Chapter 2
The Second Dagger

I pressed the button to stop the playback and sat in silence, staring down at the recorder. The whiskey in the tumbler a foot away didn't hold any solutions, and the millions of dollars worth of airplanes just beyond my plexiglass window couldn't help me. One of the voices inside my head roared for me to play the tape while another beseeched me to light it on fire and watch it burn. No matter what was on the rest of the tape, I couldn't come up with any good that could come from hearing it, but the same voice asked, "What harm can come from hearing a simple message recorded years ago?"

Anya had been a part of my life I would've undone if it were possible. She'd stalked, tracked, and finally caught me during, and immediately following, my first real assignment. Ours had been a relationship filled with lies, deceit, and ultimate pain. Her physical beauty was undeniable, but the monster behind the mask of allure terrified and repulsed me. I'd once been in love with the person I wanted to believe lived inside that irresistible shell, but time revealed that person was purely a creation of my own design. I had long since moved on and found the magnificent, truly good woman I both needed and wanted. I no longer wrestled with the ghost of Anya Burinkova. She was little more than a lesson and a memory the world gave me when I was young, naïve, and vulnerable. Having spent nearly a decade facing some of the worst monsters society could produce, I was no longer young, naïve, nor vulnerable, especially when it came to the former Russian assassin who nearly destroyed the man I was destined to become.

The decision was made. I didn't care what was on the rest of the tape. It would change nothing, so I scooped the recorder from my desk and tossed it—tape, new batteries, and all—directly into the metal trashcan at my feet. Before the device hit the bottom, my tumbler was in my hand and headed for my lips when the forces of the natural world aligned against me.

The collision with the inside of the bin somehow pressed the play button, and Anya's voice blared, amplified by the acoustic geometry of the empty can. The whiskey continued its course to my mouth, and masochistic curiosity kept me from digging the recorder from the trash and crushing it beneath my heel.

"Is difficult for me to say to you everything, but this is best way for me. I once believed I knew everything about you, and perhaps this was true before night in Saint Thomas. This is first time we touched each other, but I saw you many times before this, and I think also you saw me. Of course, I touched you many times while you slept inside boat, but you did not know I was there. I feel bad for this and also for cutting your tongue when you would not give to me answers I needed. I need for you to know I was not going to kill you inside water. I was only trying to weaken you so we could talk. This is when you shot me and left me without toe. I think many times at night before falling asleep, maybe it would have been better if you had killed me that night instead of only shooting foot. I could have never hurt you if you had done this."

I listened intently, surprised by her admissions, but unchanged in my resolve for her to be only a memory. My life without her, though still often chaotic, was better than it would've ever been with her.

I swallowed another mouthful of whiskey and listened as she continued.

"So much has now changed since night you shot me—so many good things for you, and for me also many changes. My heart is happy for you because you now have love of beautiful woman who is wife and is kind to you. You are also kind man, and this means for her she is happy, also. I must now tell to you something that is strange and impossible, but also many nights when I am falling asleep I dream of maybe being her. She will never see and do horrible things I have seen and done. This means she can sleep with peace inside heart when I cannot. I am envious of this peace, but also I am envious because you give to her love I will never feel from anyone. This is good and how everything inside marriage should be. I want to say this is lucky for you and for her, but this is, I think, not true. Is not luck. Is something more than this, but I do not know word."

My tumbler required refilling, so, out came the bottle as Anya continued.

"There is one more thing you must know. When you came for me in Russian Black Dolphin Prison, this was wonderful day for me. You and others risked life to bring me back to freedom outside of prison, and you wanted nothing in return. You gave to me on that day and night something so beautiful and perfect it is impossible for me to thank you, even if I could say it a thousand times. This is reason for message. I do not know how to say to you this thing. Maybe is better if I do not. I think maybe is best if only I say . . ."

The office door swung inward, and I looked up to see Penny standing in the door way, staring toward me as Anya said, "Because of this, our lives will forever be connected, and even if you do not believe is true, I will forever love you, my Chasechka."

Hearing those words, Penny slowly lowered her gaze to the floor, stepped back outside, and closed the door.

I leapt to my feet and rounded the desk to give chase, but by the time I reached the landing outside the door, Penny was already crossing the hangar floor thirty feet below.

"Penny! Wait!" Bounding down the stairs, I caught her before she reached the exit door. "Penny, listen to me . . ."

She spun to face me with tears tracing their way down her perfect face. "Listen? Is that really what you want me to do? I've been listening, and let me tell you what I heard. First, you get an assignment that can't be put off three days before the most important day of my life. No one else on Earth is good enough to go save the world. It's up to you. You're the only one . . . like you're Superman or something."

I reached for her, but she pulled away.

"Oh, no! I'm not finished. After you take this assignment, what do I hear next? Would you like to guess?"

She paused, but I stood in silence.

Wiping away the tears, she said, "I heard your airplane. *The* airplane with *my* picture and *my* name on it, Chase. I heard you playing with your million-dollar toy, but none of that can top what I heard up there." She pointed toward the elevated office. "I saw you getting drunk and listening to your beloved little Russian, who you apparently can't live without, telling you how much she'll always love you." She landed her hands on her hips. "What else do you have to say that you so badly want me to hear, huh?"

I reached out to take her hands, but she took a step backward and smiled.

"You want to hear something funny, Chase? I'm not mad. Getting mad at this point wouldn't accomplish anything. What I am is awakened—awakened to the reality of where I really fit in your world." She started counting with her fingers. "One, your work.

Two, your airplanes. Three, your whiskey. And four, your Russian." She paused and held up five fingers. "Fifth, Chase. Fifth place. That's where I stand. And that's not how successful marriages work."

She held up two fingers, but it was definitely not a peace sign. "Do you see this? That's where I'm supposed to be . . . second. You're supposed to put God first. Just ask Singer. He'll tell you. Then me, Chase. That's where I've always put you, and I'm ashamed to say there have been times when I put you first. When was the last time you put me above fifth place?"

I couldn't answer.

"Thank you, Chase Fulton, for showing me where I stand. Now it's up to me to decide if I'd rather be in fifth place with you or if I'm better than that and want to be in second place with someone else."

If the look she gave me on the back gallery at Bonaventure was the first stab into my chest, her last line was the killing blow from the second dagger.

Chapter 3
A Higher Calling

My handler and former partner, Clark Johnson, picked up the phone in South Beach on the second ring. "Yeah, I know. We're moving fast on this one, College Boy. I've been on the phone all morning. How much do you know?"

"I know a lot more than you about the far greater problem than a kidnapped Supreme Court Justice," I said.

He groaned. "What could be a greater problem than that?"

I cleared my throat. "Me. *I'm* the bigger problem. You and the team can move as fast as you want, but it'll be without me. I'm not deployable until Monday."

"What are you talking about? This isn't a take-it-or-leave-it as-signment. We're going to war today . . . the whole team. And that includes you."

"No, I'll go, and I'll give it a hundred percent, but not until Monday. Penny's screening is Saturday night in L.A., and I'm not going to miss it. I have commitments that have to come first."

"Yeah, you do. And one of those is following the orders of the president of the United States."

"Remember when you were in the Army and it came time to reenlist?" I asked.

"Sure. I did it four times, but what's that got to do with this?"

"Do you also remember that part about obeying the orders of the president of the United States and the orders of the officers appointed over me?"

"Of course I remember. Everybody who's ever enlisted remembers."

"That's exactly my point," I said. "I didn't take that oath. I don't live my life under that obligation. But . . . I've never refused a mission, and I'm not refusing this one. I'm simply refusing to go before Monday. Not including the dozens of active-duty military teams, I know for a fact there are at least twenty other teams just like ours—"

Clark interrupted. "That's where you're wrong. There are other teams with similar capabilities, but none are like our team . . . your team. What you're talking about isn't possible."

"Here's the bottom line. I'm available for deployment to anywhere on the planet for any mission the Board—or the president —can dream up on Monday. Until then, I don't exist."

Clark paused, presumably considering my position. "You don't know what this decision will do to the remainder of your career, Chase. You need—"

"No one, not even you, gets to tell me what I *need* to do. What I *need* to do and what I *will* do is support my wife and stand beside her the first time her name appears on a movie screen. There's one more thing you *need* to consider. Our team is not my career. I don't need a job. I've made more money than I can ever spend, and the same is true for every member of this team, except for maybe Disco, but the point is this . . . Threatening me with damage to my so-called career is an empty and laughable threat. I don't have a career. What I do have is a wife who loves and supports me through the limitless hell I put her through every time the phone rings. It's her turn to be the most important person in my life."

A long silence filled the telephone before Clark said, "Okay, I'll send it up the chain, but there's nothing I can do to protect you from the fallout."

"I've got a twenty-million-dollar umbrella spread across a dozen banks all over the world. Fallout doesn't scare me." I glanced down at my phone to see a blank screen. The line was dead.

I jogged up the stairs and retrieved the mini recorder from the garbage can and headed for the door. With the touch of a button, the oversized hangar door closed and locked itself in place.

My walk back to Bonaventure took me beside the North River at low tide. The mud and muck left on the banks of the river when the Atlantic Ocean was leaning toward the other side of the world revealed the dark truth about what lay beneath the brackish, placid waters of the river where it became the sea. Animals crawled in the sludge, and filthy broadleaf vegetation bowed and swayed in the wind as if beckoning the tide to return. Perhaps the tide of my life had just turned, revealing things I'd refused to see. My priorities, when uncovered and laid bare for me to see, were impossible to justify. Penny had been right to feel the way she did, and every ounce of her anger, pain, and emptiness was my fault. That meant the healing of those wounds could only come from me . . . or so I thought.

As I continued my walk along the river, I stepped inside the gazebo and laid my hand atop the eighteenth-century cannon I'd unearthed from the bottom of the Cumberland Sound as a gift to my great-uncle, Judge Bernard Henry Huntsinger. Somehow, that three-hundred-year-old weapon of war reminded me of the sickening truth of how mankind would never stop fighting until the hand of God claimed His children and crushed our lust to be right. Perhaps I was as much to blame for that crime against humanity as anyone. Perhaps the arrogance born of victory had implanted in me a false sense of infallibility. I was nothing more than a man saddled with the same doubts and fears as every other. I just happened to have more checks in the win column than most. Over time, those checks tend to make a man believe the loss column will forever remain empty. Penny's horrible pain was proof that my loss column had just been filled to overflowing.

I stepped from the gazebo toward the back stairs of Bonaventure, where she and I had taken our vows and become one flesh in the sight of God and man. How wicked and weak must a man become to torture half of himself the way I'd tortured the woman I claimed to love without end?

To my surprise, that other half of me came running down those stairs and threw herself into my arms with tears streaming from her face. I embraced her as if we'd been apart for an eternity, and she melted into me.

Through the strain of weeping, she said, "I love you, Chase. I shouldn't have jumped to conclusions. I'm sorry."

I leaned back and held her at arm's length. "It's okay, Penny. I understand why you're upset, and I'm the one who's sorry."

"No, Chase. You have nothing to be sorry for. I just got off the phone with Clark. He wants me to convince you to go on the mission. That means you told him you're not going. I made a stupid assumption, and I'm sorry."

"I'm still going on the mission, but I'm not leaving until we get back from California. My promises to you will never again be subject to the requirements of the rest of the world. You're the most important thing to me, and I'm never going to let you forget that again."

She stepped back into my arms, and we held each other in silence until I said, "Come sit with me. I want you to hear something."

She looked up at me and narrowed her gaze. "What is it?"

I motioned back toward the gazebo, and we slid into a pair of Adirondack chairs. Pulling the tape recorder from my pocket, I said, "I want you to hear the whole message Anya left. I have nothing to hide from you, and it's important that you know that."

She pulled the small recorder from my hand and stood. I'd thrown thousands of baseballs to second base from behind home plate, but I'd never made a mini-cassette recorder sail like Penny Fulton did that afternoon. It bounced twice on our floating dock between *Aegis* and our Mark V patrol boat, shattering into hundreds of plastic shards with every bounce. Finally, each piece found its way into the North River and would, in time, wash into the cold North Atlantic.

After demonstrating her throwing prowess, she sat back into the chair beside me and took my hand. "I don't need or want to hear it. I have you, and I trust you."

I yearned to tell her what Anya had said on the tape. I wanted to understand it, and Penny was my one and only link to the possibility of ever understanding women. I decided it would be better to run it through the pitiful decipher machine in my head than pour it out for anyone else.

"You know, the other side of that tape had a conversation between me and the president."

She shrugged. "So? You've got his number. You can have a conversation with him anytime you want."

"I'm not sure that's how it works," I said.

She held out her hand. "Give me your phone, and I'll prove it to you."

"I think my phone will stay right where it is, and we won't test your theory on my access to the leader of the Free World."

We held hands and stared at the cannon.

She lifted her foot and pointed a toe toward the gun. "Wouldn't it be cool if that thing could talk?"

"It does talk," I said. "You just have to be willing to listen."

"You're a strange man, Chase Fulton, but I love you."

A ladybug landed on her knee, and we watched it walk in slow lines, traversing the denim of her jeans.

"Isn't it supposed to be good luck if one of those lands on you?" she asked.

"I don't know, but I like the fact that you're not freaked out by a ladybug."

"That's silly. Ladybugs are harmless, but let a roach crawl across my foot, and you'll hear me scream from miles away."

I gave her hand a squeeze. "So, are you going to do what Clark asked?"

"What? Talk you into going on the mission?"

I nodded.

"Hah! Not a chance."

Before I could explore the question further, Singer, our Southern Baptist sniper, came around the corner of the house and headed for the gazebo. His upper arm still carried the bandage from the surgery to reconstruct his bicep after he took a round in the arm on our most recent mission.

"How's the arm?" I asked as he propped up on the wooden railing.

"It'll be fine," he said. "It just takes time. What's this I hear about you turning down a mission?"

I grinned. "I guess good news travels fast, huh?"

"Yeah, I guess so. I just got off the phone with Clark. He says they're tasking us on the missing Supreme Court justice thing and you turned it down."

"That's not entirely true," I said. "They aren't exactly tasking us. They're ordering us."

"The Board is ordering us to do something? That's new."

"This one isn't coming from the Board," I said. "It sounds like it's coming straight from the White House."

"The White House? When did that start happening?"

"I've not been fully briefed yet, but they seem to believe the justice has been kidnapped, and we're—"

"Kidnapped?" he said. "Somebody kidnapped a sitting Supreme Court justice? What kind of idiot would think that's a good idea, and why would we get involved? That's exactly what the SEALs do best. We don't need to get tangled up in this. Clark didn't say anything about that."

"So, what *did* Clark say?"

"He wanted me to come over here and talk some sense into you, but I'm starting to believe he left out a few details."

I laughed. "He does that sometimes. The truth is, I told him we'd go, but not until Monday. The screening for Penny's movie is on Saturday, and I'm not going to miss it, no matter how many people get kidnapped between now and Monday."

He held up one finger and pulled his phone from his pocket. Covering the mouthpiece with his hand, he whispered, "Can you score another ticket to the screening?"

Penny smiled and nodded.

"Hey, Clark. It's Singer. I'm over at Bonaventure talking with Chase just like you asked me to do, and I just wanted to let you know that he and I will be in L.A. for the weekend, but we'll be back in time to go save the judge on Monday."

I couldn't hear Clark's side of the conversation, but it wasn't hard to guess what he said based on Singer's reply. "Yeah, you can probably count Hunter and Mongo out, as well. Disco may be available, though. He kinda strikes me as a scab who might cross the picket line for you."

Singer chuckled and slid the phone back into his pocket. "Hmm . . . I guess he didn't want Disco, after all."

Penny beamed her mesmerizing smile and pulled herself from the chair. "You boys have fun planning your strike. I've got packing to do." She stepped from the gazebo and turned back to face us. "Oh, and one more thing. We'll probably need Disco if we're taking the Citation, so tell him he'll have to wait 'til next time to bust up a strike."

Chapter 4
Neighborhood Watch

As it turned out, Disco, our chief pilot, wasn't a scab. With him occupying the driver's seat and me in the other, our Citation jet kissed the Earth goodbye and climbed into the western sky.

The airplane was loaded to her maximum gross takeoff weight with Penny, Hunter, Singer, our resident giant, Mongo, and all the fuel we could squeeze into the tanks. It wouldn't be possible to make L.A. without a fuel stop, but even with the stop, the Citation outclassed commercial airline travel by leaps and bounds.

With the Rockies behind us, we touched down at Hollywood Burbank Airport and taxied to the ramp where Penny's car service waited with a pair of black Town Cars. Penny's house we'd purchased in the Hollywood Hills proved not only to be a great investment in her career but also a nice financial decision, as well.

Only seconds after we stepped through the door, Penny took my hand and led me to the bedroom, closing the door behind us. I liked where I *thought* the morning was headed. It turned out I was wrong, but I'm wrong a lot, so I listened while she whispered.

"Is everyone crashing here for three days? I mean, we only have two bathrooms and two beds." She pointed to her four-poster. "You and I get that one. And it sounds like Disco is camping out in the guest room."

"Would you prefer that I get them a hotel?"

"It's fine with me if they stay, but it's not going to be very comfortable for six people."

I laughed. "Sweetheart, compared to some of the places those guys have made their home sweet home, this place is the Taj Mahal. They're knuckle-draggers. They'd be happy in the bed of a truck, but I'll talk to them about a softer place to sleep."

She grabbed my wrist. "I don't want them to think I don't want them here. It's not that at all."

"Relax," I said. "You worry too much. Everything will be fine, but we need to rent something to drive. We're not exactly car-service people."

"We have a garage. Why not buy a Suburban or something like that to keep out here?"

"Are you okay driving a big SUV around L.A. while you're out here alone?"

"Unlike you and your knuckle-draggers, I *am* a car-service girl. The service will send a driver, and he can drive the SUV. I don't think I'll ever learn my way around this town anyway."

"Sounds good to me. We're obviously not locked in the bedroom for the reason I hoped, so we might as well go car shopping."

She gave me a playful slap. "You're terrible, but now you're catching on to the reason I'd like it better if we were here alone."

The lightbulb came on, and I declared, "Hotel . . . then Suburban."

She smiled and pulled off her blouse. "I think I'll get a shower and make a salad while you boys are doing guy things. I'll be here when you get back . . . alone."

I kissed her and lingered a little longer than the typical goodbye until she pulled away. "Go! Have fun. I'll see you when you get back. I love you."

The pair of Town Cars dropped us off at the Falconer Resort and waited while I secured a three-room suite for the team.

"Oh, I see how it is," Hunter said. "You're kicking us out so your fancy Hollywood friends won't see the riffraff."

I tossed him a key to the suite. "No, you're welcome to sleep on the floor at the house and wait in line behind Mongo for the bathroom."

He caught the key. "Well, since you put it that way, I guess you two could use a little privacy. This looks like a nice place."

Disco scoped out the bedrooms and claimed the one with what he declared to be the perfect mattress firmness. "I think I'll grab a nap while you guys are shopping. Unless you're buying a bigger airplane, my opinion is pretty much useless."

I said, "I like the bigger airplane idea, but this trip should cost me a few million less than a new plane. Enjoy your nap. We'll do dinner someplace nice tonight, so don't screw up your appetite if you wake up hungry."

Consolidating down to one car, Hunter, Mongo, Singer, and I slid into car number one.

The driver asked, "You want to visit the Chevrolet dealer. Is that right?"

"Yeah, but let's do a little sightseeing first," I said.

He nodded. "Sure. What would you like to see?"

Hunter spoke up. "Take us to *The Beverly Hillbillies* house."

The driver stifled a chuckle. "I'm afraid that was on a soundstage and wasn't real. What else do you have in mind?"

Hunter palmed his face. "My whole childhood was a terrible lie. I guess you're going to tell me the La Brea Tar Pits aren't real either."

"No, those are real. They're at the corner of Wilshire and Fairfax. If that's where you want to go, just say the word."

Hunter gave the thumbs-up. "I've heard of Wilshire Boulevard. Let's check it out . . . if that's okay with you guys."

I said, "Whatever you want, Jethro, but you can't be a double naught spy."

He pretended to pout. "I never get to have any fun."

Several blocks north of the tar pits, the driver pointed across a massive intersection. "Check it out. That lady's getting carjacked."

He probably expected us to peer through the glass in awe at the spectacle, but peering isn't what we do. Before he could finish his sentence, the four of us were out of the car and sprinting through traffic to the tune of horns blowing and drivers shouting obscenities. I remember thinking how strange it was for them to yell at us instead of the carjacker, but I didn't have time to psychoanalyze the whole City of Angels.

When we reached the scene of the attempted crime, Mongo nodded to the lady backpedaling across the street. "Don't worry, ma'am. We'll take care of this."

I hit the passenger door at full speed and leapt into the car beside the would-be jacker. Singer slid behind me onto the back seat, and Hunter took the seat of honor right behind the potential driver. Mongo leaned against the driver's door as if relaxing and enjoying the midday sun. Obviously realizing the error of his ways, the thief grabbed the door handle, but neither man nor beast could open that door with Mongo on the other side.

I said, "Hi. We're here from the auto club. We thought you might need a little instruction on the finer points of stealing a car."

With a look of utter terror on his face, he lifted his shirt and reached for the tool he thought would solve his problems. As he raised the pistol, Hunter slipped his belt from his waist and slid it around the thief's neck, pinning him to the headrest. I attacked his bicep with a knuckle strike, sending explosions racing down his arm. My second blow to his wrist convinced him he didn't want to hold the pistol any longer.

"No, no, no," I said. "We never steal a car while carrying a firearm. That means a minimum sentence of twenty years. Think of that as lesson number one."

He strained against Hunter's belt around his neck. "Look, man. I don't want no trouble. Just let me out, and you'll never see me again."

"Oh, no, that'll never do. You obviously accepted the consequences of getting caught as soon as you decided to steal that nice lady's car, and you still have so much to learn. We're just getting started."

I gave Hunter a nod, and he laced his belt through the headrest and fastened the buckle. Unable to escape Hunter's improvised restraint device, our new friend flailed and twisted like an animal caught in a trap.

I reached across him and grabbed the shoulder strap. "Rule number two is, always wear your safety belt. There are crazy people out here on the streets, and you wouldn't want to get hurt."

I wrapped his wrists with the seatbelt and handed the buckle to my partner, who quickly secured it to the headrest alongside his belt.

"Now that we're good and safe, we want to make sure you practice proper cleanliness inside someone else's car." I lifted his pistol from the floorboard and pressed the muzzle beneath his ear. "Don't tell me you're about to soil this lady's beautiful leather seat. It's one thing to ruin your own pants, but this leather is really nice, and you'd never be able to get the smell out."

He tried to speak, but the belt wouldn't allow enough air across his vocal cords. Ignoring him, I press-checked the pistol and discovered the chamber to be empty, so I laid the top of the slide against the bridge of the thief's nose and shoved the pistol forward, racking the slide with the rear sights digging into his nose.

"Rule number three is, always carry your pistol with a round in the chamber. You never know when you'll need to use your weapon to defend yourself against a hardened criminal on the street. The extra second you saved by keeping one round in the pipe might be the second that saves your life. Always remember . . . safety first."

Blood ran down his nose and pooled on his shirt. "Oh, look," I said. "Another bodily fluid. You're making quite the mess of yourself. You're going to have to pull yourself together. No self-respecting car thief would ever let himself be seen in public with soiled pants and a bloody nose. You're embarrassing yourself, man. Get it together. We're having class here, and you're making a mockery of the proceedings."

Sweat poured from his brow as he trembled at the realization of his predicament.

I said, "Free his hands. We're going to do a little self-defense training."

Hunter unwound the seatbelt and let it fall.

I grabbed the man's wrists. "Now, make a fist with each hand."

He groaned an uncooperative sound and tried to pull his hands away from my grasp. "No, no. You came here to learn, so you need to cooperate. Now, make a pair of fists. I'm sure you've done it before."

He balled up his hands.

"Good. You're catching on. Now, hold your fists up like this to protect your face. You always want to protect your head and face in a street fight." I moved his hands into position. "Good. Just like that. Now, I can't hit you in the face, but there is one little vulnerability built into this defense." I threw a thundering right fist to the two lower ribs on his right side, and the breath left his lungs.

I lifted his chin. "Calm down. It's okay. Pain is the feeling of weakness leaving the body. Just relax and let it out. Trust me. You're going to be a better man when we get finished here today." I handed the pistol across the seat to Singer. "Clean that up, will you?"

Singer understood my meaning instantly and silently unloaded the weapon, wiped it clean of our fingerprints, and held it between the thief and me.

"Go ahead," I said. "You brought the gun to the party, so it's only right that you leave with it."

He shuddered in fear, disbelief, and pain as he stared between the pistol and me.

"Do I look like I'm joking around, friend? The correct answer is no. Now, take your pistol."

He tried to shake his head, so I grabbed his wrist again and forced his hand around the butt of the weapon. "Good. You're catching on. Now put the muzzle in your mouth."

If he'd been afraid before, he was now mortified.

"Okay, I guess I have to do everything for you." I twisted his wrist and pressed the muzzle against his tightly drawn lips. "Open him up."

Hunter grabbed his chin and forehead. Soon, the muzzle of the nine-millimeter automatic was pressed against his tonsils, and he dropped his hands.

"No! I thought we covered this. Always protect your face. Get your fists back up here."

He didn't move, so I threw an uppercut that would've made Mike Tyson stagger. The sound of breaking teeth echoed through the car, and blood from his mouth joined what was still flowing from his nose."

"Here you sit with a pistol in your mouth, your nose is probably broken, and your teeth are definitely broken.

I thought you were just a wreck on the outside, but I was clearly wrong. I hate it when I'm wrong. Do you know how it feels to be wrong?"

He slowly nodded with a look of pleading in his eyes.

"That means we're making progress. I'll bet right about now you're wishing you'd stayed in bed this morning or at least picked a different car to jack. I'd win that bet, wouldn't I?"

He continued nodding.

"Get the pistol out of your mouth, you suicidal maniac. Nothing good can come of that kind of behavior. You clearly need some counseling. Lucky for you, I studied psychology in school, so I may be able to help. Do you want my help?"

He nodded again.

"That's it. The first step to recovery is admitting we have a problem. Look at you. You're ready for step two. Do you know what step two is?"

He squeezed his eyelids closed and shook his head. I took that as his way of saying no.

"Oh, I'm sorry. I guess you didn't know there would be a pop quiz today, did you?"

He sobbed with blood still pouring from his face and sweat cascading like rain from his forehead.

I reached across and gave the driver's side window a gentle knock. Our beast of a man turned and opened the door, and I grabbed the man's chin and forced him to look at Mongo. "See that guy? He's not as nice as I am. He likes it rough, and he's going to teach you a little more about broken ribs while we wait for the police to get here. How does that sound?"

He whimpered, and I gave Mongo a wink. With the flip of his wrist, Hunter unfastened his belt buckle, freeing the man from his restraint, and Mongo yanked him from the car and deposited him not-so-gently onto the street.

A pair of LAPD officers flanked the man, and I climbed from the car, pulling my Secret Service credentials from my pocket. By the time I'd rounded the car, the would-be car thief was cuffed and on his knees.

I handed the man's pistol, butt-first, to the officer, and flashed my badge. "Supervisory Special Agent Fulton. I'm here on an assignment that doesn't need the publicity of something like this, so do you think you guys can handle it from here?"

The cop inspected his new prisoner. "Yeah, I think we can manage, Agent Fulton. He looks like he's in quite the cooperative mood."

I gave a sideways glance to the thirty-something owner of the car as she stood, trembling on the sidewalk with her cell phone pressed to her ear. She caught me looking and gave me a pained smile. My nod was my team's way of saying you're welcome.

Back inside the Town Car, our driver was still shaking his head. "What were you thinking? Nobody gets involved with things like that on purpose. Who are you guys?"

I popped open the glovebox and withdrew a paper napkin. Wiping my hands, I said, "You can think of us as your friendly neighborhood watch."

Chapter 5
Glitz and Glamour

Our driver seemed to ponder our limited claim. "You can't be doing stuff like that out here. You sound like you're from the South. It's a different world here in Cali. If you confront the wrong person, he's likely to shoot you before anything else."

"Thanks for the advice," I said. "We certainly don't want to get shot, do we, guys?"

Singer shuddered. "Oh, man. I hate guns. They scare me to death."

The driver shot a thumb toward Singer. "See? He knows. Just be careful out here. I don't want to see any of you get hurt."

"We'll keep that in mind," I said. "Let's get to that Chevy dealership. We've got a dinner date with a big-shot screenwriter tonight, and we can't be late."

"So, you've changed your mind about seeing the La Brea Tar Pits?"

"We'll hit that another day."

We pulled into the dealership, and the driver said, "I'll wait here in case you don't find what you want."

I pointed toward a row of black Suburbans. "I don't think we'll have any trouble finding what we need, but we've got your card. We'll call if we need you."

He reached to shake my hand. "Whatever you say. It's been a pleasure."

I slipped a folded bill into his palm and climbed from the car.

An hour later, we were the proud owners of a brand-new, 2005 blacked-out Suburban. We elected Hunter as our chauffeur and headed back toward the flat in the Hollywood Hills.

My phone chimed, and I pressed the speaker button. "Hello, Clark. How are things in South Beach?"

He said, "Oh, how I wish I were in South Beach. Thanks to your little insurrection, I'm in D.C. suffering death by briefings."

"I'm sorry to hear that. What can we do for you?"

"We? Am I on speaker?"

"Yes, but we're inside the Suburban. It's Hunter, Singer, Mongo, and me."

"What Suburban, and where's Disco?"

"Disco is catching up on his beauty rest. You know how it is. Old guys like you and him need an afternoon nap before you hit the four-thirty buffet at Golden Corral."

"Keep at it, College Boy. You'll be lucky to live so long. Now, shut up and listen. This thing is bigger than we thought, and you were partially right. We're not the only team on it. I can't brief you about the other players, even on a secure line, but we're going to be in good company."

"That sounds encouraging. What's our role going to be?"

"That's still up in the air, so to speak. Remember when I said there were other teams but none like ours?"

"Sure."

"Well, I was more correct than my usual degree of correctness. Apparently, the other teams, at least the ones on this mission, need a well-defined plan before they ship out."

I laughed. "A plan? I'm not familiar with that word."

"Exactly. That's why we're so valuable on this one. We work the problem, adapt, and overcome. Apparently, we're the only ones with enough brains for all of us to have one of his own."

"Are you keeping Skipper in the loop?"

"Nope. She's keeping herself in the loop. She's been in every briefing I've been in all morning, plus some extras. No one will be as well-informed as your analyst."

"That's why she's the best," I said.

"No, she's the best because she's doing exactly what she's meant to be doing. Sound familiar?"

I rolled my eyes. "Yeah, yeah. That's what you keep telling me, but I think I'm meant to be lying on a beach somewhere with a cocktail waitress making sure my glass is never empty."

"The fact that you're not living that life is proof you're doing exactly what you're supposed to be doing."

"Whatever. Surely you didn't call just to complain about being briefed to death."

"Actually, I called to do a little begging."

"I already told you I'm not missing the screening, and there's nothing you, or anybody else, can say that'll change my mind."

"I know. I'm not calling to ask you to miss the screening, but do you have to go to the after-party?"

"What do you know about after-parties?"

"Nothing, but it sounds like something you glitz-and-glamour Hollywood people would do after a screening."

I ignored the jab. "When do you need us back in the saddle?"

"Yesterday! But I'll take whatever I can get. The sooner you get back to Georgia, the better."

"We'll be home Sunday afternoon. But there's one more thing we need to talk about."

"What is it?"

I glanced at Singer with his arm still bandaged and mostly useless. "We don't have a sniper."

Singer bowed his head. Apparently, hearing us discuss his place on the disabled list was too much for him.

I gave his knee a punch. "Hold your head up. You're not off the team. You're just on injured reserve until you're back in gunslinging shape."

He nodded, but the look on his face said the truth still hurt.

"Don't worry about that," Clark said. "I'll go with you. I'm no Singer, but I can still shoot."

Before responding, I eyed our sniper, and he gave me a firm nod.

"Okay, then. We'll see you on Sunday afternoon."

He said, "Plan to be wheels up at daylight on Monday morning."

"Anything else?" I asked.

"Nothing that can't wait until Sunday, but you might want to check on Skipper this evening. Her head has to be on the verge of exploding, so I'm sure she'd appreciate a little love from her boss."

"If you think I'm her boss, you're more delusional than I am."

"Regardless, I'm sure she'd like to know you care."

"I'll give her a shout," I said.

"There's one more thing before I go. This screening thing of Penny's . . . Can you score some more seats?"

"How many?"

"Can you get four?"

"Sure. Let me know when and where you'll be arriving, and I'll have our chauffeur pick you up."

Without another word, he was gone, and I shoved the phone back into my pocket.

"Who do you think he's bringing?" Hunter asked.

"I suspect he's bringing at least one person you should've brought. The other two have to be Skipper and Maebelle."

He said, "I guess I should've invited Tina, but I didn't know if it would be cool to assume."

"It's always cool for you to assume, Hunter. You're family."

Hunter dropped me off at Penny's flat and picked up our chief pilot. He said, "We're heading back to the hotel to get cleaned up for dinner. Let us know when and where."

Penny stepped out the front door. "I see you bought a Suburban. Surprise . . . surprise. How was your first day on the streets of L.A.?"

"Pretty boring," I said. "Nothing exciting unless you're into car shopping."

She lowered her chin. "I don't think it's possible for you to have a boring afternoon—especially not in L.A."

I reached for her hand, and unlike her reaction the previous day in the hangar, she not only let me take it, but she also pulled me close and let her eyes explore the house. "Do you hear that?" she whispered.

"Hear what?"

She nibbled at my earlobe. "The sound of the two of us alone in an empty house."

"Well, yes, Mrs. Fulton, I do hear that. And I suggest we take full advantage of that sound."

She agreed, and we did.

* * *

Dinner was at Spago at 8:30, and it was the epitome of country-comes-to-town. Although the net worth of the six of us likely outweighed any other table in Wolfgang Puck's prestigious restaurant, nothing about our appearance would stand in support of that fact. Penny, of course, rocked a gown fit for royalty and caught the eye of every man, and most of the women, in the room —even in a town where beauty is a commodity for sale beneath the scalpels of more cosmetic surgeons than anywhere else on Earth. The practice of transforming average into exceptional was nothing short of wasted time, money, and effort when my North Texas knockout floated through the room. The queen of the screenwriters made it impossible for anyone to notice or care what the man whose arm she held was wearing.

Disco tried, but after spending twenty years dressed in what the Air Force ordered him to wear, he still hadn't mastered civilian attire. Hunter and Singer looked almost like they belonged in such an elegant establishment with their dinner jackets and pressed slacks . . . until closer examination revealed they were both wearing well-seasoned Danner boots because they'd forgotten to pack what they called "party shoes."

At six foot eight and approaching three hundred pounds, finding anything to fit Mongo was like trying to dress an elephant at Baby Gap.

To Singer's great disappointment, sweet tea wasn't an option on the expansive drink menu, and when the waiter asked if he'd like sparkling or still, our dead-eye sniper replied, "Tap."

I was no more sophisticated than my team, but when Hunter leaned in and whispered, "What's tartare?" I recommended ordering *anything* else.

His finger continued down the menu until he froze and gasped. "Chase, there's a pizza on here for seventy-eight bucks. For *one* pizza!"

"If we can't afford it when the check comes, I'm sure they'll let us wash dishes to settle our tab."

That seemed to settle his nerves, but Disco appeared to be entranced by something or someone at the next table. I tried to follow his line of sight, but there were too many heads in the way.

"Hey, Disco," I stage-whispered. "What are you staring at?"

When he answered, he didn't do so in any type of whisper—stage or otherwise. "I think that's Diane Lane and Josh Brolin."

The actress looked up and flashed him a smile, and our chief pilot melted in his seat.

I gave him a nod. "Now you know how I feel every time Penny smiles at me."

My stunning wife rolled her eyes. "That was cheesy, even for you, Chase Fulton."

The appetizers arrived, and Mongo stared down at the single scallop in the center of his plate with a twig of something unfit for human consumption draped across the top. The whole team covered their mouths in a fruitless effort to avoid laughing at our jolly giant.

What the appetizers lacked in quantity, the main course more than made up for in quality. I suddenly wished Maebelle were at the table with us. Aside from her cooking, I'd never tasted anything better than what Wolfgang Puck's executive chef sent to our table that night.

Just when I believed the experience of dinner with my team couldn't get any better, dessert arrived. The waiter presented Penny's first and declared it to be European hot chocolate. He described the beautiful creation as a pair of steaming chocolate chip cookies beneath perfectly whipped heavy cream and house-made marshmallows. He placed a second plate in front of me. "And for you, sir, a dark chocolate soufflé with Madagascar vanilla gelato, crème fraîche, and complexite guittard chocolate."

Immediately behind the waiter, the sommelier presented a port glass. "And of course, a nineteen ninety-five Ramos Pinto port to accompany the soufflé."

The remaining desserts were at least as impressive as mine, and we turned the final course into a family-style buffet, passing our plate to the left after every bite so the whole team could enjoy the grand finale.

When the check arrived, I pulled a card from my wallet to cover the extravagance, but a gentleman stepped around the waiter and lifted the leather binder containing our check from the waiter's hand.

Penny immediately stood and took the man's arm. "Hey! I didn't know you would be here tonight." She turned to me. "Chase, meet Trevor Bastogne, our executive producer."

I stood and extended a hand. "It's a pleasure to meet you, Trevor. I'm Chase Fulton."

He shook my hand, shot Penny a look, and let out a chuckle.
"I know who you are, Chase, and the pleasure is mine. I saw a bit of your handiwork earlier this evening, and I insist that you allow me to pick up the check. You and your . . . friends . . . have more than earned it."

I narrowed my eyes. "I'm afraid you have us confused with someone else, but I appreciate the offer."

He laughed, slapped my shoulder, and slid the check binder into his jacket. "Fearless and humble. Those are two character traits we're lacking in this town."

Trevor walked away, and Penny asked, "What was that all about? What did you guys do this afternoon?"

I eyed my team. "I told you, sweetheart. It was just a boring day in the city doing a little car shopping."

Chapter 6
Standing Ovations

After a beautiful November Friday in Southern California spent exploring and sightseeing, Penny's big day—the day she'd waited for most of her life—finally arrived. Limousines, and at least one blacked-out Suburban, lined the drive, depositing their perfectly quaffed, manicured, and overly adorned occupants beneath the portico of the Excelsior Theater.

After the photos were taken and hands were shaken, the seats filled, and the film's director took the stage.

"Good evening, ladies and gentlemen. For those of you who do not know who I am, my name is Robert DaSilva, and I had the good fortune to make a remarkable picture from a breathtakingly beautiful screenplay with some of the most talented and gifted people not only in Hollywood, but anywhere in the world. Thank you for joining me for the first screening of *The Essence of Time*."

A round of applause sounded and then gave way as the lights went down and the screen came alive. We sat in astonishment as the story of timeless love, sacrifice, and integrity played out on the silver screen. The audience wept, laughed, and undoubtedly found themselves enraptured by the story.

Ninety minutes later, the closing credits rolled, and the theater came alive with raucous cheers and applause as everyone rose to their feet. The director reclaimed the stage. He spoke for several minutes, congratulating the actors for their splendid performances, and called the names and titles of two dozen people I'd never heard of.

Then he said, "Now that you've all seen the finished product and tasted the cake, so to speak, I'd like to introduce you to the immensely talented writer who gave us the recipe for such a magnificent cake. Ladies and gentlemen, it is my great honor to introduce to you, first-time screenwriter extraordinaire, Mrs. Penny Fulton!"

Penny pulled her hand from mine, stood with tears in her eyes, and waved to the adoring crowd. Someone handed her a microphone, and she nearly leapt from her shoes. She accepted the microphone as if it were a cobra ready to strike, and the crowd laughed.

After testing the best distance from her lips to the microphone, she said, "Oh, my goodness. I'm a writer, not a talker, so please forgive me for what I'm about to put you through. When I originally wrote this story, I was traveling the East Coast. Yes, America does have an East Coast for those of you who think the whole country is California. Anyway, I was traveling aboard a beautiful sailboat with some dear friends. I had a lot of time on my hands back then, and choosing how to spend that time is what gave me the early idea for this story. Like most stories, mine grew and changed. The best change came in the form of a wonderful man whose last name I now share." She whispered down at me. "Stand up, Chase."

I obeyed.

"This is my perfect—well, mostly perfect—husband, Chase Fulton. Without his support, none of you would've ever read my screenplay, let alone turned it into this." She held up both hands as if presenting the screen. "By the way, if any of the financiers are here, I've got another story in the works that'll soon be for sale."

The laughter grew until a man in the back yelled out, "I'll buy it today!"

Penny blushed. "It's not finished yet, but I'm certainly open to offers. It's going to be much better than this *thing* we turned into a movie."

Penny was the belle of the ball and adored by all until Trevor Bastogne claimed the stage and the microphone. "Thank you, Mrs. Fulton, for such a wonderful story to turn into a picture. I have no doubt you have a long and glorious career ahead of you, and the way you look tonight, no one here would be surprised to see you in front of the camera instead of behind a laptop."

Cheers and whistles rose from the crowd until Bastogne called the room back to order. "Thank you for that. I've known Penny long enough to know she is both flattered and even a little embarrassed by your adoration, but she's more than deserving. And now I'd like to take a moment for something deeply personal. Penny not only brought a brilliant story into all of our lives, but she delivered one other surprise none of us could've expected. If you would indulge me a moment, please take a look at this astonishing footage captured two days ago, only a few blocks north of Wilshire Boulevard."

There were rumblings of conversation in the crowd until the screen came to life with low-quality cell phone camera footage of a thwarted carjacking, in which a woman was pulled from her car at an intersection by a would-be car thief. Seconds after climbing behind the wheel, the thief was surprised to discover four men appearing out of nowhere. Three of the men climbed inside the car while a fourth man of enormous stature held the driver's door firmly closed.

I closed my eyes and lowered my chin as the video of the amateur videographer played out.

This is supposed to be Penny's night. None of this should be happening. She's going to kill me. Clark is going to kill me.

When the footage ended, it froze on the face of the young woman whose car we'd saved.

Bastogne said, "The woman in the clip you just saw is not an actress. She's my beautiful wife, Lacy. Stand up, Lacy."

The crowd clapped while she waved, and Bastogne said, "That's not all, ladies and gentlemen. The men you saw in the video are here tonight. They are the friends and family of Penny Fulton, our screenwriter. Stand up, guys. Let us have a look at you."

Thankfully, none of my team stood. We kept our butts planted firmly in our seats, but the rest of the crowd rose in a standing ovation.

When Bastogne finally got everyone back in their seats, he said, "So, if there are any casting directors here looking for real-life, bad-ass heroes, I think Penny can point you toward a few."

The director spoke up again. "What a night this has been already. But I'd like to invite everyone to join us next door in the ballroom for cocktails, champagne, and hors d'oeuvres."

As we filed out, Penny pinched the underside of my left arm. "A boring afternoon, huh?"

I shrugged. "Nobody got shot, and we didn't blow anything up."

She rolled her eyes and kissed my cheek. "I love you, you crazy man."

The next sound out of her mouth was a squeal that could be heard all the way to Texas. She kicked off her high heels and ran into Clark's arms. Maebelle and Skipper joined the embrace, and Tina Ramirez stood staring at Hunter, the man she'd just watched on the screen. She stepped to him, and they embraced.

Penny's excitement couldn't be contained. "I can't believe all of you came. This is so amazing. Thank you so much!"

Maebelle squeezed Penny's hands. "It was a beautiful movie. I cried through the whole thing, but when she died, oh my! I fell apart, girl. I knew it was going to be good, but it's better than good. It's amazing. Who knew you were so talented?"

While Maebelle was fawning over Penny, Clark took me by the elbow.

I said, "I know what you're going to say, and you're right. We shouldn't have gotten involved in the attempted carjacking. The last thing we need is our faces on TV. I get it."

"I don't care about any of that. Nobody outside this room will ever see that footage. Don't worry about it. You did a good thing, and it sounds like you guys have a career in the movies if the whole save-the-world thing doesn't pan out."

I pulled my arm from his grip. "If you're not going to yell at me for that, what's on your mind?"

"It's gotten worse, Chase. It's not just the Supreme Court justice anymore. They've got two congressmen and the governor of South Carolina. They're threatening to kill them on national television if their demands aren't met."

"What demands?"

He checked the environment. "Not here. I'll brief you on the plane, but we have to move, now."

"Okay, you round up the others. I've got to tell Penny."

Inside the ballroom, my wife was the star attraction. She was getting more attention than the movie stars, and the look on her face said she loved everything about it.

As badly as I hated to interrupt her, I had no other option. I stepped beside her and whispered into her ear, "They've kidnapped two congressmen and the South Carolina governor. I'm sorry, but—"

She spun to face me and pushed me away from her crowd of admirers. Grabbing my face with both hands, she planted an unforgettable kiss exactly where kisses belong. "I understand. Go save the world, but don't you dare get killed. Thank you for making tonight so special for me. I love you."

"I love you, too," I said. "And I promise to be careful. I'll call when I can. We're taking the Citation back to Saint Marys, but I'll send it back out for you."

She glanced over her shoulder and then back at me. "Don't worry about that. I'll stay here in L.A. for a few days. It sounds like I may have a few offers to attend to."

We kissed once more, and I fought my way through the crowd in search of my team.

I caught up with them as they headed out a side door. "What's the plan?" I asked as I fell in step.

Clark said, "Getting our butts on the airplane is the immediate plan. Beyond that, things are a little foggy."

* * *

Our drivers dropped us at the Hollywood Burbank Airport, and I counted heads. "By the time we put all of us aboard, I'm afraid we'll be pushing the limits for the Citation."

"Relax, College Boy. I've got it handled. The State Department was nice enough to lend us a white top. Your cute little Citation can stay here while a real airplane puts us in the fight."

Clark's white top turned out to be a Gulfstream that not only had plenty of seats but also crossed the country without so much as the thought of a fuel stop.

"We've got to get one of these," I said.

Clark laughed. "You don't have the bankroll for one of these."

I shrugged. "Maybe someday."

When we pulled into Bonaventure, I checked my watch only to discover the sun would soon be showing its face over the eastern horizon.

I pulled Clark aside. "I think we should get some sleep. If we hit the ground running, we'll burn out pretty quickly."

He glanced at his watch. "You're probably right. You put the kids to bed, and Skipper and I will fire up the ops center. Meet us up there in ten."

I made the announcement, and no one resisted the opportunity to hit the sack for a few hours.

Chapter 7
Out of the Frying Pan

When I walked into the ops center, it was impossible to ignore the man with the shaved head on the screen. He appeared to be in his mid-thirties and spent a little too much time in the gym.

Skipper looked up. "Good, you're here. Chase, meet Master Chief DeAndre Lewis, Special Boat Team Twenty, Naval Special Warfare Group Four out of Little Creek, Virginia."

I locked eyes with the SEAL on the screen. "Good morning, Chief Lewis. It's a pleasure. I'm Chase Fulton, but I don't have any fancy titles before or after my name. I just run this little team of ne'er-do-wells down here at Kings Bay."

"The pleasure is mine, Chase, and fancy titles don't impress me much. Just call me Dre. We've been tasked to support your unit in waterborne infiltration and exfiltration, but I'll be honest, we're not big on supporting. We'd rather be out front with the trigger-pullers, if you know what I'm saying."

"I'm going to be upfront with you, Chief. I've never worked with SEALs. My team fell together when the Army shook the SF tree, and we picked up a couple of boys in blue along the way."

"Let me interrupt you, Chase. I think I know where this is going. Despite what you may have heard, you don't have to teach us to read and use a fork. We're team guys. Of course, we're SEALs first, but we understand the value of other operational styles. On, in, or under the water, I'm in charge . . . nonnegotiable. But when we put you on the beach, it's your show. If you take us with you into the tree line, we'll adapt—unless the SEAL way is better. In which case, we'll teach your guys the better way. It's that simple."

I gave his speech some thought. "Like you, we're pretty good at being autonomous, but I'm not going to turn down a dozen SEALs who want to help me kill the bad guys."

Dre said, "Commander Lattimore made it clear that we're the subordinate unit until you or one of your guys does something stupid to get us killed. At that point, if we get there, it becomes my operation, and I'll make the decision for my team to either press on or retreat." He lowered his chin. "Chase, I've been a frogman for twenty years, and I ain't never retreated. You feel me?"

The time would come when I'd butt heads with Chief Lewis, but that wasn't the time to arm wrestle.

I said, "I would've liked it better if we could've done some training together before stepping out of the frying pan and into the fire with each other, but when this thing turns into a train wreck in a swamp, I think I'm going to be glad to have you and your team on that train with us."

Clark slapped the table. "Okay, that's enough growling and butt-sniffing. We've got work to do."

Dre said, "Let me guess . . . Green Beret, right?"

"To the core," I said.

Clark snarled. "Don't be jealous just because neither of you two earned your SF tab."

"Now who's growling?" I asked. "I thought you said we've got work to do."

Clark cleared his throat. "So, here's what we know. This group is likely operating out of The Bahamas. That's only about seven hundred islands and twenty-four hundred cays spread over five thousand square miles. Skipper is on the satellite imagery train, but we simply don't have enough analysts to scour the pictures."

Skipper is impossible to explain. Essentially, she was my little sister who fell into the hands of an intelligence analyst and found her calling. She was the best naturally skilled analyst I'd ever met, and brilliant beyond description.

Dre said, "We can likely disregard most of the cays. There's little growth and even less elevation on most of them. These guys are too smart to kidnap and house an HVT on a sandbar a foot above sea level."

Clark turned to me. "HVT is a high-value target, in case you didn't learn that in college."

I ignored his shot over my bow. "What makes us so sure they're operating out of The Bahamas?"

Skipper said, "I'll take this one. It's two things. First, your call from the U.S. Ambassador to The Bahamas made us believe the embassy may have received some kind of communication from the group responsible for the kidnapping. And second, so far, all of the snatches have occurred on the east coast of Florida."

"Forgive me for asking the obvious questions," I said, "but hasn't someone investigated how the ambassador became involved in any of this?"

"That's the thing," Skipper said. "We tried, but he's gone."

"Gone where?" I asked.

"We don't know. He's just gone."

I scratched my head. "We'll come back to that. In the meantime, how did we learn about the two congressmen and the governor being nabbed?"

Skipper said, "This one falls in my area, as well. The three kidnappings were reported by the three families, all within thirty minutes of each other, and all under similar circumstances."

"What kind of similar circumstances?"

Skipper continued without checking her notes. "Each of them was walking on the beach just after sunup yesterday morning. They all left their beachfront houses around seven thirty and never came home."

"Have there been any ransom demands or comms with who-ever's doing this?"

"This is where it gets weird," Dre said. "Their demands are all over the place. They want the release of two dozen prisoners around the world that seem to have no connection. They want a commitment from either the U.N. or the U.S. to provide the country of Gabon with five billion dollars in non-specific foreign aid."

I held up a hand. "I'm sorry I'm not up on world politics like the rest of you seem to be, but where is Gabon, and what is non-specific foreign aid?"

Dre said, "Gabon is a country of just over two million people in Equatorial West Africa, just west of the Congo and south of Cameroon."

"That's interesting," I said. "How about my second question?"

Dre flipped through several sheets of paper. "Oh, yeah. Non-specific foreign aid is money with no caveats, meaning the recipient can do whatever they want with it without any responsibility to the provider."

"Five billion dollars is a lot of money to give away without getting anything in return," I said.

Skipper held up a finger. "If I may, we would get something for our money, and if it happens, it will absolutely be *our* money because the U.N. isn't volunteering to write any checks. We'd get our Supreme Court justice, two congressmen, and a governor back."

"What about the prisoners?"

Dre said, "That one has all of us stumped, but we're working on tying them together."

"So, let me see if I've got this straight. Four—and maybe five, counting the ambassador—high-value targets have been nabbed, and whoever has them wants both the release of a bunch of prisoners with no connection and a huge paycheck for some place called Gabon that nobody's ever heard of. Have I got it all right?"

"Not exactly," Skipper said. "We don't think the ambassador was kidnapped."

"Why not?"

"Because his disappearance is nothing like the other four. He vanished with his passport, a quarter million dollars in cash, and his cell phone. The others had nothing on them when they were grabbed."

I laid my chin in my hands. "Okay, so the ambassador is running. Surely you're pinging his phone, right?"

Skipper shook her head. "He ditched it in Havana two hours after he disappeared."

"Havana? Like Havana, Cuba?"

"Exactly like that," Skipper said. "We've got a couple of State Department assets poking around down there, but so far, they've come up empty. I traced all the calls he made before ditching the phone, and three of them came back to Swiss banks. The other two were to you, Chase."

"Me? Are you saying the call I got on Wednesday was one of the last calls he made?"

"Yep. He actually called you twice—once at eleven thirty-eight a.m., and he tried again at twelve fifty-seven, but you didn't answer the second call."

I replayed the day in my head. "I was up in the Mustang when he called the second time, and that's why I didn't answer. But that doesn't tell us why he would've called me. I understand the calls to the bank. He's obviously planning a vanishing act and wants to make sure he can live comfortably for the rest of his days."

Silence overtook the ops center as we pondered the situation.

I tapped the table. "Does the ambassador have any ties to Gabon?"

Skipper hit a few keys on her laptop. "Not that I can find, but we're still exploring that possibility."

"How about ties to any of the prisoners?"

"Same answer," Skipper said.

I closed my eyes to let the jumble of information roll around inside my head. When I opened up, everyone was looking straight at me. "What?"

Skipper said, "We're waiting to hear what's going to fall out of your mouth when you rejoin us."

I said, "There are more demands, aren't there?"

The little pigtailed girl I'd watched grow into a woman and ultimately into my intelligence analyst slowly nodded her head.

"Let's hear them," I said.

Skipper glanced at Clark and took a deep breath. "There's actually one more demand *and* a caveat. The demand is that Justice Mateo resign from the Supreme Court, immediately."

"Has he done it?" I asked.

"No, not yet."

"What do you mean, not yet? The United States doesn't negotiate with terrorists."

On the screen, Master Chief Lewis stepped aside, and a woman stepped into frame.

I pointed up at the display. "Who's she?"

Before Skipper could answer, the woman said, "She, being me, is Simone Tolliver, undersecretary for Arms Control and International Security Affairs. It's nice to meet you, even if electronically, Mr. Fulton."

I turned to Skipper. "That doesn't even sound like a real thing. Undersecretary to whom?"

Simone said, "You can talk directly to me, Mr. Fulton. I'll answer any questions you have, and the first one is this . . . I am an undersecretary to the secretary of state, and I assure you my department is quite real, regardless how it *sounds* to you."

"I meant no disrespect, Ms. Tolliver. It's just that I'm more of a door kicker than a handshaker, so my familiarity with the organizational structure of the federal government is one of my weaknesses."

"No offense taken. Some days I wish my department wasn't necessary, but unfortunately, in today's world, a great many agencies and departments are essential that would've been things of myth only a few years ago. But that isn't why I'm here. You mentioned that the United States doesn't negotiate with terrorists."

"I certainly did. And I stand by that policy. We're the most powerful nation on the planet. If we'd flex that muscle a little more, these terrorists and many others would likely have a second thought before they started grabbing up our citizens."

"I understand your position, and from your perspective, that's exactly the position I would expect you to take. As you said, you're a door kicker."

"No offense taken," I said.

She huffed. "That wasn't the offensive part, Chase. Your belief and opinion of what the policies of the United States should be are naïve and simpleminded."

"Well, Ms. Tolliver, you were right. I am now well offended."

She ignored me. "The time has come for us to stop worrying about who we offend and to get busy getting our American victims back. I may not know how to kick down a door, Mr. Fulton, but I assure you, I know exactly how diplomacy works. Not only does the United States routinely negotiate with terrorists, but we're also better at it than anyone else in the world."

"If that's the truth, then why do you need me and the SEALs?"

"We need you—and the SEALs—to be our eyes and ears in the field while we get our hostages back with appropriate degrees of diplomacy and negotiation."

I smirked. "You may know everything there is to know about diplomacy, Ms. Tolliver, but there's clearly one thing you don't understand about Master Chief Lewis and me."

"And what is that?"

"We're the people *your* people call when that beloved diplomacy of yours fails. You don't have the power to give these people what they want. No one does, and that's what they're counting on. These people are obviously a lot brighter than we are. They're smart enough to put a wide array of demands on the table that can't be met. That puts you and your diplomatic corps in a tailspin trying to figure out what the kidnappers are willing to concede so you can make that golden offer. I don't think they care about those prisoners, so you can start by taking that off the table. That'll give your people a ring of plastic keys to chew on while Master Chief Lewis and I go get your hostages back . . . because that's what we do."

As if considering my position, she let her eyes wander to the ceiling. "Let's say you're right and these people want to wreak havoc on powerful Americans. What's their end game, and why did Ambassador Woodford call you directly . . . three times?"

"Three times?"

"Yes, Mr. Fulton, three times. He called you the first time while you were in California, and the second and third time while you were back on the East Coast. Why do you think he would do that?"

"I have a theory on that," I said. "Ambassador Woodford did me a huge favor while I was in The Bahamas a couple of weeks ago, and I think—like a good diplomat—he was calling in a favor from a guy who owes him one."

"What favor?" she asked.

"I've not had time to think this one completely through, but I believe Ambassador Woodford knows I'm the kind of man who doesn't kick butt and take names. He believes I'm the kind of man who leaves a string of dead bodies in my wake to accomplish my mission—and that's exactly what he's counting on."

The undersecretary cocked her head. "I'm not sure I'm following you. Can you elaborate?"

"I think it's the classic double-cross. Woodford got in bed with these guys for some reason. It doesn't matter why, yet. He got in over his head, and now he's on the lam. Whoever these people are, they're not going to let him live when they find him. He's not running from us, Ms. Tolliver. He's running from his teammates."

Her light came on. "Oh! So, he makes sure you're part of the response because you owe him a favor and because he believes you'll kill the people he's afraid of. Mr. Fulton, you may have a career in the diplomatic corps, after all."

"No, thank you, ma'am. I'll stick to gunslinging and door kicking. I'm a lot more comfortable with people shooting at my face than stabbing at my back."

Chapter 8
Wheels Up . . . Sort of

With the early morning conference accomplishing little, I declared the meeting adjourned, and I crashed. I don't know how long I slept, but it wasn't long enough. I smelled the beautiful morning aroma of coffee brewing when I stumbled down the stairs and found everyone except Clark gathered around the table.

"We have rooms other than the kitchen in this house, you know."

Singer looked up. "Good morning, Chase. Coffee's on, and Skipper was just filling us in on what little is known."

I pulled my favorite mug from the shelf. "Let me get some caffeine in my body before I try to digest any more intel." Holding my mug beneath the stream of dark, black coffee pouring from the machine, I said, "What time is it, and do we know any more than we knew when we hung up on her majesty, the undersecretary?"

"It's almost eight thirty," Skipper said. "And there's been no additional verified intel since you went to bed."

"Speaking of going to bed . . . Did you get any sleep?"

Skipper pointed to herself. "Me? No, of course not. I'll sleep later. There's too much work to do right now."

I blew across the mug and took my first sip. By the time the cup was half empty—or half full, depending on one's perspective—I was feeling almost human again. Hunter pushed out a chair for me, and I joined my team at the table.

"Okay, Skipper, please continue."

"Even though we don't have any official news, I've been digging around in the telephone system of The Bahamas. Let me tell you —that is an antiquated system, to say the least. It's too complicated for me to explain. Besides, it would just put all of you back to sleep. But I'm more convinced than ever that the demand calls originated in Nassau."

I've learned many things by listening closely when Skipper speaks, and that morning was no exception. I took another sip and asked, "Did you say calls, plural?"

"I did, and thank you for paying attention. The same electronically modified voice made two calls."

"Two calls to whom?"

"That's the fascinating part. They called the U.S. Embassy in Nassau both times, but the calls were routed through fourteen countries before the station chief's phone rang at forty-two Queen Street in Nassau."

"Wait a minute," I said. "They called the CIA chief of station's direct line?"

"Yep, both times. And before you ask, I'm piecing together a call log, both incoming and outgoing, from not only the station chief's office, but also the whole embassy. As you might imagine, it's a herculean task. The smaller the needle, the bigger the haystack."

I drained my cup and headed for more coffee. "We're in way over our heads on this one. Can you give me a rundown of the agencies involved in this thing?"

Skipper shuffled some papers. "Sure. Do you want the official list or just what I can remember?"

"Just the major players."

"State, of course. SOCOM—they're running the SEALs. Defense Intelligence Agency. I don't think I have to tell you why DIA is involved. DOJ is on board because of the Supreme Court justice being one of the victims. Oh, that reminds me! But you and I will talk privately about Justice."

"Hang on a minute. I don't need any information the rest of the team doesn't have. We're one unit on this, so give it to me."

Skipper scanned the table. "Uh . . . are you sure?"

I returned to the table with the coffee pot and topped off mugs all around. "I'm sure."

She shrugged. "Okay, here goes. Your little Russian girlfriend is still working with Justice, and I have a theory that this is exactly the kind of mission they want her on. It wouldn't surprise me if she showed up, or at least, some evidence of her having been there shows up. If that happens, you've got to keep your head on straight."

"You were right. We should've had this conversation privately, but now that we're in it, I'll make the same promise to you I made to Penny."

Silence befell the team, and I said, "Anya is behind me in every way, and she's not going to screw me up again. I *will* admit one thing, though. If I were tasked with the job of sending one, and only one person to take care of this situation, it would be her. She'd make a mess of things, and bodies would pile up in her wake, but she'd get the hostages back, and I doubt any of you would disagree."

Clark strolled through the door as if he'd been eavesdropping. "I've seen her work. Most of us have, except maybe Disco, and she's one of the best individual operators I've ever seen. She's *shite* when it comes to teamwork, but on her own, she's practically unstoppable."

Mongo seemed to let his mind drift back in time. "Yeah, I'd agree with that. If I were tied up in a hole someplace and I could have only one person coming for me, she'd definitely make the short list—along with everybody at this table, including Skipper. I've seen you shoot."

That earned a chuckle, but it wasn't a joke. In addition to being a world-class analyst, Skipper was at least as good as anyone at the table when it came to natural shooting talent. The team had burned through millions of rounds on the range and tens of thousands in real-world ops, so they had the advantage of experience, but Skipper had talent.

"Speaking of crackpot shots," I said, "who taught your little Eastern Bloc beauty to shoot?"

"She's got a name," Mongo said.

"I know. I just wanted to pull your chain a little. But the question still stands."

He said, "Irina—that's her name—claims her father taught her and her brother to shoot when they were children, but I'm a little dubious about that story."

Skipper knocked on the table. "We're getting off track, boys. Try to focus."

Appropriately scolded, Mongo and I returned from our mental vacation to Stalingrad.

"Sorry," I said. "Let's get back to the demands. Obviously, most of them are bogus and designed entirely to give the diplomats the false sense of accomplishment when they negotiate them away."

Clark pointed a finger-and-thumb pistol at me. "And that's the key to this whole carnival. If we can find out what they really want, we'll be well on the road to finding out who these guys are."

"I think you're right," Skipper said. "If I were placing a wager, I'd hang my hat on the five billion to Gabon. How about you?"

I chewed on the number. "I'd make a different bet."

"You don't think they really want the money?" Skipper asked.

"No, they want money, but probably not that amount. That's probably another planned concession. If the negotiators can whittle five billion down to one, they'll be heroes in the hostage negotiation world."

Skipper nodded. "I can see that. You're probably right. Okay, enough about the money. What else do you need to know before you go wheels up?"

"Do we have dossiers on the congressmen and the governor yet?"

Skipper's fingers came to life on her keyboard. She dragged out the word "Yeah . . . but they're incomplete. You want medicals and financials, right?"

"Medicals, first," I said. "I'm sure the financials will be slow in coming."

Skipper leaned back in her chair. "Here's what we know so far. Justice Matthew Caputo was the first hostage taken. We are calling them hostages, right?"

Everyone turned to Clark.

"I don't care what we call them as long as we get them back. Pick a name, and stick with it."

Skipper said, "We'll go with hostages until somebody up the chain comes up with a different moniker."

Heads nodded, and she continued. "Justice Caputo is sixty-eight years old, been on the court for six years, and he's center right, politically. Here's what you wanted to know . . . He takes blood pressure and cholesterol meds. Neither condition is life-threatening in the short term, but the stress of being kidnapped and held for ransom isn't going to do his heart any good."

She looked up for questions, and I asked, "Family?"

"Oh, yeah, sorry. He's married for forty-one years to the same woman. Two kids, both attorneys. Total family net worth around six million dollars. The bulk of that was an inheritance from his wife's parents who died in an airplane crash on Martha's Vineyard ten years ago."

I pulled a sheet of paper from Skipper's stack and made some notes. "That sounds benign enough. Let's hear about the congressmen."

She clicked a few more keys. "Congressman David Solomon, age sixty-four from Nashville, Tennessee. He's on his second term and leans just left of center, politically. He's pro-choice but not a militant. Excellent health. Runs at least two marathons every year. He did twelve years in the Tennessee Air National Guard as a C-One-Thirty pilot. Left the National Guard after getting shot in the left hand in an undisclosed conflict with the rank of major. Married, no kids, wife is an OB-GYN."

Again, she looked up, and I gave her the signal to continue.

"Here's the one you've been waiting for. Congressman James 'Jimmy' Paige. Before you ask, no, not that Jimmy Paige. As far as I know, this one can't play the guitar, but he can run a campaign. He's from Pennsylvania and on his sixth term, sixty-six years old, on his second marriage, and is an insulin-dependent diabetic. He's also on blood thinners and thyroid medication. He weighs two hundred ninety pounds."

Mongo grunted. "Two-ninety isn't so big."

Skipper glared at him over the rim of her glasses. "It is when you're five foot seven."

"Ooh, yeah. I've got over a foot on him."

"Any questions before we move on?"

I raised a finger. "Has anyone spoken with his aide?"

Skipper looked back with confusion in her eyes. "His aid? What are you talking about?"

"If he's a diabetic, the aide probably knows more about his condition than his wife does. The aide will know how long he can live without the insulin."

Skipper's eyes lit up, and she scribbled on a pad beside her computer. "Brilliant. I'll get on that as soon as we wrap up here." Without giving us a window for more questions, she moved on. "Now, for Governor Laura Holcombe. She's thirty-eight, widowed, she leans further right than any of the other hostages, but that doesn't appear to be the reason she was nabbed. I think she, just like the congressmen, was an easy target. She's healthy, and by all indications, not in a romantic relationship."

"Children?" I asked.

"None."

Mongo cocked his head. "Tell us about the dead husband."

Skipper typed until the computer couldn't take any more. "I'm not finding much. That's weird."

Suddenly, Mongo's question had everyone's attention.

Skipper said, "He died in nineteen ninety-nine, and she ran for governor in two thousand. She won by eight percent, and by all indications, she's done a good job for the state of South Carolina."

The table fell silent for several seconds until Clark said, "It sounds like good ol' Jimmy Paige is the weakest link in the chain. I've not formed an opinion on the intellect of the kidnappers yet, but I doubt they want a hostage in a diabetic coma or worse."

"I have a theory," I said. "If they have a brain at all, they would've never chosen to kidnap a sixty-six-year-old diabetic. Taking him was, likely, a mistake of opportunity. I think he's the hostage we can most easily negotiate a release for."

Skipper pulled her glasses from her face. "What makes you think we're doing any of the negotiating? That's way outside our lane."

"Are the FBI negotiators on this one?"

She leaned back and thought about the question. "That's something we should probably know. I'm ashamed to say I don't have an answer, but I will soon."

I clapped my hands together and checked my watch. "I think we have enough to get started on the recon. Let's be wheels up in thirty minutes."

Hunter scratched his head. "Wheels up to where? And which wheels?"

Chapter 9
SEALs Are Great, But . . .

I had instantly become the center of attention. "What? Why is everybody looking at me?"

Clark said, "Probably because you seem to have a recon plan we haven't briefed. How about letting us in on the secret?"

"Maybe I'm oversimplifying things, but it makes sense to do some aerial recon and maybe get lucky spotting something that doesn't look right."

Hunter pointed toward our analyst. "Skipper said the calls came from Nassau. Aerial recon over a city of a quarter million people and tens of thousands of tourists probably isn't going to yield any meaningful intel."

I turned to Skipper. "That's not exactly what you said, is it?"

"No, I said I was convinced the calls originated in Nassau through an antiquated system."

I gave her the thumbs-up. "Exactly! And I just happen to know that there's a network of underwater communication cables connecting Eleuthera, Crooked Island, Long Island, Georgetown, Cat Island, San Salvador Island, and the West Side islands to Nassau."

Skipper nodded. "That's right, and Grand Bahama and Great Abaco are routed through Freeport via the new wireless system that's being constructed. Over the next ten years or so, all of The

Bahamas will be wireless, but for now, everything south of Bullock Harbour is still being run through underwater trunk lines."

Clark let out a sound like a wounded cat, and I couldn't resist chuckling.

"What was that about?"

He swallowed a drink of coffee. "I remember last time we messed with underwater trunk lines. That was way back in the day when it was just Chase and me . . . before the rest of you came on board."

"We really don't have to tell this story," I said.

"Oh no, I'm telling it. Me and College Boy were in Panama, southwest of the Miraflores Locks, looking for explosives on the trunk line connecting North and South America."

Hunter leaned in. "Did you find them?"

Clark laughed. "Oh, we found them, all right. In fact, your fearless leader let one blow him out of the water from about eighty feet. He was lucky to be alive. By the time I found him, he looked like a wadded-up glob of unbaked dough. Thank God there was a research ship loitering in the area skippered by an old crusty Agency guy named Stinnett. They had a recompression chamber and a decent doctor who put our hero back together, and we finished the mission. That wasn't the first time I pulled his butt out of a bear trap, but it was one of the scariest."

I held up a hand. "Okay, that's enough show-and-tell. Let's get back to The Bahamas."

Skipper said, "Wait a minute. Before we move on . . . That was the mission when I learned I wanted to be an analyst when I grew up."

I smiled. "Yep, that was the one. And I think I can speak for all of us when I say we're thankful to have you."

A round of agreement rose from the table until I tapped my pen against my coffee mug. "Back to business. What we know about the telephone system in The Bahamas leaves a lot of ground and even more water for us to cover. I think the best way to pull that off is with two airplanes and a helicopter."

Disco cleared his throat. "You'll have to forgive me, but I'm a little slow on the uptake. I'm not an international man of mystery like the rest of you. I'll fly anything you put me in, but what are we looking for out there?"

"That's where it gets interesting," I said. "There are only two ways to get to The Bahamas—boats and flying machines. Our Caravan qualifies as a combination of the two. We can prowl around in the chopper, the One-Eighty-Two, and the Caravan without attracting too much attention, but I need to know one more piece of information before we blast off." I turned to Clark.

"What?" he said.

"Who's in charge?"

"In charge of what?"

"The whole thing. Are we reporting to somebody, or are we autonomous?"

He clicked his tongue against his teeth. "That's still up in the air. As you know from last night's briefing, they've tasked a SEAL team to provide infil and exfil for us."

"SEALs are great," I said, "but they're not great at being subtle. If we're on our own, I think we can get this done without getting anybody hurt. Except maybe a few of the bad guys."

Clark grunted. "I don't know how willing they'll be to let us run amok."

"That's my question. Who are *they*?"

He chewed on his bottom lip for a moment. "Officially, we report to the Board, but this tasking came straight from the White House. Give me ten minutes in the ops center, and I'll have an answer for you. In the meantime, pre-flight the aircraft in case they give us—me—an answer we don't like."

I narrowed my gaze. "You used a lot of interesting pronouns in that sentence. I want to make sure I understand exactly what you're saying."

"Oh, you got it, College Boy."

While Skipper and Clark headed upstairs to the ops center, the rest of us piled into the microbus and set out for the airport.

Disco towed the chopper out of the hangar on its dolly behind the John Deere tractor, Hunter pulled the Cessna 182 out by hand, and I used the ancient airport tug to drag the Caravan out of her cave and into the sunlight.

Without interrupting each other, we conducted thorough preflight inspections on each of the aircraft. With everything perfectly airworthy, we sat on the Caravan's portside float, waiting for Clark's arrival.

Disco said, "You still didn't answer my question. What are you looking for out there?"

I sighed. "There's no singular definitive answer. We're looking for something that doesn't fit. If they're taking hostages from the east coast of Florida, they have to have an airplane or a boat. Any airplane can make the crossing to The Bahamas, but not every airplane can carry three hostages and their captors. Boats are a different story. The Gulf Stream isn't exactly gentle with wind out of the north, so if they're using a boat, it's a boat big enough to handle the seas and carry a payload."

"So, we're looking for big boats and big airplanes that don't look like they belong in The Bahamas. Is that right?"

"As vague as that sounds, that's pretty much what we're looking for. It's irrational to believe they'd land at a real airport and move three hostages from an airplane into a van or SUV. There's too much opportunity to get busted. That leads me to believe they have a seaplane or a fast boat."

He nodded. "You're against the SEAL escort, aren't you?"

"It's not an escort. They believe that they are our primary means of egress and exfiltration. We've built this team around the concept of being autonomous. The more people we get involved, the less likely it is that we'll complete the mission successfully."

Disco made a face as if uncomfortable.

"Say it. Whatever it is, I need to know what's going on inside your head."

He grunted. "I'm not trying to be argumentative, but our last mission was exactly the opposite of autonomous. Earl's magic container and Kenny's truck got us in, and the Navy got us out."

"There's something I need you to understand, Disco . . ."

He swallowed hard.

"We're a team, and every thought, opinion, idea, fear, and concern have to be group knowledge. Never—and I mean absolutely never—keep quiet when you have something on your mind. You're right about the last mission. We would've lost Singer's arm and maybe our lives if the Navy hadn't been involved. They delivered the explosives we needed, and they gave us a ride out of there."

Disco looked relieved. "I thought you were going to give me a lecture about when to shut my mouth."

"I don't give lectures. Surely you've learned that by now. We're a team, and everybody's ideas are valuable, but here's why I think being autonomous is best on this mission. The SEALs show up in boats like our Mark V and helicopters that are undeniably military. I've not been privy to the phone calls, but I'm sure the kidnappers are demanding no police or military involvement. We don't know how willing they are to kill a hostage, but they're bold enough to snatch three of them off the beach in broad daylight, so I have to believe they're committed. If we can get in and out, especially in the recon phase, without drawing attention to ourselves, we'll be a lot safer, and more importantly, we won't risk the lives of the hostages."

Hunter nodded. "I agree. If we show up, even in a SEAL small boat, we're going to get a lot of attention. What do you think Clark's doing?"

I said, "I think he's listening to a set of orders we're going to ignore."

Almost before I'd finished my sentence, Clark pulled up to the hangar. He stepped from his Suburban and made circular motions with his index finger above his head, signaling us to go to work.

I slid down from the float and turned into the operational commander. "Hunter, you put the Caravan on the dock at Bonaventure. The rest of us will meet you there."

Hunter looked bewildered. "By myself?"

"It's a two-minute flight. I don't think you'll get lost."

He shook his head. "No, I mean, you've never let me fly it solo."

I waved him off. "Last time you flew it, you crashed into the river in Montana. I'm not getting back in that thing with you."

The rest of the team piled into Clark's Suburban and headed for the Bonaventure armory. We pulled the weapons we thought we'd need and twice the ammo we guessed.

I secretly crept to the corner of the house and watched Hunter glide the Caravan onto the North River as gently as a baby's kiss.

Clark whispered from behind me. "I like what you did there."

I looked back at him. "What are you talking about?"

"Hunter needs to know you've got faith in him, and you just proved that you do."

We jogged to the dock to help tie up the Caravan, and Mongo drove the gator loaded with arms and ammo down the yard.

Hunter shut down the Pratt and Whitney turbine and climbed down from the cockpit.

I tossed a backpack to him. "That was a lot better than your last so-called water landing."

He rolled his eyes and caught the pack. "What's this?"

"Groceries for you and Singer. I'm sending him with you in the One-Eighty-Two, and I know you guys like to snack."

He unzipped the bag and peeked inside. "Well done. Good looking out."

Clark looked up. "Do I get a goody bag?"

"Of course. I wouldn't leave you out. I want you and Disco to bring the chopper down. Are you okay with that?"

"Sure. I guess that leaves Mongo with you, huh?"

"Yeah. I thought I'd let him get a little stick time on the way down."

"Are you going to teach him to fly?"

"I'd like for all of us to have at least the skill, if not the license."

"Agreed. Perhaps we'll have some time off when we clean up this mission, and you can get Mongo started. I'd like to take the One-Eighty-Two down to Miami at some point to get Maebelle a few hours at the controls."

"It's yours anytime you want it. I thought about starting Mongo in the chopper, anyway. It'll be a tight fit for him in the front of the Skylane."

Clark checked his watch. "We can work all that out later. Let's get underway."

"Good plan," I said. "We'll rendezvous at the Ocean Reef Club Airport on North Largo."

Chapter 10
Lead Dog

The string of islands lazily stretching their way to the southwest, delineating the Gulf of Mexico and the Caribbean Sea, came into view.

The giant beside me with his hands on the controls of the Caravan sighed. "You know, I've been all over the world doing things nobody will ever know about, but some of the most beautiful sights I've ever seen have been right here in the States."

I followed his gaze through the windshield. "I couldn't agree more. That turquoise water and those green islands look like they were made to be together."

He disengaged the autopilot and let the big airplane begin her descent into the airport at the Ocean Reef Club. "Have you ever been into this airport before?"

I nodded, remembering Hank, the airport manager, who'd flown with Doctor Richter during what he called "the war." The sly old dog had a way of stealing the attention of every woman I'd ever brought onto his little strip of concrete at the top of the Keys.

"I've been here a couple of times. In fact, part of the first real mission I ever worked took place in that marina just over there."

Mongo said, "That was the Cuban thing, right?"

"I guess you never forget your first, huh?"

He seemed to let himself drift back in time. "No, some things are impossible to forget. My first gig after I got my Green Beret was in Panama in December of eighty-nine. It was my first combat jump—the first time I ever shot a man. In fact, I earned my first bullet hole and my first Purple Heart on Christmas Day."

"Your *first* bullet hole? How many do you have?"

He sent his eyes searching the headliner of the Caravan. "I don't know. Maybe eight or ten. How about you?"

"Just one. But that's one too many."

He chuckled. "You're still young. You'll hit double digits if you live long enough. It's all part of the gig."

"I'm not looking forward to the next ones."

"Neither am I, my friend, but if they happen, I can't think of a team I'd rather be with when they do."

He studied the landscape beneath us and scanned for other airborne traffic. "If you don't mind, I'd like to fly the approach."

"As long as it's nice and stable, I'll stay off the controls until touchdown. Just remember to put the gear down and land it flat. Don't pitch up like we do in the Skylane."

He danced with the controls and power settings until we were perfectly aligned with runway 23.

"You're doing fine," I said. "Just fly her right onto the runway. I'm going to follow you through the controls in case we get a gust near the ground."

Never taking his eyes off the approach, he gave me a nod as we lumbered down the final approach leg.

From my seat on the right side of the cockpit, I watched a low-wing airplane taxi toward the runway. Uncertain of his intentions, I keyed my mic. "Ocean Reef traffic, Caravan two-zero-eight-Charlie-Foxtrot is short final, full stop, runway two-three, Ocean Reef."

The airport didn't have enough traffic to justify a control tower, so the pilots relied on each other to announce their positions and intentions in the traffic pattern.

Mongo apparently noticed the airplane, as well. "What's he going to do?"

"I don't know, but if he—"

Before I could finish my sentence, the pilot taxied onto the runway and aligned himself with the centerline of the forty-four-hundred-foot strip of asphalt.

Without allowing the anger I felt creep into my tone, I said, "Let's go around. Sidestep to the left, power up, pitch up, pick up in that order."

I could see Mongo's wheels turning inside his head as he followed my instructions. His massive hand pressed the throttle full forward to stop our descent. As our speed increased and our descent rate decreased, he eased the yoke back to bring the nose above the horizon. With the Caravan climbing parallel to the runway, he pulled the landing gear up as I keyed my mic again.

"Ocean Reef traffic, Caravan eight-Charlie-Fox is going around left of runway two-three for unannounced departing traffic."

I hoped the pilot, still on the ground, could hear my displeasure with his decision to pull onto the runway in front of us, but he made no radio calls and seemed oblivious to our presence.

Mongo flew the pattern as I watched the other plane take off and turn to the west.

Mongo said, "What was that guy thinking?"

"Who knows? It's an uncontrolled airport, so he didn't break any laws, but sometimes, being stupid should be against the law."

With the other airplane out of the way, Mongo greased the landing as if he'd done it all his life, and we taxied to the ramp.

As we climbed down from the cockpit, Hank ambled across the parking ramp toward us. He shielded his eyes against the sun with one hand while clutching his pipe with the other. "Is that you, Chase?"

I waved and picked up my pace. "How's it going, Hank?"

"I'll be darned. It is you. How've you been, boy? And more importantly, where's that North Texas pretty gal of yours?"

"She's in L.A. She's a big-time screenwriter now."

He stuck the stem of his pipe into his mouth. "If you ask me, she ought to be in *front* of the camera. Between her and that Russian girl you used to run around with, you've done more living in thirty years than most of us old horndogs do in a lifetime."

I gave him an elbow shot. "You're not fooling anybody, Hank. Something tells me there's a trail of broken hearts behind you all over the world."

He held up his hands. "What can I say? Some of us have the touch. Who's that behemoth you brought with you?"

"Hank, meet Mongo. Mongo, this is Hank. He flew with Doctor Richter in the good ol' days."

Hank stuck his hand into Mongo's dinner-plate-sized palm. "Nice to meet you, Mongo. Richter and me done a lot more than just flying together, and the so-called good ol' days ain't nearly as good as we like to pretend they were."

Mongo said, "It's nice to meet you, too. I'll bet you've got some stories."

Hank waved a hand. "Aww, you wouldn't believe them if I told you. What brings you boys to the island? You going to do some diving?"

"Unfortunately," I said, "this isn't a pleasure trip. We're on the clock. In fact, there will be two more stragglers behind us. The first one will be a One-Eighty-Two-RG, and a Bell Four-Twelve will bring up the rear."

Hank motioned toward the Caravan. "None of those horses are thoroughbreds, but I see you came in the least slow of the bunch."

"You know what they say . . . If you're not the lead sled dog, the scenery never changes."

"Ain't that the truth. So, is this a gas-and-go, or will you be staying on the island overnight?"

I checked my watch. "That depends on how the rest of the team feels when they get in, but I'd like to go to work if the flight down here didn't suck the sap out of them."

Hank glanced over each shoulder. "What kind of trouble are you getting into, Chase? It's been a lot of years since I strapped on a six-shooter and went gunslinging, but if you can tell me, I'd love to know whose tail you're headed out to kick."

"It's just recon, I'm afraid. Nothing exciting."

Hank closed one eye and squinted against the sun. "You wouldn't lie to an old man, would you?"

"I would, but in this case, I don't have to. We're really just doing recon out on the bank."

"The bank, you say? That wouldn't have anything to do with that missing judge, would it?"

I lowered my gaze. "What do you know about a missing judge?"

He took a draw from his pipe. "I haven't been out of the game so long that I don't still have a grapevine or two. An old man still hears things."

I glanced at Mongo, then back to Hank. "I'm not saying you're right, but if you happen to hear anything through those grapevines of yours that might make our job a little easier, I'd love to hear it."

"I doubt I'll hear anything you don't already know, son, but if I do, I'll pass it along. If you've not already made arrangements out on the Bahama Bank, I just happen to know of a little airport tucked away on Andros and a shack that'll keep the rain off your head."

"You don't say. Where might a fellow find this airport and shack of yours?"

He pulled the pipe from his mouth. "I can't claim the airport to be mine. It's Nicholls Town on North Andros. They've got enough runway—such as it is—to handle anything you'll put on it, and the little house is about half a mile south on Queens Highway. It's all yours if you think you can use it."

I watched the smile grow on Mongo's face.

I said, "I'll rent the place from you, Hank, but I'm not going to use it for free. You've done too much for me over the years, and I'm not going to take advantage of your generosity."

He waved me off. "Don't be ridiculous, Chase. You were practically a son to the best friend I ever had. By my figuring, that makes you and me darn-near family. Take a look at the place and see if you can use it. If you can, we'll work out a deal of some kind. The house belonged to my brother, and he was, well, I'll put it like it is . . . He was a bit of a scallywag, but he managed to stay out of prison most of his life. When he passed on, I inherited the house. I've been trying to sell the place, but it needs a lot more work than I can do, and it's hard to find a contractor a man can trust on the island."

The sight of an island bungalow crumbling into the sand filled my head, but I said, "Thank you, Hank. We'll take a look. And who knows? I might want to own a place on Andros, and I just happen to have a good contractor who likes to travel."

Hank laid a hand on my shoulder. "If you want the place, I'll make you a real deal on it. It'd do my heart good to know it's going to the good guys."

"Speaking of good guys and bad guys, who was that jackass taking off while we were trying to land?"

"Was it a red and white Saratoga?"

"Yes. It was a nice airplane, but I can't say the same about its operator."

Hank chuckled. "He's a real estate broker who made a little money and thinks he owns the world. We get a few of them around here every year, but it never fails. Their newfound money runs out before their ego does, and we end up selling another house in a bankruptcy auction, and the airplanes always seem to vanish into thin air."

Chapter 11
Crime Statistics

The rest of the team arrived without anyone pulling onto the runway in front of them, and we wandered from the FBO and onto the ramp.

Hunter stepped from the 182 and kicked a chock beneath the nose gear.

"How was the flight?" I asked.

"Interesting," he said. "Clark and Disco wanted to practice formation flying, and that's a skill you haven't taught me yet."

"There's nothing to it when you're the lead ship."

"You've got that right," he said, "but trying to hold speed behind a helicopter sucks."

Clark and Disco ambled up, and I said, "I hear you're teaching formation flight now."

Clark pointed back toward the helicopter. "Yeah, Hunter did fine, but the autopilot in the chopper is misbehaving. It's commanding random turns every few minutes, so we had to hand-fly the thing all the way down here."

"That doesn't sound like much fun," I said. "Maybe Hank knows a good technician. We can live without an autopilot for a while, but if there's something else going on behind the panel that's causing the problem, I'd like to get it resolved before we strike out over a hundred fifty miles of open water."

Disco said, "I've been troubleshooting for the last hundred miles, and I can't find a failure anywhere except with the autopilot, but I agree . . . We need a pair of qualified eyes to look it over."

Hank came around the corner of the terminal building in the fuel truck and headed for the 182. I flagged him down, and he rolled down the window. "I know! The Cessna takes avgas, and the chopper drinks jet fuel."

I said, "I wasn't afraid of you putting the wrong fuel in. I trust you, but we need an avionics tech. The chopper's autopilot is acting up."

He pointed toward the door of the terminal. "Go in there, and look under the plexiglass on my desk. You'll see a card for a guy named Sam. You won't be able to pronounce his last name, so I don't recommend trying. Give him a call. He's up in Miami, but he'll come down here if you want to pay him. It's cheaper to fly it back up there to him, though."

I ran a hand through my hair, and Hank picked up on my frustration. He said, "How about you leave it here with me, and I'll take care of it for you while the rest of you go play looky-loo in the Cessnas?"

"If you're sure it's not too much trouble, that would be a lifesaver."

He scoffed. "No trouble at all. I'll top off the tanks and get you the keys for the house on Andros. Just have your chopper driver write down the symptoms, and I'll get Sam on it right away."

Everyone made use of the facilities, and I briefed the new situation. "We'll leave the chopper with Hank, and he'll have his man take a look at the autopilot. The rest of us will shoot over the Gulf Stream. Hank has a vacant house on Andros a half a mile from the airport. We'll hop over and get some rest tonight before we start prowling around tomorrow morning."

Clark said, "Sounds good to me, but I think we should do the crossing together."

I nodded. "I agree. We'll pull the power back a little so Hunter can keep up. There's no need to fly close formation. Just keep the Caravan in sight. If something goes wrong, we'll all be together, and we can fish you out of the drink if you try to pull a Bermuda Triangle on us."

Hunter shook his head. "That's great if I'm the one who goes in the water, but what am I supposed to do if you go down?"

"Circle overhead and call the Coast Guard," Disco said. "In fact, I'll go with you, and we can work on formation flight and a few other little things." He turned to me. "You're okay flying lead, aren't you?"

"Sure. We'll plan for a hundred thirty knots. That'll be a comfortable speed for the One-Eighty-Two."

"One thirty sounds great, and we'll stay in comms on one twenty-three forty-five."

I left a credit card with Hank. "Fix whatever is wrong with it, and if it can't be fixed, make the replacement an upgrade. In fact, have Sam price a full panel upgrade. The radios are original."

"I'll get on it this afternoon. Are you sure you boys don't need an extra trigger puller on this one?"

I laughed. "We won't be pulling any triggers on this run, but we may take you up on that offer when things get hairy . . . and they always get hairy sooner or later."

We blasted off and joined up in a two-ship formation as soon as we leveled off at eleven thousand five hundred feet. Altitude is the cheapest insurance you can buy on an ocean crossing. The higher we are, the farther we can glide when pieces start falling off the airplane.

The airport on North Andros came into sight seventy-five minutes later, and we landed without incident.

I gave Hunter a slug on the arm. "It looks like you mastered formation flight."

"Most of that was Disco, but I'm getting the hang of it. Another thousand hours, and I'll be able to follow you without slamming into you."

Clark handled customs without an inspection of our cargo, and we got a pair of taxis to take us to Hank's house just south of the airport. What he had called "a shack to keep the rain off our heads" turned out to be a five-bedroom vacation dream home with a few missing shingles and in dire need of several gallons of paint.

We waded through the vegetation that had once been landscape and made our way inside. The property was dated and in need of an upgrade, but there was no evidence of water getting in. A decent contractor could have the place looking like a palace in a few days.

I pulled Clark aside. "What do you think of this place?"

He surveyed the surroundings. "It looks like nineteen eighty came here to die, but it could be a nice place with a little love."

"What do you think it's worth?"

He shrugged. "I don't know. Why? Is it for sale?"

"It is, and I wouldn't mind owning a place here. The airport is convenient, and the beach is just a couple of miles away."

He gave me a wink. "It's your money, Daddy Warbucks. Do what you want with it, but I think I'd rather have something on the water."

San Andros proved to be a fine island town. Pizza delivery was fast and fresh, and the local constabulary proved to be more efficient than expected. A knock on the door only twenty minutes after we arrived surprised me, but it turned out to be one of the three police officers in town.

"I jus' be makin' sure ain' nobody goin' inside empty house dat ain' s'pose be in here."

His island patois flowed, and the shine on his shoes was enough to blind a man in the sunshine.

"We're friends of Hank's," I said.

"Oh, yeah. Hank be da owner from over in da Keys. He be da airplane guy, right?"

"That's him. I'm considering buying the place. Can you think of any reason I wouldn't want the house?"

He removed his hat and peered through the door.

"Come inside if you'd like."

He stepped inside and took in the space. "I never been inside before, but it sure be better than da house I lives in."

"So, is there anything about the island I should know, like crime stats and things like that?"

"You gots childrens?"

"No, just a wife and some good friends."

"In dat case, ain' no reason not to be buyin' da house. Day ain' no good school here, but if you ain' gots no kids, dat don' matter. Day ain' no crime on da island other den what da tourist peoples do, and dat ain' nothin' to be worryin' 'bout."

We ate our pizza and explored every nook and cranny of the house before hitting the sack for a much-needed night's rest.

* * *

Sunrise came in conjunction with another unexpected knock on the door. To my surprise, the constable from the night before stood on the welcome mat beside a woman wearing an enormous muumuu and holding a basket of pastries.

The officer said, "I'm sorry to botha you, but dis is my wife, and she make a big bunch of tings for you and your friends to say welcome to da islan'."

I invited them in and set the basket on the kitchen counter. They explored the room with their eyes and whispered to each other in a dialect I'd never understand.

Finally, the officer nodded to his wife.

She said, "You eat dem goodies I makes for you, and if you likes 'em, I clean and paint better than I bake. Jus' 'member dat when you buy dis here place."

I thanked them for the pastries and promised to call if we needed the house cleaned and painted. The early morning visit turned out to be the least surprising element of my morning.

Clark came down the stairs with his phone pressed to his ear and a rare look of concern on his face.

"What's going on?" I mouthed.

He said, "Hang on a minute, Skipper. I'm putting you on speaker." He covered the mouthpiece and locked eyes with me. "Wake 'em up, Chase. This is serious."

Chapter 12
Too Far

I ran through the house sounding reveille. "Get up, guys! We've got news, and Skipper's on the phone."

Bedroom doors opened, and my team of groggy warriors dragged themselves to the living room. I slid the basket of pastries onto the center table and started the coffee pot.

Clark said, "Okay, Skipper. Let's have it."

The sound of rustling papers poured from the phone's speaker. "They've turned up the clock," she said. "A third demand call came in this morning, but this time, it didn't ring in the station chief's office in Nassau. This one rang in the White House situation room."

"How did they get that number?" Clark blurted out.

"It doesn't matter how they got it. The fact is, they're more connected than we thought. They have access like no one has ever seen, but that's not the pressing issue."

Clark huffed. "Maybe not, but it certainly changes the game. If they can ring the president's phone, they're in a whole different league of bad guys."

"We'll deal with that in a minute," she said. "For now, you need to know the new timetable."

More rustling of paper sounded. "Forgive my disorganization, but things are happening a lot faster than I expected. Okay, here it is. I've got the audio of the call, so instead of telling you about it, just listen."

She stroked a few keys, and the audio played.

A no-nonsense voice said, "Lieutenant Bell."

An instant later, a non-descript voice spoke in calm, unaccented English. "You will listen without interruption, or at least one of our guests will die. By now, you have a small idea of what we are capable of doing. We've taken one Supreme Court justice from right beneath your noses. We will admit that was slightly more challenging than the three politicians we have now added to our guest list. For every day that passes without one hundred percent of our demands being met, the body of at least one of our guests will be delivered to your door, and we will add one additional demand to your requirements."

The voice paused as if the statement was finished but soon filled the speaker again. "Today's demand is to halt trading on the New York Stock Exchange. You will not ring the bell on Wall Street this morning. If you do, we will select a guest at random, and you will be responsible for that person's death. His—or her—blood will be on your hands, Mr. President."

The chilling message sent lightning bolts down my spine, and I quivered where I sat.

Lieutenant Bell's voice sounded. "Sir, I have no authority to negotiate with you—"

"You have not been listening, Lieutenant. There will be no negotiations. Our demands, as well as our resolve, are inflexible. If the opening bell sounds on Wall Street, one of your beloved elites will perish. Now, be a good little boy and pass this information to your superiors. I am confident you will have no trouble locating a superior, as everyone in that city believes himself superior to every-one else."

The line clicked, and Skipper's voice filled the air. "What do you think?"

Clark said, "I think we're dealing with—"

Skipper interrupted. "I wasn't talking to you, Clark. What does Chase think?"

I swallowed the lump in my throat. "I first thought it was a recording, but the interaction with Lieutenant Bell quashed that idea."

"That's not what I want to know, Chase. Tell me what you heard."

I said, "Play it again."

I let the voice consume me as I held my eyes closed and listened to every syllable. The confidence in the caller's voice reminded me of how I'd felt sitting in the passenger's seat of the car in Los Angeles with the thief trembling beside me. He was powerless to harm me. I held all the cards, leaving him completely the victim of my will and mercy—a trait I doubted the terrorists possessed.

When the audio stopped, silence filled the room, and I opened my eyes. "I hear supreme confidence. These people aren't bluffing. They hold the mightiest country on Earth in the palm of their hands, and they're not going to back down."

Skipper let my words hang in the air for a long moment before saying, "I was afraid that's what you'd hear. I don't like the way that makes me feel, and worse than that, I don't like having no idea what to do to stop them."

I spoke barely above a whisper. "Stopping them requires killing them . . . All of them. Anything short of that will not end this situation. Have you heard from Wall Street?"

"No, but there's no way the president will let the exchange open, right?"

"I don't know. I have no idea how any of that works or even if the president has the authority to close the stock market."

"I know you'll be surprised, but I've done the research, and the president *does* have the authority to close the New York Stock Exchange. It's happened several times before, but I wonder if he'll do it this time."

"If he doesn't, they'll kill a hostage."

"Are you going to call him?"

"No, he wouldn't take my call anyway. I'm going to do the only thing I can. I'm going to find these animals, and we're going to make them regret the day they drew their first breath."

She let my threat hang in the air before saying, "Be careful, Chase. These people are dangerous. If all they truly want is money, it's not worth your lives to stop them."

"We're going to catch them. We have no choice. It's not about making these people pay. It's about making the next people think twice before they start kidnapping Americans and making demands."

"There's more. The National Reconnaissance Office and Defense Intelligence has tasked a fleet of satellites and at least fifty analysts. We've got a huge team on this now, and with that many eyes studying the photos, something will turn up."

"Who's running the team? Is it NRO or DIA?"

"I don't know, but why does that matter?" she asked.

"Do you know where they're working?"

"No, I didn't ask, but again, why is that important?"

I scratched my chin. "It's important because the more links there are in the chain, the more likely it is that at least one of those links is a lot weaker than the others."

She groaned. "I get that, but there's nothing we can do about that. We're just one of the links."

"That's what concerns me. We'll be airborne in half an hour, and maybe we can resolve this thing before the government turns it into a self-eating monster. Where are the SEALs?"

"Mayport."

Clark gave me a nod, and I said, "Good. Keep them there as long as possible . . . Wait! I've got an idea."

I paused to let the plan play out in my head, and the world around me turned silent until Clark said, "Let's hear it, Chase."

I held up a finger. "It's not a fully developed plan yet. It's just an idea. Skipper, can you pick a place where we know for sure the hostages are *not* being held?"

She stammered. "I'm not following. What do you mean?"

"I want to create a diversion that will, hopefully, inflate their ego enough to cause them to make a mistake."

"You're not making any sense. What are you talking about?"

"I'm talking about having the SEALs storm the wrong beach."

The light came on for Clark an instant before Skipper put it together. "That's brilliant, College Boy, but how do we do it?"

I said, "I've got an idea, but it's going to require Master Chief Lewis to be on the inside with us. He did say he's been a SEAL for twenty years, right?"

Clark nodded. "That's what he said."

I leaned back and allowed the crazy idea to bloom in my head. "Do you know anyone who knows Lewis well?"

Clark said, "I could ask around, but those SEALs are a tight-knit bunch. They're not quick to let anybody else in—Green Beret or not."

"We just need these guys to relax enough to say or do something that'll give us the key to the castle."

"I like it," Clark said, "but there's still one wildcard out there."

"What's the wildcard?"

"The Ambassador. If he's in on the scheme—"

Skipper spoke up. "I don't think he's in on it. I think he's running."

"It's possible," Clark said, "but it's also possible that his disappearance is a diversion and an attempt at misdirection. If he's in on it, the kidnappers know we're in the game, and I don't like that."

I bounced a pencil off my knuckles as my brain churned inside my skull. "So, what we really need to know is whether the ambassador is a player or a victim."

Skipper said, "I think he was a player in the early days and lost his nerve. Now I think he's scared and on the run."

"That's possible," I said, "but these people are at least as smart as we are, and probably smarter. If the ambassador running is all part of the game, that changes everything."

Clark said, "I think your plan to have the SEALs attack the wrong target is solid, no matter what part the ambassador is playing in the whole ordeal. Even if he's still inside and knows we're in play, it's unlikely that he knows the SEALs have been tasked to work with us. I think it works no matter what the truth is surrounding the ambassador."

Skipper said, "I don't know. This could backfire, and it could be disastrous. What if they use the attack—even in the wrong place—as a reason to kill a hostage?"

It was time to put my education to work. Having spent four years at the University of Georgia studying the human psyche, I'd learned a few party tricks to get unsuspecting victims to spit out the truth as they believed it to be. Most of those techniques worked best when the victim was hungover, tired, or in pain. Skipper was working on her third day without sleep. No one, not even a brilliant analyst like her, could function at their peak without sufficient rest. I was going to take advantage of my analyst's selfless devotion to duty, and nothing about it made me feel good.

"Skipper, tell me where they can't be."

"There's no way I can do that. I believe they're somewhere in The Bahamas."

"I don't care where they *are*. I want to know where they *aren't*. I think we're going to need another set of eyes on this. Should we call in Ginger?"

"What?" she demanded. "What do you mean, a fresh pair of eyes?"

Although it drove a sword through my heart to do it, I said, "I need an analyst who can do better than guessing where they might be when all I need is one island where they cannot be. If you can't do it, my next call will be to Ginger."

I could almost feel the steam rising from Skipper. "If you think Ginger can do a better job than me, you go right ahead and call her. It'll take her at least a week to get up to speed. By that time, you'll have four dead hostages and God only knows how many new ones. It'll cost human lives, and those lives will be your responsibility, Chase Fulton."

"Then tell me where they're not. Just give me a name!"

My team wore masks of disbelief as I tore into a woman I loved as if she were my own sister—a woman who'd mastered a skill set only an elite few could fathom, let alone accomplish.

"Fine!" she roared. "They can't be on Conception Island. It's uninhabited and protected as a national park for some damned sea bird and stupid rare species of boa constrictor. There! Does that make you happy? They can't be there!"

Hearing and feeling her anger broke my heart. "Skipper, I'm sorry. I shouldn't have done that, but we're getting desperate. I would never call in another analyst for any reason. I'm truly sorry I had to push you like that, but I needed a stage for my performance. It's the only way we're ever going to find them."

"Damn you, Chase!"

"Get some rest, Skipper. I would've never been able to push you far enough to explode if you were rested. I'm sincerely sorry, but I had no other choice. Please get some rest."

The line went dead, and I looked up into five faces of men who would follow me into Hell if I asked them to, but their pained expressions said I'd gone too far.

Chapter 13
The Number

Singer, one of the world's deadliest and most feared snipers, stood, stared down at me, and said, "Let's go for a walk."

I suddenly felt like a child who'd disappointed his father. I couldn't think of anything I wanted to do less than take a walk with the sniper who was the godliest man I would ever know. Hearing the sadness in his voice sickened me and left me wishing I could erase the previous five minutes of my life.

Like that scolded child, I stood and followed my friend and moral compass. Our walk ended less than ten feet from the front door. He stopped, sat on the top step of the failing stairs, and patted the spot beside him. I knew if I took the seat, what followed would be a universal truth and life lesson about how badly I'd strayed from the path I should be walking. But sometimes, what we think we know is the furthest possible thing from the reality that is staring directly into our blinded eyes.

I took the seat and stilled myself for the rebuke to come, but instead, Singer put a hand on my shoulder. "I've never seen anyone more focused on accomplishing a mission than you, and I envy and admire that ability. So few men have that drive and singular purpose. The Apostle Paul had it after his conversion on the road to Damascus. Everything in his life changed in an instant, and he became a warrior for our God, a man of ordained purpose, motivated by nothing other than direction from above. Other than Jesus himself, the Apostle Paul likely changed more lives than any single person in the history of the world. He did it because that was his calling, the sole reason he'd been born into this world. Do you ever feel like that, Chase?"

I studied his words and tried to apply them to my life—to my existence—but I fell short. "No, I've never felt like that. I've never known how it feels to be driven entirely by the source of all goodness. What we do is ugly, Singer, but it is necessary."

He grimaced and held up his right index finger. "Do you see this finger?" He touched his cheek. "And this eye?" He curled his finger, examining it as if he'd never seen it before. "Since I was eighteen years old, I've made my living with this eye and this finger. For some reason, I have a talent for finding targets with this eye and destroying them with this finger . . . my trigger finger. It's all I've ever known. It's what I know, and it's what I have. I can't fly an airplane like the rest of you can. I can't plan an operation like Clark. I can't swim or fight like Hunter. All I can really do is erase men's lives."

I wanted so badly to understand where he was leading me, but I was lost, so I sat in silence, waiting for him to continue.

Finally, he did. "We all have our own versions of this eye and this finger, Chase. Yours is invisible, though. The whole world can see my finger, but yours is behind those eyes. It's the ability to reach inside another man's head and twist and turn and push and pull until you've driven him to the brink of madness. We all have our gifts, our talents, our own brand of magic. Some of our skills are far more powerful than others. Take mine, for example. I have the skill to take a man's life from two miles away. He'll never hear the crack of my rifle because my bullet travels almost three times faster than the sound of the powder exploding. How many lives have I saved by taking the life of another man serving beneath another flag?"

He shrugged, and I continued to listen.

"Who knows? Maybe thousands, or maybe only a few. Snipers almost always keep their magic number someplace safe. They don't brag about the number of kills they've had, but they all know the number, even though they rarely say it out loud. To me, that number doesn't matter. The only number that truly matters, the number that demonstrates precisely which team I'm on, is the number of times I've turned around and fired back at the people I'm supposed to be protecting. How many shots has this finger sent toward my teammates, toward my countrymen, toward the people I love? That number is zero, and that's the only number I treasure in this terrible road I've been charged to walk."

He pressed his lips into a thin, horizontal line and laid his deadly finger against my forehead. "Don't turn your weapon on your team . . . on your family. That's not why you were given the intellect you have. That was a gift, Chase. Use it in a manner that would make your father proud—your earthly father who left you far too early, and"—he turned his eyes skyward—"and the Father you'll have to answer to when you leave this world."

I sat in silent awe of the wisdom my friend and brother-in-arms possessed, and I wondered if I would ever see the world with such clarity. How could a man who poured soul-chilling horror onto every battlefield he claimed be at such peace with himself, with the world around him, and with his Creator?

I left Jimmy "Singer" Grossmann sitting alone on the dilapidated stairs, talking to his god like an old friend, and I returned to my team, my family, and apologized for what I'd done.

In true Clark Johnson style, my handler took me by the shoulders and stared into my eyes. "Don't be sorry, College Boy. Be better."

I pulled my phone from my pocket and began dialing Skipper's number, but Mongo's massive hand covered mine. I looked up, and he said, "Not now."

* * *

At the airport, we found both Cessnas—the 208 Caravan and the 182 Skylane—fully fueled and ready for whatever lay ahead. The two golden rules of aviation, never pass up a bathroom or a free cup of coffee, sent my team inside the operations building, where they found no free coffee, but they did find a bathroom that had, perhaps, once had a door sometime in the distant past.

The second discovery inside airport operations was a black-and-white television set tuned to a 24–hour news channel.

The anchorman said, "In a decision described as necessary for national security, the president of the United States exercised his ability to cancel trading on the New York Stock Exchange today. For the first time since September eleventh, two thousand one, following the attacks on the World Trade Center Twin Towers in New York City, there will be no trading today."

The half-asleep Bahamian behind the counter ignored the television, but my team breathed a collective sigh of relief.

On the walk back to the airplanes, I said, "Let's fly the perimeter of Andros today in two teams of three. I'll take Singer and Mongo with me in the Caravan. Clark, Hunter, and Disco, I want the three of you to fly the counterclockwise route, and we'll head north on the clockwise route. The perimeter is around three hundred miles, so we should meet on the southeast end of the islands around Little Creek Settlement. From there, we'll fly the interior, looking for shallow draft boats or floatplanes on the waterways dissecting the islands of Central Andros. We'll be too far apart for radio comms most of the route, so use your sat phones if you spot anything that looks out of place. Any questions?"

None came, so we climbed aboard and began our startup check-lists. Before I'd spun the turbine, my phone chimed, and I looked down to see Skipper's number on the screen. I tossed the checklist onto the panel and pressed the green button. "Hey, Skipper."

She wasted no time with pleasantries. "Listen to me, Chase. It doesn't make it right or even okay, but I understand why you did what you did. You already apologized, so I don't want you to do that again. What I do want is a promise from you that you'll never speak to me like that again."

I swallowed hard. "I'm sorry, and it will never happen again under any circumstances."

"Okay, then it's behind us. I'm going to get a couple hours of sleep, but I have two things to tell you. First, the president closed the stock exchange for the day. Second, Chief Lewis will meet you at the Nicholls Town airport at three this afternoon. He'll be alone, and he knows what to expect."

Before I could respond, the line went dead, and I pocketed the phone. As I spun up the turbine and introduced the fuel, the other half of my team in the 182 took off and turned south. We were only minutes behind them and began our clockwise pattern.

When people think of The Bahamas, most of them think of Nassau or Freeport—the two most common Bahamian cruise ship stops. But judging the island group by those two cities is like view-ing the entirety of the United States as New York and Los Angeles. The overwhelming majority of the Bahamian geography is breath-taking, unspoiled beaches, and unbelievably blue, shallow water. Since the abolition of slavery in The Bahamas in 1834, the over-whelming majority of the population has consisted of freed slaves and their descendants. Looking down upon the spectacular scenery from five hundred feet made it difficult to believe something as sinister as the kidnapping of prominent American citizens could be a reality in the subtropical paradise.

I glanced over my shoulder. "Let's run the camera. It might see something we miss."

Mongo made his way to the back of the cabin and brought the camera system online. "Okay, it's up and running, but we've only got three memory cards on board. That won't cover the whole island."

"We don't need it to," I said. "We're only flying half the perimeter and then one track up the interior."

"We might have enough storage, but it'll be close."

While I flew the airplane, Singer, our wounded sniper, Mongo, and our camera scoured the landscape below.

Singer pulled his microphone to his lips. "It sure is beautiful down there, but I'm still not sure what we're looking for."

"I'm not either," I said, "but based on geography, if the kidnappers grabbed their hostages and ran to The Bahamas, this is the most likely place they'd land. They've got to have a relatively big boat or seaplane. I just don't think they'd take the chance of being seen at an airport. Based on that assumption, we're looking for a boat or seaplane that looks out of place."

Mongo spoke without taking his eyes from the beaches below. "What if they have a yacht—a big one—where they're holding the hostages? A boat like that wouldn't look out of place anchored out or even tied up in a marina."

"I hadn't considered that," I said. "I guess it's reasonable to suspect these guys are well funded and could have such a vessel."

The suite of electronics in the Caravan allowed me to plug my phone into the communication panel and make calls through my headset without yelling over the engine and wind noise. The Skylane didn't have such an option, but I made a mental note to do some panel upgrades when we returned to Saint Marys.

Clark picked up on the fourth ring and yelled, "Yeah? What is it?"

I briefed him on Mongo's idea of a yacht capable of holding four hostages.

Through the noise of the 182, he groaned. "I didn't think about that. If that's what's going on, there's no chance of spotting them."

I said, "That also means they aren't necessarily on The Bahamas. They could be underway at sea anywhere in the North Atlantic."

"Ouch. That's a twist we haven't considered. Do you know if we have any satellite imagery from coastal Florida when they were nabbed? If we do, we might see the boat or plane they used."

"It's worth asking the question. We'll talk to Skipper about that this afternoon."

Through the roar, he asked, "Are you having any luck?"

"No. I'm starting to think we're wasting a lot of time and fuel, but I don't know what else to do."

"Let's keep flying," he yelled. "We might get lucky."

We continued our route down the eastern side of the island until Fresh Creek Inlet in Andros Town came into sight a few miles ahead. I let my eyes follow the inlet into the interior. The wide, shallow waterways spread out as I continued my survey to the west. The landscape reminded me of the water surrounding Jekyll Island, where I'd first been recruited into my life behind the curtain of secrecy.

Perhaps it was nostalgia, or maybe it was just a hunch that made me roll to the right and follow the creek away from the Atlantic Ocean.

"What do you see?" Singer asked.

"I don't know yet, but there's something about this inlet that caught my attention."

"Do you want me to keep the camera rolling?" Mongo asked.

"Yeah, let it run. I'm just going to poke my head in here and have a glance."

My quick peek turned into a twelve-mile trek into the rising terrain of the island. When I'd seen enough, I started a slow turn to the right with the intention of returning us to the eastern coast-line, but Singer said, "Hey! Wait a minute, Chase. Take a look at nine o'clock."

I leveled the wings and rolled out on a northerly heading. The eagle-eyed sniper had spotted exactly what my gut hoped to find.

"Well done!" I said as I turned back to the northwest.

Stretching out in front of us was a body of water perhaps a quarter mile wide and two miles long, running east to west.

I offset our course to the north of the long, narrow strip that looked as if God himself had created it especially for seaplanes. With every eye pinned to the water, I flew westward as if planning an approach and landing in the opposite direction.

Singer said, "I don't know anything about seaplanes, but if I were trying to hide one, I'd do it just like that."

"Just like what?" I said, craning my neck to follow his line of sight.

"Right over there at ten o'clock, there's a draw back into the trees, and it looks a lot like camouflage netting over the tail of an airplane."

The thousands of hours our sniper had spent learning to find objects and people who didn't want to be found had paid off in spades.

I said, "Good eyes, Singer. I would've missed it."

Mongo said, "I still don't see it."

"I don't want to spook them," I said, "so, I'll make the loop around the lake as if we're just out for a Sunday afternoon joyride. That'll give the camera a chance to do its thing."

I made the loop around the lake headed for the coast. "Shut down the camera. I don't want to risk overwriting the video from that pass."

Mongo made his way back to the camera and pulled the most recent memory card. "I've got it. Do you want me to call Clark?"

I was already reaching for my phone. "No, I'll do it."

Clark answered almost immediately. "What's up?"

"I think we may have found something, and we're headed back to the house to check it out. I hope we got some decent video."

He said, "We just rounded the southern tip, and we've not seen anything meaningful. We'll meet you back at the house."

"If this turns out to be what I hope it is, we didn't find the proverbial needle in a haystack. We just found one specific needle in five thousand square miles of needles."

Chapter 14
Nature Abhors an Idiot

To say a typical childhood exists is a miserable lie, but to say my childhood had any relationship with typical is a catastrophic lie. Until well after my parents and sister were murdered in Panama, I believed myself to be the son of missionaries doing God's work throughout Central and South America. My parents were, at least to some degree, missionaries; however, their missions were often far from godly. Both had been covert operatives, not unlike me, but I wouldn't learn that until years after their slaughter. Like most American children, the tradition of Santa Claus played a lasting role in my childhood. The sleepless December nights in faraway lands, where no one outside my family spoke English, left me wondering if the jolly old elf spoke every language. The anxiety of fearing Santa may not know where I was in those formative years made Christmas Eve a torturous night with time slowing to near stopping. Ultimately, I'd never been disappointed on Christmas morning, but that didn't relieve the anxiety that would return in twelve months.

That same feeling filled my gut on the flight from Central Andros back to the airport. Would the tiny memory card in Mongo's care deliver the present I wanted so badly? Although the Caravan's Pratt and Whitney turbine pulled us through the air at 150 knots, my impatience and anticipation of what the video would reveal made the thirty-mile trip feel like a circumnavigation of the globe.

Flying the Caravan isn't a particularly challenging endeavor. She's docile, responsive, and forgiving of most mistakes in the cockpit, but she, like most flying machines, detests playing second fiddle. She can, at times, be jealous and insecure. She proved that by bouncing like a kangaroo at the bottom of the worst approach I'd ever flown. My attention was laser-focused on the video of the inland lake and the camouflaged seaplane. The pilot's term for the aerodynamic maneuver is *porpoise* because of how the airplane looks as it strikes the runway, bounces back into the air, and again dives for the surface. It can be massively destructive in airplanes with the typical configuration of two main landing gear and a nose gear, but in a seaplane, especially one the size of the Caravan, it can be catastrophic. Turbine engines, despite their massive horsepower, are slow to spool up and generate that power.

Ignoring her limitations, I added power and prayed I could arrest the snafu I'd caused. If the turbine wasn't capable of producing power to climb quickly enough, one of two scenarios would play out: either the falling nose of the heavy airplane would drive the bows of the pontoons into the asphalt runway, or I would force the nose up with elevator pressure and allow the beast to come falling out of the air onto her main gear and do more damage than could be repaired on the island.

The apparent inability for time to pass at a predictable rate left me questioning if the world around me was speeding up or if my brain was decelerating at a tremendous rate. I was left sitting in the captain's seat with both hands full of neglected, misbehaving airplane, and praying she'd start flying again before colliding with the runway.

By some miracle I didn't deserve, the old girl clawed at the air and forced herself back into flight. I kept the nose low, allowing the airplane to build the necessary speed to climb away from the airport and try the whole ordeal again. My negligence was mercifully rewarded, and the airspeed built until I raised the nose and climbed back to pattern altitude.

"What was that?" Mongo asked when we were, once again, safely in the air.

"That's what happens when a pilot loses focus," I said. "I promise to do a little better next time."

As I rolled the wings level after my turn to final, the memory stick and the video it contained were the last things on my mind. I flew the Caravan as she deserved to be flown—with attention, respect, and efficiency. She apparently forgave my previous transgression and handed me a picture-perfect landing. I taxied to the fuel ramp and shut down the turbine while silently thanking the seven-hundred-degree power plant for outperforming my lagging gray matter.

For the first time since we'd been on the island, the lineman met me beside the portside pontoon as I stepped to the ramp. He wore a look of conspiratorial mischief. "How much gas you want?"

"Top it off with Jet A. My card is on file in the office."

"No, da card is no good no more, sir. It's cash only now."

"Let's take a walk inside," I said. "I'm sure the card is just fine."

"No, sir! We do it all out here. Cash only."

Mongo descended the steps behind the lineman, and I gave him a wink.

"This guy says your card is no good and you have to pay cash. How does that make you feel?"

The lineman turned to face the man who outweighed him by nearly two hundred pounds and stood well over a foot taller. Seeing the lineman's reaction as he leaned back to look up at Mongo almost made it impossible to avoid laughing.

Our peace-loving giant laid a hand on the man's shoulder. "Let's see the cash you collected from the previous sale."

"No, sir. It was just a misunderstandin', dat's all. I'm sure your card is jus' fine."

Mongo squeezed his shoulder. "Let's see the cash."

"No, e'reting is all right, sir. 'Twas jus' a misunderstandin'."

Mongo scowled down at him. "The misunderstanding is between you and me. We both seem to be speaking English, but you don't seem to understand. Show me the cash from the previous sale." He jabbed the air with an enormous finger. "I watched you pumping fuel into *that* airplane."

The lineman looked across his shoulder toward the plane he'd just refueled while I was trying to crash the Caravan.

As soon as his head turned, Mongo grabbed his belt buckle, yanked him from the ground, and turned him upside down. "Check his pockets, Chase."

I reached inside each of the man's pockets and relieved him of several hundred dollars in cash, mostly American.

Mongo said, "You have two choices. You can walk inside the terminal with me, or I can drop you on your head. Pick one."

His terrified patois was impossible to understand, so Mongo threw the man across his shoulder and headed for the terminal. Inside the building, Mongo deposited the man onto the counter in front of the drowsy attendant.

I said, "This man says our card is no good, and he insists that we pay him cash outside for fuel. At least one of the two of you is running a scam, and I tend to believe you're both in on it. You've got ten seconds to change my mind before I unleash the big guy on you."

The attendant sized up Mongo and made the best decision of his life. He grabbed the lineman by the collar, jerked him across the counter, and went to work on the much smaller man with a fire extinguisher he pulled from beneath the console. When the beating ceased, the bludgeoned man crawled from behind the counter and scampered toward the door.

The attendant said, "Dat man don' work here, and he be a menace. I tink between da fire extinguisher and what you did to him, he won' be back, no, sir."

I laid the wad of cash I'd pulled from the man's pocket onto the counter. "He scammed this off at least one other pilot, and if you've got a credit card receipt for this amount, you're going to need a lot more than a fire extinguisher to win the fight in front of you."

The man nervously pulled open a top drawer and withdrew a stack of credit card receipts. "You can look for yourself. I ain' got no business wit dat guy."

When we walked from the terminal, Hunter was taxiing the 182 to the ramp beside the Caravan. He shut down, and Clark and Disco crawled out of the plane behind Hunter.

Clark's impatience outweighed Mongo's strength. "Well, let's hear it. What did you find?"

The half mile between the terminal and Hank's house took me only three minutes to run. Hunter was already inside by the time I climbed the stairs.

I caught my breath. "I'm going to outrun you one day. You just wait."

He tossed me a bottle of water. "I'm sure I'll be waiting a long time for that day to come."

Mongo brought up the rear with Clark and Singer only seconds in front of him. He held up the memory card as he huffed through the front door. "I may be slow, but you weren't going to start without me." He opened the laptop and inserted the card.

Seconds later, scenery from the northern coast of the island played in high resolution.

"Fast forward about twenty minutes," I said.

He followed my instructions and soon had the footage from our inbound turn at Fresh Creek playing.

Singer leaned in. "Fast forward a little more until the lake comes into view."

Soon everyone in the room was glued to the screen as Mongo froze the image on the outline of the seaplane beneath camo netting.

"Does that look like a seaplane to you?" I asked.

Clark slapped Singer on the back. "I'd bet dollars to donuts it was you who spotted that thing."

"You'd win that one, boss."

Clark said, "I rarely lose. Can you zoom in?"

Mongo manipulated the frozen image until it filled the screen.

Clark squinted. "While I'm winning bets, I'd put money on the fact that's a de Havilland Twin Otter."

"I wouldn't bet against you, and that's plenty of airplane to haul kidnappers and kidnappees from the east coast of Florida. Boys, I think we've found our bad guys. Let's have a look at the landscape."

Mongo zoomed back out, and we examined the terrain around the floatplane. He said, "It's an awkward angle, but that looks a lot like a trail from here."

We studied the barely visible impression through the canopy of trees.

Singer said, "It's hard to tell, but look farther up the slope." He touched the screen. "What do you see right there?"

Mongo zoomed in and squinted. "Whatever it is, it's definitely man-made. Nature abhors vacuums and straight lines."

Clark said, "That's way too big to be a vacuum."

I thumped him on the top of his head. "You're an idiot . . . and it looks like you're starting to lose your hair."

He smacked my hand away. "Cut it out. This is serious."

"You're right. It's definitely a serious bald spot coming on. You should think about Hair Club for Men."

It was my turn to be thumped, but former Green Berets apparently play rougher than college boys.

"Hey, be careful! I'm delicate. Pay attention."

Mongo said, "Are you guys going to mess around all afternoon, or are we going to figure this out?"

Properly scolded, I said, "Sorry, but I'm pretty sure we've found what we've been looking for."

Singer crossed his arms. "I don't know. It was too easy. I don't like how it smells."

Clark said, "You know what they say. Even a blind bird in a bush finds a hog occasionally."

Mongo rolled his eyes. "Yep, that's what they say. Leave it to Clark to put things in perspective for us."

Clark held up both hands. "That's why I'm here, boys."

I checked my watch. "Our SEAL will be on deck in half an hour. I look forward to hearing his take on the video. Has anybody heard back from Skipper about satellite footage of the abductions?"

Heads shook, and I made the call on speaker.

She answered before I heard the first ring. "Hey, Chase. Boy, do I feel better after some sleep, but I've got some bad news."

"I'm glad you got some rest, and we may have some great news."

"You go first," she said.

"We found a seaplane hidden beneath camo netting and a structure in the hills on the center of the island. We got some footage. I'll try to email it to you. We're waiting for Chief Lewis to show up so we can get a SEAL's perspective on what we found. We may have a real target to assault."

"That's great news, but what I have to tell you is going to put a damper on any piece of good news this day offers up."

Chapter 15
Fish Eggs and Fast Cars

Skipper rarely prefaced news of any kind with a preparatory state-ment, so to hear her warning took the team by surprise and left me expecting to hear her detail another kidnapping.

"That doesn't sound good. What have you got?"

"Do you know General Donald Gervais?"

"Sure. He's the national security advisor. If I remember cor-rectly, he's a retired Army three-star, right?"

"Yeah, that's the one. Technically, his title is Assistant to the President for National Security Affairs, APNSA, but that doesn't really matter. What matters is that an envelope arrived at his home in Georgetown this morning. The return address was his daugh-ter's house in Utah, so his wife opened it up, expecting pictures of their new granddaughter. There were no pictures inside, only a one-line, typed note on common, twenty-pound bond paper that read, 'Do your job, Advisor.'"

"That sounds ominous, but what does that have to do with this mission?" I asked.

"That's not all that was inside the envelope. There was a likely lethal dose of anthrax, Chase. The wife is being treated at George-town Medical Center, but it doesn't look good."

Groans rose from the team, and I said, "Is there any connection between Gervais and any of the hostages?"

"We don't know yet, but everyone is asking that same question. I'm on it independently, and, of course, I'm staying on top of the other agencies involved in case they find a connection before I do. But I'm not sure who we can trust yet."

My wheels churned for several seconds. "There's no reason to suspect the SEALs have been compromised, is there?"

I could almost hear her shaking her head. "None. There's no history of a SEAL team ever being compromised prior to a mission. They're as solid as they come."

"So was Brown's team in Montana, but it happened to them."

"They weren't an active-duty SEAL team, though. You have nothing to worry about with Lewis and his men. They're vetted at every level, and I've been given access that no civilian analyst has ever seen."

I snickered. "Were you *given* the access, or did you tunnel your way into the access?"

"That's the thing . . . I think your buddy, the president, made it happen. I didn't have to use my shovel this time. They let me in the front door."

"Hmm. I'm intrigued."

"Yeah, me too," she said. "When something that big changes, it always makes me nervous, so I've been corroborating everything I find through outside, independent sources, and so far, everything checks out. I understand your concern, though. It's a little freaky."

"Just keep your eyes open, and beware of government officials bearing gifts. Let's get back to the anthrax. Was Mrs. Gervais the only victim?"

"She was the only *human* victim. They had two Scottish Terriers."

"Had?"

"I don't know if the dogs survived, but I'm sure they're at the best vet in D.C."

I sighed. "I'm sure somebody has put some guards and guns around the daughter and new baby."

"I don't know. That's not my lane. But I'm getting the feeling we're in way over our heads on this one. You can't kidnap four prominent Americans, try to kill the national security advisor's wife, and expect that we won't respond with every weapon in our arsenal."

"I'm not so sure that's what they expect. I still think it's about the money."

She cracked her knuckles. "I'm not so sure I agree with you anymore. If it was about the money, why would they want another justice to resign and for two dozen prisoners to be released?"

"I don't know, but nothing is adding up. They keep getting themselves in deeper and deeper with every move before they give us a chance to give them what they want."

Sounds of Skipper repositioning in her chair poured from the speaker. "It's almost time for Chief Lewis to be there. Get his take on the plane and potential structure you found, and brief him on the anthrax thing if he doesn't already know. When that's done, you can give me a call if you want. I'll be right here in the ops center."

"Thanks, Skipper. As always, you're doing amazing work."

"There's one more thing before you go. I've been thinking about the threat you made . . ."

I bowed my head. "I know, and I'm sorry. As I promised, that won't happen again."

"No, it's not that. You already apologized, and we've moved on, but I think maybe you had a good idea."

"What are you talking about?"

"I think I *could* use Ginger on this. It's getting bigger than I can manage alone, and another set of qualified eyes would be nice."

I surveyed the room as everyone nodded. "Get her on the phone, and double her daily rate. Whatever you need, just do it, and I'll pay for it."

"Thanks, Chase. Talk soon. Bye."

I stuck the phone back in my pocket, and Clark let out a low whistle.

"Wow. You know it's serious when Skipper asks for help."

I shrugged. "I've never heard her ask for help before, but I'm not telling her no. As far as I'm concerned, if she needs beluga caviar and a new Maserati to get through this one, I'll write the check."

Singer tugged at the bandage on his bicep. "I'm afraid this one is going to take more than fish eggs and fast cars. We may never know what this whole thing is about, especially if we give in to their demands and they vanish."

"Unless our lucky break turns out to be their compound, they've already vanished," Clark said.

I said, "You don't think it's them, do you?"

He shook his head. "No, but I was wrong once before, so I pray this time makes twice."

I left the living room and made my way into a bedroom down the hall, where I could sit in silence and think.

How did I get here? Eight years ago, I was the best collegiate base-ball player in the world. The Atlanta Braves would've selected me as the number-one draft pick until fate and a train wreck at home plate turned my right hand into ground beef and sent me down a road I never knew existed. I'm thirty years old, in command of a team of elite commandos, and slapdab in the middle of the biggest assault on the American government since Nine-Eleven.

With butt on bed, elbows on knees, and head in hands, I sat contemplating what was to come until the man who taught me more about winning than anyone else in my life walked through the door and parked his Green Beret butt next to mine.

"How you doin', College Boy?"

"I'm struggling, Clark. Every time we get one step closer to these guys, they sprint ahead. How do you stop someone like that?"

He laid an arm across my shoulder. "Remember the last fist-fight you were in?"

"I don't fight with my fists. I carry a gun and two knives."

"You're screwing up my teaching moment. Think back to the last fistfight you had."

I gave him a slow nod, and he said, "How many people were in the room?"

"I don't know. Maybe a dozen. Where are you going with this?"

"All right. Take me through the action, play-by-play. How did you kick all thirteen of the asses in the room?"

I looked up beneath my wrinkled brow. "I was only fighting one or two of them."

"Why didn't you fight all of them?"

"Why would I even try that? Nobody fights a dozen people at a time."

He gave me that crooked smile, patted me on the back, and left me alone, wondering how many more lessons I would have to endure on the most complex mission of my short life.

Clark, as usual, was right. Finding the bad guys in The Bahamas was my fight. The anthrax, the baby granddaughter, the utter chaos in Washington D.C., and anything else that went wrong before I could find, capture, or kill the psychopaths behind it all were someone else's fight. Only a fool would fight a dozen battles at once.

"Hey, Chase! Your frogman is here." It was Disco's voice that brought me from my pity party and onto my feet.

I made it to the living room just as Mongo opened the door for Naval Special Warfare Master Chief DeAndre Lewis.

Prior to having the chief walk through the door, I'd only seen him from the shoulders up on the comms screen in the Bonaventure ops center. Next to Mongo, Chief Lewis, like most men, looked like a child.

As is routinely the case, hands were shaken with grips a little tighter than the Baptist handshake, first impressions were made, and everyone except the SEAL seemed anxious for what lay ahead.

"I'm Chase Fulton."

He shook my outstretched hand. "Yeah, I remember. Dre Lewis."

"It's good to finally meet you, Chief."

He shook me off and inventoried the room. "No. Just Dre. In this room, we're all knuckle-draggers." He bobbed his cleanly shaven head toward Disco. "Except for maybe that one."

"Don't let him fool you," I said. "He's the baddest of the bunch. I watched him T-box a bad guy in Montana with the whole building falling down around our feet."

Lewis almost smiled and gave Disco a respectful nod. With a single clap of his hands, the SEAL said, "Okay, time to go to work. Let's have it."

The next ten minutes were spent bringing Chief Lewis up to speed on what little intel we had. He watched the video and studied the still shots as if his life depended on understanding everything the camera had captured. Perhaps it did.

After apparently digesting every pixel, Lewis looked up and asked, "What else?"

"That's it on-site," I said, "but we have some news from D.C. It seems that someone is gunning for General Gervais, or at least his family."

"The NSA?"

"Yeah. Somebody delivered a letter to his house in George-town. His wife opened it up and read the four-word note. 'Do your job, Advisor.'"

Chief Lewis shrugged. "There's no way to logically connect that to any of this."

"I'm not finished. There was enough anthrax in the envelope to hospitalize the general's wife and their two dogs."

Lewis seemed to chew on the information for half a minute, then said, "Okay, I'll tuck that one away, but there's nothing we can do about it, so let's gut the bandits in front of us and let the bureaucrats deal with the inside-the-beltway crap."

I met Clark's stare, and he raised an eyebrow as if to say, "See, College Boy?"

Lewis scanned the room. "Do you guys have anything to drink?"

"Just some bottled water," Singer said. "We haven't had time to do any grocery shopping."

"Water's great, thanks. What happened to your arm, by the way?"

Singer glanced at the bandage. "I got shot by a Chinese guard in an underground bunker while we were running from the eight hundred pounds of C4 we planted."

Dre chuckled. "Been there, done that." He uncapped the bottle and swallowed the contents. "Your analyst told me you had the bare bones of a plan and you needed to brief me up, so let's hear it."

I tapped the laptop's screen. "The plan's changed since we shot that video. I wanted to talk you into assaulting a beach on Conception Island as a show of force."

He crushed the plastic bottle and recapped it. "I think you mean decoy instead of show of force."

"Maybe," I admitted, "but none of that matters now that we have a real target. I want to hit the airplane and compound, and I want to hit them hard."

Chapter 16

Sea, Air, and Land

Master Chief Dre Lewis put on his first grin of the day. "How many cigars did you bring with you?"

Covert operatives, at least the ones I'd worked with, smoked the best cigars they could buy, steal, or beg when an operation came to a successful end. If they lost a man during an op, his cigar would still be lit, and his whiskey would still be poured. It was, sort of, the missing man formation for knuckle-draggers.

I made a show of counting heads in the room. "There's six of us, so a cool half dozen should do it unless you want to come along for the ride."

Dre inspected a fingernail. "That depends on what your definition of hitting hard is."

I gave Clark an eye, and he nodded. Saying too much too early was still a weakness of mine, but I'd just been given the steal sign.

I said, "Everything is on the north shore of the lake, so their backs are against the wall to the south. There's rising terrain to the north and west and a downslope to the east. If we go in hot, we'll approach from the north and flank to the east, effectively pinning them between the rising terrain and the lake. If we play thief-in-the-night, we'll crawl in from the north, slit throats, and exfil to the east."

"That's cute," Dre said.

I lowered an eyebrow. "Cute?"

"Yeah, single-pronged assaults are cute, but if you want to make an impression, don't crawl into the compound on your belly. You gotta do it the SEAL way, baby."

"The SEAL way?"

"Yes, sir! Sea, Air, and Land. That amphib Caravan at the airport is yours, right?" I nodded, and he continued. "You got insurance on it?"

"I do."

"Good. As long as you're not afraid of a few bullet holes, that'll make a fine insertion craft. I can put six SEALs on the pontoons for a beach assault, six more on the slope to the east for an ambush, and you six on the ground from the north. What are your weaknesses?"

"Our weaknesses?" I asked.

"Yeah, your weaknesses. You know, what don't you have that you need, or what isn't your team good at?"

I motioned toward Singer's arm. "We're down a sniper, and one of us has to fly the Caravan."

"Snipers are a dime a dozen, man. I'll put one in the tree line south of the lake and one to cover the ambush site. If you want a third for overwatch from the north or west, just say the word."

It was time for one more unspoken question between me and my handler, and Clark gave another nod.

I turned to our chief pilot. "Hey, Disco. Can you land the Caravan on that lake in the dark?"

"It's against the law, but sure, I can do it."

Dre laughed out loud. "Against the law. Now, that's funny. I'm going to launch a full-blown assault on the interior of a sovereign country with a dozen SEALs and a gang of cowboys with green berets lost in their closets somewhere at home. Do I look like I'm worried about breaking the law?"

I said, "You're calling us cowboys? You're insane, but how soon can you have your team here?"

"When do you want to hit them?"

I checked my watch. "If patience is a virtue, we're the least virtuous gang you've ever met." Before he could answer, my phone chirped, and I thumbed it to life. "Chase."

"Hey, Chase. It's Hank from Key Largo. I hope I'm not interrupting anything."

"No, sir. Nothing at all. We're just planning our night out on the town."

"I remember those days," he said. "Try not to come home with gonorrhea or bullet holes in you."

I chuckled. "That's good advice. I assume you're calling about the chopper."

"That's right. The avionics tech came down and found the problem right away. It was a poor connection. He tightened it up, and we flew it for forty-five minutes without any issues."

"That's great news. I was afraid we were in for an expensive repair."

"You got off easy on this one, but as many airplanes as you have, you must be constantly fixing something."

"It's not so bad. We have a great A and P mechanic who keeps everything in pretty good shape. How much do I owe your tech?"

"That's part of the reason I'm calling. He says if you'll let him do the avionics upgrade at sixty bucks an hour plus parts, this one's on the house."

"Tell him he's got a deal. We'll leave the helicopter at his shop as soon as we finish this mission. In the meantime, I'll come get the old girl. If you'll make sure she's topped off with fuel, I'd appreciate it."

He said, "It's already done. She'll be here waiting for you when you get here, but I'm closing shop a little early today. I've got an appointment I can't miss, so I'll leave the keys in the chopper. Nobody will mess with it."

"I'll need to pay you for the fuel, and it'd be nice to top off the Caravan while we're there."

"The keys are in the fuel truck behind the FBO. Pump all you need, and we'll square up on the bill when you get finished saving the world, son."

"What would I do without you, Hank? Thank you for everything."

Almost before I hung up, Dre said, "You have a helicopter?"

"We do."

He grinned for the second time in one day. "Can it carry a sling load?"

"It can."

"How much?"

"With just crew on board, we can haul an external load of almost a ton."

He frowned. "Inches and ounces add up. How much is *almost* a ton?"

"Nineteen fifty."

He closed one eye as if running his mental calculator. "Our RHIB is nine eighty, and a kitted SEAL is two twenty-five. That gives me four frogmen and the boat. Can you leave off a second driver and the crew chief?"

I laughed. "Second drivers and crew chiefs aren't required crewmen for us, so that gives you six SEALs and a boat."

He snapped his fingers. "I love it when a plan comes together."

Clark stepped in. "You know the A-Team were Green Berets, right?"

Dre fingered his imaginary Hannibal Smith cigar. "Yep, I know. That was obvious when they'd fire ten thousand rounds and never hit anybody."

Clark rolled his eyes. "I walked right into that one, didn't I?"

Dre laughed. "Go get your helicopter. I'll have my team's boots on the ground by the time you get back."

Mongo looked up at me like a little boy who wanted another cookie, and I motioned for him to follow. "Come on, Mongo. You can go with Disco and me."

With the big man in the left seat and Disco in the right, we pointed the nose into the western sky—destination, Key Largo.

As promised, the keys were in the fuel truck and the helicopter. Disco ran Mongo through the Caravan's fueling process, and I spun up the turbines on the chopper.

With a wave and salute, I pulled pitch and lumbered out over the Atlantic. The Caravan would take another ten minutes to fuel and get airborne, but they'd catch me long before the halfway mark across the Gulf Stream.

Hank had been correct. The autopilot managed the chopper better than I could've done, and I sat back and enjoyed the ride. Disco and Mongo caught up and pulled ahead about a quarter mile. With the radio tuned to 123.45, Mongo keyed up and said, "Do you need some help finding the biggest island in The Bahamas?"

"You'll never hurt my feelings by helping me," I said. "Show me the way home!"

"Try to keep up."

Without hesitation, I said, "Try to hover . . . No, wait! On second thought, I love that airplane, so don't try to hover."

When we arrived back on Andros, a CASA 212 rested on the parking apron with its rear ramp deployed. By the time we parked and shut down, fourteen SEALs, a desert patrol vehicle, and a trailered rigid hull inflatable boat waited behind the boxcar of an airplane.

Though dressed more like college kids on their way to play paintball than hardened warriors, Chief Lewis's SEALs were unmistakable. As we approached the beehive of special warfare activity, a pair of Lewis's men stepped toward us and slid their hands beneath untucked shirts.

I threw up my hands. "Easy, guys. We're on your team."

Neither man flinched until Dre jogged to their side and ordered, "Stand down. They're with us. Meet Chase, the team leader, and Mongo, the team mongo. That's Disco over there. Don't shoot him, either. I hear he loves to shoot back."

The two SEALs relaxed their posture and turned to rejoin their teammates unpacking gear.

Dre looked across my shoulder, taking in the chopper. "You didn't tell me it was a Huey."

"Technically, it's not, but with a different paint job, they'd be hard to tell apart. That one was in the logging business in Montana when we picked it up. I think it's safe to say she prefers her new life to dragging logs off mountains."

Dre nodded with unspoken respect. "Retirement's drawing closer every day if you guys happen to have an opening for an old frogman."

Mongo sized up the Naval Special Warfare veteran. "I don't know if you could hack it on a hardcore team like ours. I had to bench-press my weight before they'd even look at me."

Dre scoffed. "I weigh one ninety, and I can throw that around like a child's toy."

Mongo smiled. "I didn't say you had to bench *your* weight, Chief. I said you had to bench *mine*."

Dre gave his own bicep a squeeze. "You know, I'm thinking I may stick with the Navy for another hitch."

I asked, "Can your team be ready to hit the compound by midnight?"

"They're ready right now, but I'd love to show them the site if that Caravan of yours can handle the weight."

"It came from the factory with fourteen seats, so it can handle the weight. The problem is, we took most of the seats out."

"Even better," Dre said. "Seats are for Air Force butts. We prefer the deck."

I turned to Mongo. "Keep an eye on this gear while we're gone. And by 'keep an eye on,' I mean, see if there's anything we want."

Dre threw up his hands, "Hey, gear gets lost and destroyed on every deployment. Take all you want. We'll buy more."

Mongo pointed toward the desert patrol vehicle. "Dibs on the dune buggy."

Disco said, "Dibs on the airplane."

* * *

With the Caravan loaded to the gills with SEALs, I climbed out with the bulky airplane clawing its way to a thousand feet. The flight to the interior lake took only twelve minutes. I made my first pass well south of the lake, and every eye peered out the portside windows, committing the terrain to memory.

A pass directly down the lake would make it impossible for anyone who wasn't in the cockpit to see anything meaningful, so I made a wide arc over the eastern end of the lake and flew westward at a thousand feet.

One of the SEALs yelled, "There's definitely a structure under the canopy, but I can't make out the size."

I nodded to Dre. "That's the same thing we said the first time we saw it. I couldn't find an angle that would give us a better look."

"Don't worry about it. Let's get out of here before they get nervous down there."

As I flew the downwind leg of my approach back to the airport, someone from the back yelled, "Hey, are you sure your guys aren't frogmen?"

I glanced over my shoulder. "Yeah, I'm sure. Why do you ask?"

He wordlessly answered by pointing out the left side of the airplane. I scanned the airport and couldn't control my laughter. Mongo's enormous body was squeezed into the desert patrol vehicle, and he was sucking every ounce of speed out of the machine with the trailered RHIB still connected behind it. Disco was at the wheel of the boat, his hair pinned to his scalp in the sixty-mile-per-hour wind.

Chapter 17
Find a Way

With Mongo and Disco finally wrangled in from their joyride, we positioned the RHIB, still on its trailer, beside the chopper, and a pair of Air Assault qualified SEALs rigged the sling load.

Master Chief Dre Lewis asked, "Are you the only chopper pilot?"

I laughed. "Hardly. We have no shortage of pilots on this team. Why?"

Dre pointed at Disco. "In that case, I like that guy. Can we have him?"

I stuck two fingers in the corners of my mouth and gave a shrill whistle. "Hey, Disco. Come here."

He jogged across the tarmac with his hair still out of control from his wild RHIB ride. "Is this the part where you yell at me for playing with the boat?"

"The only reason I'd yell about that is the fact that you didn't invite me to come along. Actually, Dre wants you in the driver's seat tonight when we splash the RHIB. Are you okay with that?"

Disco drove a thumb into his own chest. "Me? I'll do whatever you want, but being dragged around the airport behind Mongo is the most time I've spent at the controls of a RHIB. Anybody else, especially any of your SEALs, would be a better choice."

I tried not to laugh but failed. "No, goofy. He wants you flying the chopper."

"Oh! Yeah, in that case, I'm your guy. I thought you meant . . ."

Dre flipped the switch and instantly became all business. "We'll brief the assault plan to everyone before we move out, but here's your role. That reminds me . . . Wait one."

He turned and motioned for a tall, slim SEAL, and the man appeared by the chief's side. He said, "Take Mongo and the DPV, and find out how deep the eastern end of that lake is."

"You got it, Chief."

In seconds, Mongo, the SEAL, and the desert patrol vehicle vanished to the south, and Dre turned back to Disco. "Sorry, but that was a crucial piece of data."

Disco shook him off. "No worries."

Dre continued. "You'll stage off the eastern end of the lake out of sight of the compound with the RHIB beneath the chopper. If the water is deep enough, I'll put six men in the chopper with you. When you drop the RHIB, they'll follow it into the water, and you'll hang back to scoop up anybody who gets hurt. You're okay under nods, right?"

Disco nodded. "Yeah, I've got plenty of time under night vision."

"Great. If anybody doesn't make it into the boat, you pick them up and put them back in the fight—unless they need medivac. From there, everyone on the boat team except the driver will hit the beach beside the camouflaged airplane. They'll join the fight while the RHIB driver tows the plane off the bank to eliminate one avenue of escape. Are you tracking so far?"

"Yeah, I got it," Disco said, "but I can give you an extra trigger puller if you want."

Dre paused. "What do you mean?"

"Instead of having the RHIB driver tow the plane off the beach, you could beach the RHIB and attach a cable from the chopper to the tie-down on the tail of the seaplane. I can tow the plane off the beach, no matter how hard aground she is, and stick it anywhere you want. That'll give you an extra SEAL on the ground, and it'll leave your RHIB available for exfil, if necessary."

Dre looked at me and shot a thumb toward Disco. "You were right about this guy. He's hardcore."

I shrugged. "I told you."

Dre waggled a finger. "I like your plan better than mine. By the time we hit the water, the gig will be up, and everyone in that compound will know the cavalry's coming, but I'd like to mask the noise of the RHIB with your rotor blades. If you can run up the approach from the east to dissuade anybody from trying to escape in that direction, that'll put you over the beached airplane roughly at the same time we hit the beach in the RHIB. The timing should be perfect."

"Sounds good to me, but what's the contingency plan if the water's not deep enough for your guys to jump?"

Dre said, "In that case, you'll land wherever you can near the east end of the lake, and my SEALs will dismount the chopper and load up in the RHIB. You'll put the boat and the bodies in the water at the same time, but do it gently. It's impossible to know which way the boat will be heading when you splash it, so keep the forward speed down as much as possible."

"No problem," Disco said.

Dre eyed the chief pilot. "How many times have you splashed a RHIB?"

Disco pulled off his sunglasses. "Including this time?"

Dre shook his head, turned, and walked away.

Disco looked at me. "How hard can it be?"

* * *

Back at the house, fourteen SEALs and the six of us made the massive house feel like a camper. The island kid at the pizza joint made me pay for the dozen pies over the phone. He couldn't seem to grasp the idea that it would take twelve pizzas to feed the guests of one house. By the time the gang of animals finished off the last slice, I was afraid they were going to eat the cardboard boxes.

"Calories are important before a night op," one of the SEALs said as he shoved the last bite into his mouth.

Dre swallowed the last of his Mountain Dew and tapped the plastic cup on the table. "All right. Listen up, you bunch of scavengers. It's time to brief the mission. Chase is the operational commander, but he's not familiar with our tactics, so I'll be at his side. If he goes down or makes a bad call, I'll step up. His voice on the radio has the same weight as mine. Got it?"

Thirteen heads nodded, and a hearty round of "Got it, Chief" followed.

"Good. Here's the op order. Boat crew two, that's your team, Miller. You're in the chopper with Disco. Swimmer checked the depth an hour ago, and it's between eight and twelve feet. That means you're getting wet. Disco will splash you and the RHIB as far east as possible before running up the slope through the ambush site. By that time, we'll have team one on the western flank and moving hard while the rest of us move in over the ridge to the north. We're hitting hard and fast, but nobody fires until fired upon. Got it?"

Another grunt of understanding came, and Dre continued the briefing. "Miller, you're going to beach the RHIB beside the camo-netted airplane and take the compound from the south. Pick one man to catch the cable from the chopper and secure it to the tie-down on the rear of the beached seaplane. If there's no tie-down, wrap the cable around the tail, and lock it back onto itself. We have to get that airplane off the beach, and I don't care if we cut it in half doing so."

Miller drove a finger toward a short, stocky man. "Larry, you're the cable guy." Groans of disapproving laughter rose, and Miller said, "I've been waiting two years to use that line."

Dre said, "Repeat after me. Don't fire until fired upon." They did, and he said, "Too easy. Now, you should know that these guys are unlikely to fire on us. They have no idea we're coming, so they'll be surprised and unpredictable but unlikely to shoot. Keep that in mind. If it becomes necessary to rough somebody up to get them under control, do it, but use only the force required to subdue. There could be up to four hostages. They are three men, all in their sixties. One is heavy, diabetic, and hypertensive."

He scanned the room until he found the man he was looking for. "Silver, you're the primary medic, so you're on the big guy unless one of us goes down."

"Yes, Chief. What's his name?"

Dre closed one eye in an obvious attempt to remember the man's name, but it wasn't coming.

I said, "Congressman James Paige, but he'll answer to Jimmy."

Silver furrowed his brow. "Congressman? I thought we were picking up a Supreme Court justice."

"We are," Dre said. "Two congressmen, one judge, and the governor of South Carolina, Laura Holcombe."

A SEAL from the back of the room jumped up. "Laura Holcombe? Are you serious?"

Dre said, "Yeah, why?"

The man said, "My momma works for her in Columbia. She's our governor."

Dre lowered his chin. "You know the rules, Hotdog."

"Yes, Chief. I'm not making any phone calls, but if we pull her out, she's gonna tell my momma about it when she gets back to Columbia."

"There's nothing we can do about the stories the governor tells, but we keep our mouths closed."

I cleared my throat. "We're getting off track. Let's talk about the exfil."

Dre nodded toward me. "You brief it, Chase."

"Thanks, Chief. When we liberate the four hostages, if they're ambulatory—"

A SEAL yelled out, "That's a fancy word that means they can walk, for you Green Berets."

Clark raised a make-believe rifle, and the SEAL took cover.

I said, "So, anyway . . . If they can walk, we'll marshal them to the RHIB and get them to the east end of the lake, ASAP. Silver, you're on the exfil team unless one of us goes down. If that happens, you'll care for the wounded, and Carter will be the flight medic. Disco will meet you there, and you'll load them onto the chopper. As soon as they're safely aboard, Disco is headed for Florida to repatriate the hostages. Any questions on that?" Heads shook, and I continued. "We'll roll up the bad guys and march them out to the trucks."

"What trucks?" came a voice from somewhere in the room.

"I forgot to tell you about the trucks," I said. "Hunter . . . Raise your hand, Hunter." He did, and I said, "He acquired four pickup trucks this afternoon. Those will be our horses in and out. We'll bring the rolled-up kidnappers back to the airport and pin them to the floor of the Caravan. I'll have them in Guantanamo Bay before the sun comes up." I gestured toward Chief Lewis. "It's all yours, Chief."

"Thanks, Chase. The only thing left is sniper locations. Mittens, you're in the tree line south of the lake. Pick your tree. And

Robin Hood, you're upslope from the ambush team. That leaves Clark. We want you on the west flank so you can cover my troopers and yours. You good with that?" Clark nodded, so Dre said, "Questions?" None came, and he turned to me. "Let's walk outside and have a talk."

At the top of the stairs beyond the front door, Dre stared off into the distance.

As much as I wanted to watch him squirm, I started the ball rolling. "Let me guess. You've never worked with a tactical team like mine, and you're afraid we're more bad-ass than you, so you want me to make sure my guys don't do anything to show up your boys. Is that it?"

He didn't want to laugh, but he couldn't stop it from coming. "You're all right, Chase. You know that?"

I looked him straight in the eyes. "My guys in there, they may cut up and joke right now, but wait until you see them when the bullets start flying. They're solid . . . all of them. They earned their stripes in the down and dirty. I'm a civilian. I never wore the uniform, but I'll dig a foxhole with any one of them and fight until we're out of bullets and blood. You don't have to worry about us, and I know I don't have to worry about you. We may not be SEALs, but we're not afraid of the dark."

"I get the feeling you guys aren't afraid of anything."

I huffed. "Ah, we had this Russian operative with us for a while. She scared the stuffing out of us."

"She? Oh, really? I think I'd like to hear that story."

I shoved him toward the door. "Get Clark to tell you. His version is better."

He said, "Hey, wanna have a little fun with the guys inside?"

"Sure. What do you have in mind?"

"When we go through the door, you put your finger in my face and straighten me out. Let's see what they do."

I twisted the knob and pushed the door inward. "After you . . ."

He stepped inside, and I gave the door my best front kick. He spun with fire in his eyes, and I stepped into his space, looked down at the man who could probably rip me in half with one hand, and growled, "Let me tell you one thing, you deck-swabbing frog. You try that garbage with me one more time and see what happens!"

He gave me a stage shove that I overplayed and bounced off the door as if he'd tried to push me through the wall. Before he could react, eighteen battle-hardened warriors leapt to their feet like New York Yankees clearing a dugout, and we barely recovered before we found out if thirteen SEALs could kill five black ops guys.

Dre threw up his hands and stepped in front of me. "Relax! We're just messin' around! Nice reaction time, though."

Knives returned to sheaths, and fists came unclenched while Dre and I laughed like kids on the playground.

When Dre regained his composure, he held up one finger. "We were just playing this time, but if me and Chase get in a real tussle, don't worry about Chase. I can handle him. But you better find a way to keep that Mongo guy off me."

Chapter 18
Envision Success

Darkness fell on Andros Island as our combined teams suited up, checked gear, and prepared for whatever the night would deliver. I had no way to know what Master Chief Dre Lewis was thinking, but he and I wore the same expression as we watched our men transform themselves into warriors who would become the darkness and plunge themselves, once again, into the face of evil, to pluck innocents from its sinister grasp.

In my junior year at the University of Georgia, my coach, Bobby Woodley, pulled me aside after four hours of practice in which I'd taken batting practice for ninety minutes, run the bases backward in full catcher's gear for half an hour, gunned down imaginary baserunners from behind home plate for an hour, and taught technique to a pair of incoming freshman catchers for the remaining hour.

Coach Woodley said, "Get out of that gear, and let's have a talk."

"But Coach, I'm not finished with the new catchers. We've still got to—"

In his soft-spoken tone, he said, "They'll be fine, Chase. Rome wasn't built in a day."

I tossed my mask and mitt onto the bench in the dugout and followed my coach into the locker room. We sat on a workbench in the equipment manager's shop with no one else within earshot. What he said next would leave an indelible mark on my twenty-year-old mind for the remainder of my life.

"Chase, I spent thirteen years playing professional baseball. I spent eleven of those years crouched behind home plate in the Major League, and you're better at this game right now than I was in my prime. You're the kind of player every Major League manager dreams of having behind the plate. You practice just as hard as you play, and that's why you'll likely be the first overall pick in the draft next year. They're going to throw more money at you than you've ever seen, and it'll be the most temptation you'll ever endure."

"Coach, don't worry. I'm going to finish school."

He smiled, shook his head, and hooked two fingers behind my chest protector. "You already have, son. Your career is behind these pads, so don't risk getting hurt playing ball with me for another year. I don't have anything else to teach you, but I do have one last thing I want to give you before you turn in your Bulldog gear for whatever big league team is lucky enough to get you."

"Are you telling me to enter the draft next year, Coach?"

"What do you want to do, son? Teach psychology your whole life like Richter? Look at that old man. He's going to die in that classroom of his because he never did anything except teach. That's all he knows. I don't want to see that happen to you. I want to see your picture in Cooperstown, Chase, right beside Yogi Berra and Roy Campanella. Do you think those guys looked back at the end of their careers and said, 'Man, oh man. I wish I'd finished college'?"

I hung my head. "I don't know, Coach."

"That's not why I called you in here. I have somebody I want you to meet. Get cleaned up, and meet me up in my office."

Because of my injury the next year, I never played professional baseball, but I did finish school. The person Coach Woodley wanted me to meet played a role in both of those life-changing events.

After a shower, I jogged to my coach's office and met Dr. Marylin Morgan.

"She's a sports psychologist, Chase, and she's going to teach your brain to be the winner your body's already proven it knows how to be."

I shook her hand and showed her the respect she deserved, but until that day on Andros Island watching my team alongside the SEALs, I never understood what she'd tried to teach me a dozen years before.

Seeing the two teams interact flawlessly side by side only hours before the action phase of a mission that could change the face of American politics for decades to come gave me the confidence to envision inevitable success. I closed my eyes and saw us moving as one through the subtropical jungle and across the shallow inland lake. I watched us power through the compound, overwhelming the unsuspecting kidnappers and freeing the hostages as if we'd worked, trained, and fought together for a lifetime. And I believed Dre was envisioning exactly the same.

With everyone fully kitted out, Dre assigned the boat team and left them in Disco's capable hands. It would take the ground-based teams nearly two hours to get into position for the assault before the chopper needed to be airborne.

Communications checks took only seconds before the action began. I patched Skipper into our comms so she could run analysis from the ops center back at Bonaventure.

She was unusually quiet, so I asked, "Is everything okay, Skipper?"

"I don't know. Something about this feels different, like it was all too easy or something. I guess I'm overthinking it. Just be careful, okay?"

"We're always careful."

She laughed. "That's a lie, and you know it. I'm here if you need me."

"Thanks. And don't be afraid to speak up if something isn't going how it should."

"Don't you worry. I'm a lot of things, but shy isn't one of them. Go get 'em, Chase."

Singer drove the first truck with Clark and the two SEAL snipers ahead of the rest of us. Although Singer's injury kept him out of the fight, no one in this world was more qualified to put the snipers into position.

We filled the two remaining trucks, me in the passenger seat of the first and Dre in the second, and headed south. The old logging road feeding toward the lake was far from a thoroughfare. Downed trees required six and sometimes seven men to clear them out of the path. Ruts and ditches deep enough to bury a horse made traversing the trail in the trucks not only slow but extremely challenging. Operating in the dark without headlights required that we wear night vision goggles that turned the world around us a ghostly green and made spotting and avoiding the ditches a constant task.

Ninety minutes after leaving the house, the snipers were in place, the ambush team was situated on the eastern approach, assault team one under my command was in position to the north of the compound, and Dre and his team were in place to the west and awaiting my command to move.

With the witching hour drawing near, I keyed my mic and performed one final comms check. Everyone was in place, and comms were loud and clear. It was time to rock and roll.

I keyed up. "Disco, bring us a boat!"

His tinny voice played in my earpiece. "Airborne now. We'll be on-site in seventeen minutes. Will advise two minutes out."

The next fifteen minutes felt like an eternity enshrouded in a mist of green with the sound of my heartbeat thundering in my head. As the minute hand crept forward, my gut kept churning as if trying to tell me to call the whole thing off, but we'd come too far, and too much was at stake to turn back now. With the SEALs by our sides, we'd never been stronger or more capable than we were beneath those trees only minutes away from liberating four hostages whose lives meant more than our own in that moment.

"Two minutes out!" came Disco's call.

I gave the order. "Hit 'em!"

My team sprang from cover and started down the northern slope with weapons at the ready. Through my nods, I watched the SEALs approaching from the west. Our timing was perfect. We'd both hit the compound in sixty seconds.

As if we were an enormous noose, we closed on the compound, tightening the perimeter with every stride. The sound of the chopper echoed across the lake, and I turned to watch the RHIB hit the water a mile away, followed by six shadows slipping from the skids of the helicopter and gliding into the water. Seconds later, the white spray from the RHIB's bow wake flashed in my nods. The compound was two hundred yards away, and we were closing fast.

Disco swung a long, graceful arc through the air to the left, no doubt eyeing the men he'd deposited into the drink. His sweeping turn continued until he rolled out along the north shore of the lake with the RHIB slicing across the water to his left. The ambush team would hear the churning rotors only feet above their head as Disco spurred his horse westward.

Four powerful floodlights illuminated the grounds around the compound, and I was instantly blinded by the blast through my night vision. Everyone threw their nods upward, folding them onto the tops of their helmets. We shielded our eyes against the assaulting beams as we continued our approach. The lights meant they knew we were coming, but nothing about our mission changed. Our charge continued as the RHIB struck the beach beside the covered seaplane. A SEAL dived from the boat, grabbed the dangling cable from the chopper, and clipped it to the tie-down on the tail of the plane.

With the boat crew joining the assault, we crushed the meager fencing around the structure and continued inward.

The sound of the chopper's blades digging into the air with the added weight and resistance of the seaplane filled my head. As my eyes adjusted to the lights, faint silhouettes of motionless figures formed in the windows. Something about the figures felt wrong as I studied them.

Why aren't they moving? They have to see us. Why would they stand in the windows like . . .

The terrible reality of the instant hit Dre, me, and Clark simultaneously, with the boat crew hitting the front of the structure.

Dre's voice filled my ears. "Abort! Abort! Abort!"

My team and I turned and hit the ground less than fifty feet from the building. I raised my head to see Dre's team doing the same, but the boat crew was committed.

The crackle of the detonation cord rang in my ears an instant before the world erupted in billowing orange flames and black smoke. The concussion of the blast felt like I'd been hit by a freight train.

I scampered to my feet in a desperate effort to put some distance between myself and the explosion. Mongo grabbed Hunter's arm and threw him to his feet.

The whole world felt like it was on fire, and I suddenly remembered Disco over the shoreline tugging desperately on the seaplane. The fire and smoke blocked my line of sight, and the roaring flames and ringing in my ears drowned out the sound of the rotor blades.

I raised my head to see the ambush team charging in from the east with their rifles at the ready. The training, discipline, and mental fortitude to run toward gunfire or an explosion is foreign and impossible to understand for those who've never seen their brothers' bodies twisted, burned, and ravaged by evil and hatred.

Once we'd gathered our wits, we joined the charge only to find the six soulless corpses of the boat crew who'd endured the fury of the horrific explosion at their fingertips. As if programmed to do so at their very core, the remaining SEALs hefted the bodies of their fallen brothers and ran for the safety of the water.

Hunter, Mongo, and I followed as the SEALs led us down the slope and into the waiting lake. They laid the bodies into the RHIB that had been blown off the beach.

Waist deep in the lake, Dre made his way to me and grabbed my vest. His face was inches from mine, but I could barely hear the words he yelled. "Can you fly that?"

I turned to follow his outstretched hand pointing at the de Havilland Twin Otter float plane bobbing in the water with Disco's severed cable dangling from its tail. Then I threw my eyes skyward to see the outline of the chopper moving south. The thought of Disco running from the scene was impossible to believe until I saw him touch down and the form of the first sniper crawl aboard.

I turned back to Dre and nodded, believing his ears were as worthless as mine at that moment. He shoved me toward the airplane, and I dragged myself from the water onto the portside pontoon. There was no way to know how much structural damage had been done to the airframe by the explosion and the stress Disco had put on the tail before the cable severed, but as long as it would make one more flight, I'd never ask for more than that from the old workhorse.

The engines came alive, and the fuel gauges read more than enough to make the Florida coast. I turned the plane away from the fire and taxied toward the men still in the water. Two SEALs mounted the RHIB and accelerated to the east with the bodies of their teammates covering the deck. Disco picked up the two remaining snipers and landed at the east end of the lake.

Men crawled from the water and aboard the Otter as I taxied as slowly as possible. I tried counting them as they came aboard, but it was a wasted effort. My brain was incapable of calculating how many had been in the water and how many Disco plucked from the Earth.

Dre leaned across my shoulder and yelled, "Go, go, go! We've got 'em all!"

I turned into what little wind was blowing and shoved the throttles to their stops. My first takeoff in an Otter was lumbering and clumsy, but she flew in spite of my unfamiliarity with her, and soon, the orange, belching flames and towering black smoke were astern, and the east coast of Florida lay 150 miles and another lifetime ahead in the silent, unforgiving darkness.

Chapter 19
Heads and Souls

The only thing I knew about the airplane in my hands was the number of engines it had and how fast it would cruise. The other thing I knew had nothing to do with the Twin Otter and everything to do with the most catastrophic mission failure of my career.

Dre crawled his way into the cockpit beside me as my hearing slowly returned. "Do you have comms with Disco?"

I yelled, "I do."

"Find out where they are, and get a count of heads and souls."

Dre's order felt like a kick in the gut, but I made the call through the borrowed—or stolen—headset in the borrowed—or stolen—airplane.

Disco said, "We're fifteen miles west of Andros with six souls and twelve heads."

Dre spun and counted men behind us. "We're nine! We're short one! Who's missing?"

I spun in my seat and found Mongo, Hunter, and five SEALs in the cabin behind the cockpit. Dre's count was correct. He and I made nine.

My throbbing head finally arrived at the answer. "It's Singer, my wounded sniper. He wasn't in the fight."

"Where is he?"

"He was in the vehicle on the northern side of the ridgeline."

Dre gave me a nod as his gears spun behind his eyes. "Can we make MacDill?"

MacDill Air Force Base in Tampa, the home of Special Operations Command, was the logical choice for Dre, but I said, "*We* can make MacDill, but the chopper can't. How about Homestead?"

Dre closed his eyes. I could only assume he was drawing a map of southern Florida in his head. When his dark eyes opened again, he said, "I don't like it. Have you got any other options?"

"We can't go to anything in Miami. We'd never be able to explain . . ."

I paused, and he grabbed my shoulder. "What? What are you thinking?"

"There's a private field in North Largo run by a friend of mine who happens to be an old Agency guy."

If Master Chief Lewis would've been capable of smiling in that moment, he would have, but the slow nod said it all.

I keyed the mic. "Disco, we're going to Largo."

With the rotor blades echoing in the background, he answered with a single word. "Roger."

As my pounding heart returned to its normal rhythm, my mind calmed enough to begin putting the pieces together, and I called Disco again. "If you can raise Singer, get him to the airport and find the CASA crew. We need to get that airplane back to the States before this thing turns the world inside out."

Again, his one-word reply came. "Roger."

The flight from Andros to Key Largo was the longest short flight of my life. So much had gone wrong—not only wrong, but unthinkably wrong. I'd gotten men injured before that night, but I feared I would forever carry the unbearable burden of six dead SEALs on my back. I'd led nineteen men into a fight that couldn't be won—a fight that was nothing more than an un-survivable death trap.

As I thought of the coming agony for the families of the men who'd given their lives under my command, I wanted to trade places with the bodies lying cold inside the helicopter. It should've been me. I made the call. I developed the plan. I led the charge. I was responsible for their lives . . . and especially for their deaths.

As the agony of the night behind us tortured my soul, I tried to focus on the tasks of flying the foreign airplane, finding Key Largo, and getting the souls of the living safely back on the ground.

The airport appeared on the horizon north of Jewfish Creek, where I'd lain at anchor on my first boat, christened *Aegis*, and received my first official mission. That day felt a thousand miles and a million years distant, but everything in my soul told me I'd never accept another assignment. I'd never again hold the lives of warriors in my hands. Every time I thought of the six SEALs who'd sacrificed their lives in the name of liberating innocent civilians, their faces became those of Clark, Hunter, Singer, Mongo, Disco, and Skipper. Had it been their bodies lying on the cold deck of the helicopter, every breath I took would sting of a thousand razors slashing at my heart, leaving me in an eternal hell of my own creation.

Returning to the reality and responsibility of the lives behind me in an airplane I'd never landed, I pulled the power back, flattened the props, lowered the landing gear, and added flaps. The runway lights fell into alignment ahead, and the Twin Otter began her descent. Her speed on final was different than the Caravan, but the airplane handled beautifully and nestled itself onto the runway with little input from me.

Having kept the airplane and its passengers alive, I taxied to the parking apron and shut down the engines. Someone opened the door behind me, and soon, the cabin was empty. If checklists existed, there was no evidence of them in the cockpit, so I completed the shutdown procedures as if I were in the Caravan, except with a pair of turbines instead of just one.

With the instrument panel in darkness and the engines silent, I sat, alone, with my heart breaking and my mind reeling.

Dre grabbed a handful of my shirt. "Get out. We need to talk."

The agonizing anticipation of what he would say tore at my gut like the claws of a ravaging animal. He would blame me for the loss of his men, and he would be right. He would likely put his pistol in my face and send me to the Hell I deserved.

I followed him down the ladder to the tarmac of the deserted airport, and he extended a finger toward the terminal. "Over there, now!"

I did as he ordered and hung my head as I tread, step after un-thinkable step, toward the building. We rounded the corner of the concrete structure to find a picnic table with a filthy ashtray perched at one end.

"Sit," he ordered.

I planted myself on the edge of the table and looked up at the career SEAL.

He stuck a finger in my face. "Listen to me, and listen good. What happened out there tonight was not your responsibility, and it damned sure wasn't your fault. Is it your first time?"

"First time for what?"

"For losing men."

I nodded and swallowed hard. "We've had injuries, but not losses."

"That's what I thought. That makes it even more important that you listen to every word I say. Don't talk. Don't think. Don't even blink. Just listen."

I froze in place.

"You'd trade your life for the life of any man on that mission tonight. I see that in you. I hear it when you talk to them. I see it when you watch them move. You're a leader, and that's exactly what my men, your men, and every other ground-pounder on the planet needs and deserves. Don't you dare let the thought of robbing them of that leadership enter your mind. It's a gift, and you've got it in spades, boy."

He leaned in, grabbed two handfuls of my shirt, and gave me a shake. "Do you hear me? Those thoughts inside your head are the most selfish thing you could possibly be thinking. If you think it's up to you whether or not you keep leading those men into the fire, you're a selfish ass, and if you quit, you're turning your back on those six men who gave their lives fighting for what's right—fighting for those who can't fight for themselves—fighting because that's what they were born to do. Don't you dare turn your back on those men. You carry them with you every time you put on your boots, and you keep fighting because that's exactly what every one of those men would tell you to do."

He gave me another shake and stepped back. "They deserve better than you quitting on yourself and quitting on them." He lunged toward me and delivered a two-handed shove, knocking me backward onto the table. "Don't quit! Get out there and lead. No matter how bad it hurts, it's what *you* are, and it's what *they* deserve."

I stood to follow him, and he spun on a heel.

"And another thing . . . That sniper of yours, Clark, he's going to give you the same speech when he gets here."

"He's not my sniper. He's my handler. Singer is the sniper."

He took an aggressive step toward me. "Tonight, Singer was a truck driver, and Clark was your sniper. It doesn't matter what they'll be when this is over. What matters is what they are right now, and right now, you're in charge. That isn't going to change tonight."

We rounded the corner of the terminal in locked step, and he said, "Check on your men, and give them something to do. It doesn't matter what it is. They don't care as long as they have a task. Then, find a way to get in touch with your analyst. The last thing she heard over the sat-com was an explosion. You think she might be pacing the cage by now?"

Leadership comes in every shape and size, but at its core, it's always the same. It's compassionate when required, stern when necessary, and selfless without fail, and Master Chief DeAndre Lewis was its epitome.

I jogged to Mongo and Hunter, and before I could speak, they both asked, "Are you all right?"

"Don't worry about me," I said. "Are you two okay?"

Hunter said, "We're not hurt, but we're wet and cold. When you calm down, you will be, too."

For the first time, I felt the water dripping from my clothes, but I ignored the discomfort. "We need to secure the airport. We can't have somebody driving up while we're regrouping. I want the two of you on the gate. The SEALs will disable the lights after Disco lands. He should be here any minute."

Without hesitation, both men climbed to their feet. "Yes, sir."

Sir? They've never called me sir. Why now?

I reached for my phone, only to discover my pants weren't the only thing wet. I pulled the waterlogged, worthless implement from my pocket and stared at the black screen. Making the call was not optional. It had to be done, so I knelt in front of the terminal building's front door and inserted my picks.

It took longer than it should have, but it finally surrendered to my tools. Hunter had been right. As I came down from the shock of the night, I shivered beneath my wet clothes. My trembling finger bounced across the telephone as I dialed the number.

It rang twice before Skipper's voice filled the line. "Ops center."

My teeth chattered as I spoke. "Skipper, it's Chase."

"Chase! Are you all right? What happened?"

I tried to steady my chin, but it was no use. The involuntary trembling would only stop when I could get out of my wet clothes and into something dry and warm. "It was a trap. There was nobody in the compound—just some silhouettes in the windows and enough C-Four to jumpstart Hell."

"Is anybody hurt?"

I knew that wasn't her real question. "We lost six SEALs. Everyone else survived."

She spoke before thinking. "Oh, thank God. I mean . . . not that anybody is dead. I meant . . ."

I rescued her. "It's okay, Skipper. I know exactly what you meant. We're on deck in Largo, and we're waiting for Disco and the rest of the team."

"That explains the call."

"What call?"

She shuffled some papers. "Sixty-six minutes ago, the War Room at the Pentagon received a call that appeared to originate in the Cayman Islands. It was an electronically altered male voice with only twenty-two words. 'Your arrogance and disobedience have cost the lives of six men tonight. You will soon know their names and regret your actions.'"

Chapter 20
Gris-Gris and an Albatross

The unmistakable sound of a multi-engine airplane approaching from the east sent me running from the terminal. Although I couldn't see it, the sound came from an aircraft at least the size of the Twin Otter, and probably bigger. The runway lights were dark thanks to the handiwork of Chief Lewis's SEALs, but the aircraft continued its approach, apparently undaunted by the darkness.

As I considered bouncing a pair of nine-millimeter rounds off the skin of the approaching airplane, the sound of footfalls momentarily turned me from the night sky to see Dre sprinting across the tarmac and waving both arms in the pale light of the ramp. "Don't shoot. It's our CASA!"

Relieved beyond words, I sighed as the main landing gear of the CASA 212 chirped as they touched down on the pitch-black runway.

"They must've been on nods," I said.

"I'm sure of it," Dre said. "They're some of the best pilots I've ever flown with. Sometimes, I think they've got night vision devices hardwired into their skulls."

With exaggerated hand signals, Dre marshalled the twin turbo-prop to the ramp alongside our commandeered Twin Otter, and the engines fell silent. The rear door swung open, and a single pilot stepped from the cabin. He crossed the parking apron, and Dre asked, "Where are the other two?"

The pilot motioned toward the east. "They'll be along soon. Chris has the Caravan, and Buckshot's bringing the One-Eighty-Two. We figured you wanted all the air assets off the island, so there were three airplanes and three of us. I made a judgment call. If it was the wrong decision, I'll eat it."

Dre shot a thumb toward the pilot. "I told you they were some of the best I've ever seen."

"No doubt," I said. "But how did you get my airplanes started without the keys?"

The pilot eyed Dre as if I'd asked him to explain nuclear fission, and the SEAL said, "They're special ops pilots. They can steal the Space Shuttle if you need it."

"Enough said."

Almost before I'd finished my sentence, the telltale *whop-whop* of the Bell 412 rang from the sky, and Disco set the helicopter on the ramp like laying a baby in its crib. Men poured from the chopper as the rotors wound down and whistled to a stop. Clark and Disco were the last two out of the helicopter and hung their heads as they crossed the ramp. The looks on their faces said more than any words could've expressed.

We stood in humble silence for a long moment before Clark laid a hand on my shoulder. "Let's go have a conversation."

I glanced at Dre, and he said, "We've already had the talk. I screwed his head back on straight. He's gonna be fine."

Clark locked eyes with me, and I gave him a barely perceptible nod.

Dre stepped away, motioning for his pilots to follow.

Clark asked, "Are you good?"

"I will be," I said. "It's a tough thing to swallow, though."

He shot a glance over his shoulder as one of the pilots climbed into the CASA. "What's about to happen is going to be the most sickening feeling you'll ever experience, Chase."

The pilot started the CASA's turbines, and Dre directed him until the tail of the airplane faced the side of our helicopter. The ramp opened, and everyone except me scampered toward the aircraft. As much as my team had become a family, there would always be a thin, barely visible line separating me from them. The uniform they'd worn while honing their craft weaved them together into a brotherhood I would never know or fully understand.

As I stepped to follow them, the landing light of the 182 and the headlights of an approaching car came into view simultaneously. I knew the sound of my Skylane as well as the beating of my own heart, but the headlights on the access road concerned me.

Clark spun and slid his hand to his pistol. "Didn't you secure the perimeter?"

"I put Mongo and Hunter on it," I said, copying Clark's movement toward the sidearm.

Before we drew our weapons, the headlights flashed five times in rapid successions, and we relaxed. Hank, the airport manager, pulled the car to a stop, and he, Hunter, and Mongo stepped from the vehicle.

"Thanks for not shooting me," he said. "I double-locked the gate and brought your men back. Nobody's going to get through the gate."

"Thanks, Hank. I'm sorry to drag you out of bed like this."

He scoffed. "You didn't drag me out of anything. I hear your little op turned into a soup sandwich."

"That it did," I said. "We lost six men tonight."

"Yeah, that's what Skipper told me on the phone." He surveyed the scene. "Listen, Chase. The airport is yours 'til daybreak, but after that, I have to open the gate."

The 182 touched down and taxied to the ramp. Singer and the pilot they'd called Buckshot climbed from the cockpit. The Southern Baptist sniper slowly walked across the tarmac in reverent respect for the dead. When he reached the helicopter, he knelt beside the aircraft and laid a hand on the threshold of the sliding door. Although I couldn't hear him, I had little doubt he was talking with God.

As Singer continued kneeling and praying, the SEALs and my team stood in a pair of lines between the CASA 212 and the helicopter with their heads bowed. Having no understanding of what was happening, I stood on the parking apron, staring in wide-eyed wonder at the scene unfolding in front of me.

Clark caught my eye and motioned for me to join him, so I silently slipped into position beside my friend, mentor, and handler. Singer's prayer ended with an "Amen" that was echoed by each of the warriors. When Singer stood and gave a nod, a pair of SEALs broke from the formation, lifted the body of one of their fallen brothers into their arms, and carried him onto the CASA while the rest of us stood in silence with our hands raised, knife-blade sharp to our foreheads, in a silent salute. The expression of love between brothers and the respect for the sacrifice continued until each of the six bodies was carried from the helicopter to the waiting airplane. When the two SEALs had carried the final body onto the CASA, they stood at attention at the foot of the ramp, raised their salute, and finished the memorial gesture with the same precision they'd carried each of their fallen comrades.

No one spoke, but my team drifted away from the SEALs as they loaded onto the CASA, the division between us now clearer than ever.

Dre broke from his team, approached, and grabbed my shirt. "Stay in the fight. We have to bury our fallen brothers, but we'll be back if you need us. This may be your responsibility, but it's not your fault . . . brother."

The CASA 212 taxied to the runway, climbed out, and disappeared into the relentless darkness of the western sky.

"Where are they going?" I asked no one in particular.

Clark threw an arm across my shoulder. "They'll go to MacDill, first, and then the mortuary affairs troops will prepare their bodies to be returned to their families in flag-draped coffins."

Regret is impossible to describe, but everyone has felt it. The gnawing, stabbing, unrelenting agony in my heart made me replay every moment of the assault, every decision I'd made, every order I'd given. Hearing the soul-jarring explosion echo inside my head both sickened and rejuvenated me. The animals who'd laid the trap would pay for murdering six of America's finest warriors, and I would forever carry their burden. But although they were the first, theirs would not be the last lives I would lose, and I prayed when the day came that my blood would stain the ground on some foreign soil and my soul would depart my flesh, that my sacrifice wouldn't stop those around me from continuing the fight. To honor my death, I would want my brothers to dig in their heels and return fire until the sounds of foreign guns fall silent in the preservation of freedom.

Hank broke the solemnity of the moment. "Come inside, guys. I'll either make you some coffee or put you to bed. It's up to you."

"I won't speak for everyone else, but I'll take you up on the coffee. I've got a lot of work to do."

Clark kicked at a pebble. "I'll speak for the rest of us. Make that coffee for six."

"That's what I figured." Hank led us to the mirrored glass door and pulled out his keys.

"Those won't be necessary," I said. "It's already unlocked."

He grinned. "Of course it is. I should've known."

The coffee was strong, black, and exactly what the doctor ordered.

Skipper answered almost before the phone rang. "Hey, Chase."

"How did you know it was me?"

"Who else would it be? I guess it's time to come up with a new plan, huh?"

"It certainly is, but we have some housekeeping to do before we jump back into the mission. We'll get you the names of the lost SEALs, and I want you to find out how much debt and how many children each of them had."

"Why would you want me to do that?"

I cleared my throat. "The Navy will pay each family a quarter million dollars, but I want to make sure everyone is debt free and that every child has a fully funded savings account for college. I'll eat the cost, no matter what it is."

Clark jumped in. "No, you won't. The Board will eat the cost. Their pockets are deeper than yours."

"Okay, that settles that," Skipper said. "What's next?"

"I need you to run the registration and history on a de Havilland Twin Otter we *borrowed*. I need a full dossier on whoever owns it." I gave her the registration and serial number.

"I'm on it. That won't take long. What else?"

I ran through my mental checklist. "Free up about a million dollars. We're going to buy and remodel a house on Andros and make it available to the SEALs' families absolutely free anytime they want it."

Clark did it again. "Belay that order. The Board will cover that one, too."

I found a notepad and pen in the pilot's lounge. "That's it for housekeeping. Let's get back to the mission."

Skipper's fingers rattled the keys back at Bonaventure. "I've never pulled off of it. In fact, I've been putting pieces together. The first big mystery—well, obviously, except for who and where they are—is the fact that they have access. They know how to call the White House Situation Room, the station chief in Nassau, and now the War Room at the Pentagon. Those aren't exactly public numbers, and some of the most advanced tracking software in the world can't trace the calls. These people are well funded and extremely well connected."

I took a long drink of my coffee. "Would a U.S. ambassador have those numbers?"

"Maybe, but I'd have to talk to somebody over at the State Department to know for sure."

"Don't do that yet," I said. "I'm working a theory, but it's not complete yet. For now, see if you can get me a number for the ambassador to Russia or Ukraine. They're far enough outside this thing to give me the answers I want."

She stopped typing. "I think I see where you're going with this, and I like it. You still think the ambassador to The Bahamas is the ringleader, don't you?"

"I'm just exploring possibilities here. He's involved at some level, otherwise, he wouldn't have run. There's nothing he could've done that would've made him look guiltier. Him running away either means it's his scheme, or he's at least privy to it."

"That's exactly how I've approached it from here," she said. "If I had to guess, I'd say he was involved in the planning and got scared when it got a little too real for him."

"You may be right, but that doesn't get us any closer to finding the hostages."

"Here's the private lines for the ambassadors to Russia, Ukraine, and Finland."

"Why Finland?"

"Because that's the least likely of the three to be tapped by the SVR, and I didn't think you wanted Russian foreign intelligence sticking their noses into this one."

"Good thinking. That's why you're worth your weight in gold. While you're poking around, put out a few feelers for former Ambassador John Woodford."

"I'm way ahead of you on that one, but I don't have anything to report yet." She gave me the numbers. "It's around noon over there, so you might get lucky if you call now."

"I could use a little luck right about now. I feel like I'm wearing a voodoo gris-gris with an albatross circling overhead."

Chapter 21
Eastern Bloc Burritos

Sleep should've come, but much like serenity, it was not to be mine. Instead, ghosts of the dead marched in endless columns through my tortured mind. Logic and reason intertwined with madness wound their way through my efforts to piece together the puzzle that'd been dumped onto my lap.

Why did Ambassador John Woodford insist I become involved with the investigation into the kidnappings? How did he convince the president I was the key to solving the unthinkable scenario? Is Woodford's disappearance somehow related to my involvement? Should I have the SEALs return, or should my team and I step back into the ring of fire and tear the situation apart from the inside?

Lying in the borrowed bed in the borrowed house, wrestling with the details of the borrowed mission, I watched the shadows produced by the climbing sun as they traversed the floor and walls like the relentless hands of time against which I was racing. Ignoring the cruelty of the four time zones separating me from the only true anchor in my life, I dialed her number with my sat-phone—the only phone I had left—and waited as the ringing phone three thousand miles away drew her from the sleep I so desperately envied.

"Chase? Is that you?" came Penny's sleep-soaked voice.

"Good morning, sweetheart. I'm sorry to wake you, but—"

"No, no, don't be sorry. I'm glad you called. Are you okay?"

"Not really. The team is okay, but we lost six Navy SEALs last night in an operation in The Bahamas."

The pain in her voice echoed my own. "Oh, Chase, I'm so sorry. What happened?"

"I can't tell you over the phone, but the *Readers Digest* version is we walked into a trap."

She sighed. "I don't know what to say. I'm just so sorry. You're not finished, are you? You're going back in, right?"

"Yeah, we're going back in, but not today. I have to get my head straight and spend some time with Skipper and Ginger."

"Ginger? It must really be serious if you've called her in."

"I didn't call her. Skipper did. This is, by far, the most complicated case we've ever been on, and we need all the help we can get."

"Do you need me to come home?"

"No, enjoy your moment. I wish I could be there with you, but this thing . . ."

"That's sweet, but you'd be bored out of your mind, and I understand. I've been keeping up with it on the news, but of course they didn't mention you guys or the SEALs."

I shook my head. "I can only imagine what they're saying."

"Trust me, you don't want to hear it."

"Okay. I need to go, but I wanted to hear your voice. I'm sorry for waking you."

"No, Chase. Never be sorry. I always want to talk to you, no matter what time it is. I love you."

"I love you, too. I'll see you sometime soon . . . I hope."

Something about hearing Penny's voice calmed the screaming inside my head, and I crawled from beneath the cover. I staggered down the stairs, uncertain whose house I was in and whose coffee I smelled. The mystery was solved when I followed my nose to the kitchen to find the rest of my team and a woman I didn't recognize.

"Oh, good morning," she said, dusting her hands on her apron. "I'm Margaret, Hank's wife. And you must be Chase."

I shook her offered hand. "Yes, ma'am. It's nice to meet you. Thank you for letting us camp out here for the night. We've had . . ."

She waved a dismissive hand. "Say nothing of it. Trust me, I understand. I lived the life for fifty years wondering when or if my husband would come home."

"My wife feels the same, I'm sure."

"Oh, do you have a proclivity for Eastern European whores, too?"

I was taken aback, and I tried not to laugh. "That's not exactly what I meant."

She wadded up the dishtowel she'd been holding and tossed it at me. "I'm just messing with you. Of course I worried about Hank getting killed, too, but I always kept plenty of penicillin on hand. There's no telling what kind of cooties those Russian girls were sending Hank home with. Alas, though, such is the life of the wife of a spy."

Clark bit his lip to maintain his composure, but it didn't work. He finally succumbed and burst into raucous laughter. When he could finally speak again, he said, "Chase has already been through the Russian cootie phase of his life, and we believe he's finally settled down."

Margaret grinned. "I don't think my Hank will ever settle down, but I'm glad to hear you learned your lesson early. Those Eastern Bloc girls may be pretty on the outside, but they can't make a breakfast burrito like I can." She stuck a plate in my hand and landed a monster burrito on it before I could flinch.

Mongo leaned toward me. "If you don't think you can finish that, I'll be glad to come in around the seventh inning to be your closer."

I pulled the plate close to my chest. "Not a chance. I've got a no-hitter working, and you can stay in the bullpen."

Margaret plated another enormous burrito and slid it across the table to our equally enormous Mongo. He grinned, and she said, "It's nice to have boys in the house to eat my cooking again. You don't know how much you're going to miss certain little things until they're gone. All of our boys are grown with kids of their own now."

My first bite of her burrito confirmed her claim. I wiped my mouth. "This is, without a doubt, the best burrito I've ever had."

Margaret dusted invisible debris from her shoulder. "From your lips to God's ears, Chase. I give all my recipes to my daughters-in-law. The boys never know I'm the secret source behind all the insider information their wives seem to magically know."

I froze with a forkful of burrito halfway between my plate and my mouth. I dropped the fork, stood from the table, and kissed Hank's wife squarely on the forehead. "Margaret, you're a genius!"

Clark eyed me for several seconds while he replayed the tape in his head. The look on his face when it hit him was priceless. "Give me your sat-phone," he demanded.

I slid it across the table, and he caught it on the way to his feet. I followed him from the kitchen onto the back deck of Hank and Margaret's beautiful home.

When the connection was made, he said, "Dad, it's Clark. I need some information without anyone knowing I asked."

I couldn't hear Dominic Fontana, Clark's father, responding, but I had little doubt he'd jump in with both feet.

Clark said, "How many people know the direct number to call the war room at the Pentagon, the Situation Room at the White House, and the CIA station chief in Nassau?"

He listened for a moment and said, "Hang on a minute, Dad. I'm putting you on speaker. It's just me and Chase." He pressed the button and laid the phone on the banister. "Okay, Dad, say that again."

Dominic said, "Hello, Chase. It's good to talk with you again. Is your new handler cutting the mustard?"

"He had some big shoes to fill, Dom, but I guess he's doing all right."

Dominic chuckled. "Clark asked about access, and he apparently wanted you to hear my answer. The list of people who'd have all that access is extremely short. Generally, it would be limited to the first seven or eight people in the presidential line of succession. The VP, speaker of the House, president pro tempore of the Senate, secretaries of state, treasury, and defense, as well as the attorney general, and maybe the secretary of the interior. The director of Central Intelligence probably has the numbers. Oh, and the new one, the secretary of Homeland Security – whatever that means."

"So, an ambassador wouldn't have those numbers?" I asked.

"Well, ambassadors would have the chief of station numbers in their own embassies and could get other COS numbers from his fellow ambassadors, but unless they were the ambassador to Russia or China, I can't imagine them having access to the war room and Situation Room numbers."

"Thanks, Dom. That gives us a pretty good starting point."

"What's all this about, boys?"

"Haven't you been watching the news, Dad?"

"I don't even have a TV."

Clark chuckled. "Go ahead, Chase. You tell him."

"Well, it seems somebody has kidnapped a Supreme Court justice, two congressmen, and the governor of South Carolina. Whoever they are, they have the phone numbers we asked about. They're demanding five billion dollars ransom be given to the country of Gabon, among other things."

"Gabon? Gabon is the armpit of Africa. They've never seen five dollars, let alone five billion. Who are these clowns?"

Clark said, "That's what we're trying to figure out, but we've run into a little resistance, so to speak."

Dominic's tone turned somber. "Are you guys operational on this thing?"

"We are," I said.

He asked, "How quickly can you be on a secure line?"

Clark said, "We're in Largo, but we can be in my office in an hour."

"Get to the office, and call me on a secure line. I don't have all the answers, but I do have some questions you'll want to ask. I'll wait here for your call."

Back inside Margaret's kitchen, Clark gave the order, "Police-up the area, wash your dirties, and get on the airplane. We've got work to do."

I turned to Margaret. "Thank you so much for your hospitality, but we have to go."

She patted my hand. "I know the game, Chase. Leave the dishes. I'll take care of everything. You boys go save the world. Just don't bring home any cooties."

We piled ourselves onto an oversized golf cart with Clark behind the wheel, and in five minutes, we were back at the Ocean Reef Club Airport, where Hank met us on the tarmac.

"Good morning, boys. Where are you headed in such a hurry?"

"We have to be in South Beach at Clark's office, ASAP."

He said, "I topped everything off with fuel, and you're welcome to leave any or all of the airplanes here as long as you need."

"We'll come back for the chopper and the Skylane as soon as we can. Charge the fuel and any tie-down charges to my card you have on file."

He waved me off. "Don't worry about any of that. There'll be plenty of time for that stuff when you get back. Oh, I almost forgot. Do you want to do the avionics upgrades on the helicopter?"

"Yes, definitely, but it'll have to wait. We may need the chopper in the next few days. Tell your man to order whatever he needs, and pay for it with my card."

Clark and Disco already had the turbine spinning in the Caravan by the time I joined the rest of the team aboard the flying machine. We splashed down at the Miami Seaplane Base beside a long row of cruise ships twenty minutes after blasting off from Largo. It took two taxis to carry the six of us, but we pulled into Clark's driveway on South Beach less than fifteen minutes after taxiing out of the water and onto the parking ramp.

Dominic picked up, and the telltale clicks followed, indicating the electronic switching making the lines secure. "Okay, we're secure on my end."

Clark tapped the glowing green light on his console. "We're secure here, as well."

Dominic said, "When we spoke earlier, I was in the pool with the rest of the world a million miles away, but since then, I've done a little digging, and my memory proved to be at least somewhat accurate."

The six of us huddled around the console, listening intently as he continued. "About eleven or twelve years ago, Clinton appointed Michael Gallagher as the U.S. ambassador to Gabon. Gallagher was married to a woman named Tiffany. Are you taking notes? This is going to get convoluted."

Although I couldn't read his chicken scratch, Clark said, "I'm writing it down. Keep going."

The sound of Dominic sipping something with ice cubes rattled through the speaker. "Tiffany was Gallagher's second wife, but he was *her* first husband. They divorced while he was assigned to the embassy in Gabon, and everyone assumed Tiffany would return to the States, but that didn't happen. They hadn't been married long enough for her to qualify for any of his pension, and the judge who signed their divorce decree was a circuit court judge in Washington D.C. named Ronald Mateo. He went to law school at Harvard with guess who? Michael Gallagher. Needless to say, the marital dissolution agreement and ordered settlement went Gallagher's way."

I interrupted. "Is that the same Ronald Mateo who's now a Supreme Court justice?"

"The very same."

Clark palmed his forehead. "Oh, this is too much. One of the kidnappers' demands is that Mateo resign his seat on the Supreme Court."

Dominic said, "Follow the money, boys. It's always about money, power, or sex. And sometimes . . . all three."

I scratched my head. "You said Tiffany didn't come back to the States. Where did she go?"

"Nowhere. That's the thing. She went to work in a French bank in Gabon and crawled in bed with a guy named . . . Ah, it's not coming. I'm on my third or fourth Bloody Mary, so I'll remember at some point, but for now, suffice it to say he was a mover and shaker in African banking. I don't know if that means anything in your case, but it sounds like something you might want to look into."

Suddenly, panic struck me, and I yanked my sat-phone from my pocket.

Thankfully, Skipper answered quickly. "Hey, Chase. What's up?"

"Have you talked with anyone at the State Department yet about who has access to the telephone numbers we were worried about?"

She grunted. "I'm sorry, but I haven't gotten that far down my list yet. But I promise . . ."

I almost yelled. "Good! Don't do it! Scratch that one off your list. I got the information I needed from Dominic."

"Dominic? What's he doing back in the game?"

"I dragged him back kicking and screaming, but he's already been worth a billion times what I paid him."

"Let me guess," she said. "You paid him nothing."

"Yeah, but that's not the point. Just don't call the State Department for any reason before you talk with either me or Clark about it. We'll call back on a secure line and give you a full briefing, ASAP, but for now, suffice it to say I'm extremely glad you didn't display your typical efficiency on this one."

"Whatever you say. Ginger is here, and she loves the ops center so much she wants you to build one just like it in her house."

"Tell her to scrape together a couple million bucks, and I'll send the contractor to Silver Spring. That's all for now. Talk soon."

Before she could respond, I shut down the phone and re-pocketed the tool.

Clark gave me the thumbs-up. "Good catch. If we're playing sleuth on this one, we want to stay as far beneath the radar as possible."

Dominic said, "That's all I have for now, but when I think of the French banker's name, I'll send it your way."

"Thanks, Dom. You've been more help than you know. I have a feeling Skipper and Ginger will have the banker's shoe size in thirty seconds. We're sorry to have pulled you out of the pool, but we really appreciate your help."

"No problem. But don't start expecting it. I usually ignore the phone when it makes that ringing noise."

Chapter 22
Summa Cum Baseball

Clark disconnected the line and spun in his chair. "Well, College Boy, it looks like this hands-on circus just turned academic. You should feel right at home. What's going on in that summa cum laude brain of yours?"

"You've clearly not seen my transcripts. I graduated summa cum baseball."

"That may be so, but you did graduate, so that makes you the smart one."

I turned to find the real brain on our island of misfit toys. "Mongo, what do you think?"

He scratched his chin where a week's worth of stubble had piled itself. "I think there's no such thing as summa cum baseball, but I also think our brains are headed down the same alleyway. The money is clearly the real play. The trap was a test, and we failed. I don't think we're going to settle this one with bullets and blades. If we're still in the game . . . We *are* still in the game, right?"

I nodded. "Oh, yeah. We're neck-deep in the game."

Mongo continued. "I hate to agree with Clark, but I think he's right this time. We're going to solve this one with our brains and some good old-fashioned detective work."

166 · CAP DANIELS

The look on Hunter's face grew sourer by the minute until he couldn't hold his tongue any longer. "You big-brained people may find these guys, but somebody still has to kick down their door, and that's my favorite part. I, for one, am not going to miss it."

"Don't worry," I said. "When it's time to bust some heads, we'll all be there, but we have to figure out which door we need to kick. We are not walking into another trap."

Mongo said, "Let's walk through the players. First contact came from Ambassador Woodford in the form of insistence that you return to The Bahamas to solve this thing, right?"

I replayed the events of the past few days. "Yes, but apparently, Woodford had spoken with the president before he called me because Clark got the tasking nearly simultaneously with Woodford's call to me."

Clark jumped in. "Yeah, that's right. But now that I think about it, what makes us believe any of this has anything to do with The Bahamas other than Woodford's call?"

"The exploding house, for one thing," Hunter belted out.

Clark raised a finger. "Yes, that sounds damning from the outside, but think about it. We would've never searched in The Bahamas without Woodford's call."

My sat-phone rang, and I tapped the speaker button. "Go ahead, Skipper."

Her tone said nothing good was coming next. "You're still at Clark's, right?"

"We are."

"I'm sending you a video, but I'm warning you, it's not easy to watch."

"Okay, we're standing by," I said.

Clark pulled up his secure email account and downloaded the video. The image that filled the screen was gruesome, disturbing, and depraved. Text-like rolling credits passed above the image of

Congressman James Paige's decapitated body. The text read: Please don't make us do this again.

We sat in utter silence before Clark said, "We knew this was coming, but it still sucks. Has Paige's family seen the video?"

Skipper said, "Not to my knowledge. It's not been released to the media, and I hope it never is."

I said, "They'll get their hands on it, and when that happens, everything changes. We have to get to these people before it gets worse. I've got two questions. First, do you believe the video is authentic, and second, where do we stand on negotiations?"

She said, "I thought exactly the same thing. I ran the video, frame by frame, and it looks authentic to me, but I'm not an expert. I wish Penny were here. She could get some of her Hollywood friends to take a look at it."

"That's not a bad idea," I said. "Why don't you give her a call and see if she knows anyone who can take a look without running their mouth?"

"Sure, I can do that, but I don't love the idea of an outsider getting their hands on the video."

"You've got a point there," I said. "How about the National Reconnaissance Office?"

"I'm sure the NRO is tearing into it, but it might be tough to get our hands on the results."

"I thought you said you think the president opened up a few doors for you."

"I still think that, but I've not tried to get into the NRO. I'll give it a try, and we'll see what happens. If all else fails, I'll go the Hollywood route."

"Great. Now, how about the second question?"

"Oh, yeah . . . the negotiations. Believe it or not, the kidnappers made a concession. Well, part of a concession. Remember the twenty-four prisoners they wanted released?"

"Sure."

"They cut that number down to eight, but it's not really a concession."

"Why do you say that?" I asked.

"The other sixteen are in prisons all over the world. Even if we wanted to release them, the U.S. doesn't have the power to do it. The eight remaining names on the list are all housed in federal prisons here in the States."

Mongo asked, "Do you have the list?"

Skipper riffled through some paperwork. "Yes, and before you ask, I'm already running the list. So far, five of the eight are in so-called country-club prisons for financial crimes. One of the remaining three is only days away from dying of cancer in the prison infirmary in Victorville, California. The other two don't seem to exist—or at least I can't find them. But I've handed that off to Ginger."

"That reminds me," I said. "Have you run the registration on the Twin Otter yet?"

"On the what?"

"The airplane from The Bahamas."

"Oh, yeah, that. I didn't know what a Twin Otter was. Anyway, that's freaky, too. It's not registered to anybody. It's like it doesn't exist."

"It exists," I said. "I flew it from The Bahamas to Key Largo."

She huffed. "Yeah, I know the airplane exists, but there's no record of it anywhere."

"Run the serial number instead of the registration and see what you get."

I could almost see her rolling her eyes. "Do you need me to tell you to put bullets in your gun before you shoot it? No, you don't, and I don't need you telling me how to do my job. I ran both, and there's no record of the airplane ever being built. The serial numbers one before and after yours exists, but yours does not—not even in the de Havilland manufacturing records."

I said, "Okay, let's not spend any more energy on that one. We need to brief you on what we learned from Dominic."

We spent the next ten minutes laying out the West African soap opera, and Skipper typed furiously as we spoke.

When we finished, she asked, "How does Dominic know all that stuff?"

Clark fielded that one. "It was his job to know everything that happened in every corner of the world when he was operational. Now, he floats around in his pool and drinks Bloody Marys 'til noon. Believe it or not, he doesn't even own a TV."

"Sometimes I wish I didn't have one, either, but in this business, current events tend to matter. I'll get to work on this, and I'll have the name of the French banker for you in a few minutes."

I said, "Thanks. Do you need anything else from us right now?"

In a rare moment of timidity, she said, "There is one thing I need to ask you before we hang up."

"Sure, name it," I said.

"I need to do something a tiny bit illegal, but it'll be worth it. The problem is, no matter what I find, it'll never be admissible in any court. Will you approve that?"

"When did you start asking permission?" I said.

"This one is a little over the top . . . even for me. It was actually Ginger's idea, but I think it's a great plan."

"Is this something any of us will go to jail for doing?"

"No way. No one will ever know we did it, but it's likely to yield some useful results."

"Okay, then. It's approved."

"You've not even heard what I want to do yet."

"I don't care what it is. I trust you. Just do it, and give us the results."

"Okay, thanks. Bye."

I asked Clark, "What do you think she's got up her sleeve?"

"Who knows? But I bet it's going to be good."

Clark leaned back and stared at the ceiling. "This is getting stranger by the minute. Has there been any news coverage of any of it yet?"

"When I spoke with Penny, she said she'd been watching it on the news, but no one mentioned us or the SEALs."

"That's good," he said as he scrounged around in search of the television remote. "Publicity is the one thing we definitely don't need right now."

The small TV in the corner of his office flickered to life, and he switched to a news channel. The talking head on the screen said, "In a rare midterm move, the president exercised his privilege to commute the ninety-nine-year sentence of disgraced financier Francis Jerome Donaldson. Donaldson had been serving his sentence in the federal prison at Victorville, California, and is reported to be near death with stage four brain cancer. Sources inside the prison say Donaldson likely will not survive the cross-country trip to his home in Connecticut. Speculations on the reasons behind the president's decision to commute Donaldson's sentence at this point in his presidency run the gamut from repayment of a political debt to possible blackmail."

Chapter 23
Rock, Paper, Scissors

As we sat in disbelief of the news of the commutation, Skipper called again. "I've got some good news and some terrible news. Which do you want first?"

I said, "Let's go with the bad news first."

"It's worse than bad."

"Let's have it."

She sighed. "The video is real, but the part we saw is only about a third of the whole thing. Apparently, the full-length video shows the actual beheading. I've not seen it yet, but I'll have it soon."

I swallowed hard. "How do you know all this?"

"It turns out I don't have access to the NRO, but Ginger found a back door, and we snuck in. She's running a program to glean the full video in pieces, downloaded out of order, and recompiled on her computer. It'll take half an hour or maybe a little longer. I'll get it to you as soon as we have it pieced back together."

"So, you're certain it's authentic?"

"No, I'm not, but the NRO is convinced."

Clark said, "You're right about that being terrible news, but at least now we know. Now give us the good news."

Her tone lightened, and she sounded animated. "Okay, so here's what we did. We know the precise times when the calls came and ended from the kidnappers. By the way, I don't want to call them kidnappers anymore. They're terrorists."

"I'm good with that—especially after what they did to Congressman Paige. Do we know if the family has been notified yet?"

"No, I don't know, but we're moving on to the good news. It's really better than good, but here goes . . . Like I said, we know the precise times when the calls came into the Situation Room, war room, and COS in Nassau."

"How's that such good news?" I asked.

"Keep your pants on. I'm getting there. There are about a billion telephone calls happening at the same times as the calls in question, and the overwhelming majority of those calls were routed through satellites. The exceptions are local landline calls. We don't care about those."

"You're losing me," I said. "You need to land the plane soon."

"I'm getting there. Just shut up and listen. As you already know, the typical traces aren't working. They're using a computerized algorithm with encryption like I've never seen, but thanks to Ginger, we don't need to circumvent the algorithm. We just need to find all the calls originating from the same point at precisely the same time and ending exactly when the calls were terminated. It gets more complex but also more accurate every time the terrorists make a call."

Mongo let out a sound as if someone had pulled his plug, letting all the air out of him. "Ah! That's genius. How many calls do you have accurate times for?"

Skipper said, "Four."

"And how many possible coincidental calls match all four in length?"

"About three hundred. But guess how many of those originated in The Bahamas."

Mongo said, "None."

"Exactly!"

I held up a hand and shook my head. "Wait. Slow down. I think I understand the idea, but there's no way we can track down three hundred people all over the world."

"They're not people," Skipper said. "They're computers. And it's not going to be three hundred after the next call."

"You've lost me now. Back up, and make me understand."

She grunted. "It's like this. The first run, we hit about six million calls that started and ended within one second of the time recorded for the terrorists' first contact. When we added in the times for the second call, that six million became just over one million possibilities. The third set of times cut that number down to slightly over one hundred thousand. And finally, the clock count for the fourth call left us with three hundred twenty-six possibilities. If the math holds true, after the next call, our pool of possibles will be down to maybe twenty. That's a number we can work with."

"What do you mean, work with?" I asked.

Mongo couldn't resist. "Don't you see, Chase? Every call makes the smuggle more accurate."

"Smuggle? What are you talking about?"

"It's simple," he said. "It's exactly the same thing as the way they used to catch smugglers back when all ships were sailboats. The authorities in harbor towns knew when the ne'er-do-wells had money because they couldn't resist making a show of spending it. They started comparing the nights when the scallywags bought every drop of rum in town to the harbormaster's logs of the ships that came and went in the days leading up to the big spending spree. When certain ships started matching up to nights when the town got out of hand, they knew those were the ships carrying and buying smuggled goods."

I turned to Clark. "Remember that big brain you accused me of having? Well, it ain't true. I'm still lost."

Skipper said, "You don't have to understand it, Chase. You just have to trust that I understand it—and I do. When they call back, we'll calculate the possible call locations down to twenty or so. Then, we'll dig into each of those until we can eliminate the ones that can't possibly be our terrorists."

"How are you going to rule them out?" I asked.

"Most of them will be scheduled electronic transactional calls like money transfers, credit card processing, and stuff like that. We'll throw those out and be left with maybe two or three possibilities. If we get lucky enough to get a nice long call from the terrorists, we might even be able to narrow it down to one. And if that happens, we'll know exactly which door to tell you to kick in."

Mongo sighed. "I'm jealous. You get to do all the cool stuff, Skipper."

"Cool stuff? What are you talking about? I'd rather be out there breaking heads than stuck in here pounding on this keyboard."

"The grass is always greener," he said. "But can I ask a question?"

"Sure, go ahead."

"Why can't you run the three hundred locations you have now against the list of scheduled electronic transactional calls and see how tight the results are?"

Skipper said, "Did you hear that, Ginger?"

Ginger's voice came on the line. "That's a good idea, Mongo, but it takes a lot of computing power to run those algorithms, and we don't have that kind of power."

Mongo grinned. "I thought you found a back door into the National Reconnaissance Office network."

The line went silent for several seconds before Ginger said, "If this works, you're a genius, and I'll want to marry you and make huge-brained babies with you."

Skipper roared with laughter. When she'd finally composed herself, she said, "Ginger, have you ever seen Mongo?"

"No, but he's smart, single—I assume—and I like his voice."

Skipper lost herself inside another fit of laughter. "You're like four feet nothing, and he's like ten feet tall and weighs a thousand pounds or something."

Ginger didn't laugh. "Oh, yeah? How soon can he be here?"

"Uh, no!" Skipper said. "He's got a girlfriend named Irina, and she's Annie Oakley with a rifle, so I'm thinking you'd better keep your hands to yourself."

Ginger asked, "Yeah, but can she make big-brained babies like I could?"

"I don't know, but they'd be beautiful babies, regardless of the size of their noggins," Skipper said.

Ginger raised her voice. "If you can hear me, Mongo, you give me a call if Irina—or whatever—breaks your heart."

The giant blushed, and I tried to get things back on track. "Excuse me, but this is supposed to be us catching a group of terrorists, not playing the dating game. Bachelor number two over here's blushing like a schoolboy."

Ginger said, "Sorry, Chase. I'm working on it, but I'm not sure I have that kind of access through the back door at the NRO. Although, I have a few ideas if it doesn't work."

"Keep at it," I said. "We'll keep hoping for another call from the kidnap . . . from the *terrorists* so you can weed out the scraps. But if you can make Mongo's idea work, that might put us a few steps ahead of the game."

Clark asked, "Is there any way the kidnap . . . I mean, terrorists could know you're running that smuggler thing on them?"

"Not unless your ops center is bugged or one of our computers has been hacked."

"Let's hope neither of those things has happened," I said. "How long should this take if it works?"

"There's no way to know," she said. "It depends on how much computing power we can 'borrow.'"

An idea came to me. "How much would it cost to build the supercomputer you'd need for something like this?"

Skipper said, "There's no way to build it in time for this mission."

"I wasn't necessarily talking about this mission, but if we ran up against something like this in the future, it would be nice to not be limited by a lack of computing power."

Ginger jumped in. "It's working, and I'm not joking, Mongo. Call me!"

"Focus," I demanded. "How long?"

Ginger said, "Calm down, Chase. It'll take a couple of hours, at least. And your supercomputer would cost around two hundred grand, and it would take a week to build it after we got all the components."

"When this is over, I want to make that a priority. Build whatever you need. In the meantime, call me the second you have a tighter list. Is there any chance this process yields only one or two locations?"

"Anything is possible, but it's not likely. We'll call you as soon as we know more. Bye for now."

The line went dead, and I threw my sat-phone at Mongo. "Stop flirting with our borrowed analyst. We need both of them to focus."

"I wasn't flirting. And besides, she started it."

"Started what?"

"The flirting."

"Exactly!" I said. "See? You *were* flirting. I'm calling Irina."

"Call Irina all you want. Just don't tell little Tatiana. She'd kill me for flirting with somebody other than her mom, and she'd kill you for letting me."

"Be honest," I said. "Do you really understand what Skipper and Ginger are doing, or were you just showing off?"

"I understand the concept, but I couldn't do it. The process really is called 'the smuggler's watch.' It's just a matter of finding all the possibilities and narrowing them down by process of elimination."

"How'd you learn all this stuff?" Clark asked.

The big man smiled. "I read part of a book once."

Clark rolled his eyes. "I think I'd like to have my own copy of that book."

Singer, who'd been quiet throughout the whole conversation, broke his silence. "I have a serious question. What are we going to do if and when Skipper finds where these calls are coming from? And on top of that, how do we know the terrorists are holding the hostages in the same place the calls are coming from?"

"We don't," I admitted, "but we have to start someplace."

Hunter said, "While we're asking questions without answers, what are we going to do with the Twin Otter that doesn't exist?"

"We'll deal with that later. Right now, the only thing on my mind is recovering the hostages safely and catching the terrorists."

"It's a little late for that," Hunter said. "We've already lost one hostage."

"I'm not so sure," I said. "I know Skipper told us the NRO authenticated the video, but these people sound too smart to risk murdering a hostage. That ups the ante and puts this crime in a whole new league. If they're savvy enough to score the telephone numbers of all those high-security facilities, technical enough to set up the trap in The Bahamas, and gutsy enough to nab four high-profile Americans in broad daylight, I think they're smart enough to fake a video. When we get the full video, I'm going to call that Bastogne guy in Hollywood. He believes he still owes us one for saving his wife from that carjacker. I think it's time to call in that favor. Don't you?"

Clark sucked air through his teeth. "I don't know. I'm with Skipper on this one. I don't like the idea of letting that video get out into the world, especially if it's faked. Imagine what that would do to his family."

When the phone rang, even though we were expecting the call, each of us jumped as if somebody had landed a grenade in the room.

Mongo was still holding my sat-phone, so he thumbed the button and slid it onto the table. "Go ahead, Skipper."

"Skipper's gone to get coffee," Ginger said. "You're stuck with me for now. And just so you know, Mongo, being stuck with me isn't necessarily a bad thing."

"You already got me in trouble once, Ginger, so I'm not risking it again. Did the borrowed computing power idea work?"

"It worked like a charm, and we've cut the list to six possibilities. I have a theory, though. I think there are only three possibilities, and the other three are mirrors of the first three. The probability of the terrorists predicting that we'd use this method to locate them is outlandish, but the times are too perfect. I think they mirrored their calls just in case we stumbled onto them. More likely, though, whoever wrote the code for them is paranoid and built in the mirroring function out of habit more than fear of us using this method to catch them."

I said, "Stop stalling. Let's have the locations."

She huffed. "Patience. I'm plotting the raw coordinates now. The first one is Kuala Lumpur in Malaysia. The second is Mexico City. And the third is Georgetown, Grand Cayman. Those are the three that I believe to be authentic. Georgetown is interesting because we got a raw hit from there, and it's easily accessible. The remaining three don't make any sense to me. One is in the middle of the Pacific Ocean, another in the Russian Arctic National Park on Severny Island, and the third is in Launceston, Tasmania."

I plotted the locations on the globe inside my head with the best recollection of world geography I could muster. "I understand why the one in the middle of the Pacific is bogus, but what's wrong with Russia and Tasmania?"

She said, "Russia is a slight possibility, but if I have the coordinates correct, it's in the middle of a frozen forest a thousand miles from nowhere, and it's November. Getting there would be almost impossible, and surviving a winter there ain't gonna happen. It won't be above zero up there until April."

"Fine, we'll rule out Severny for now, but why not Tasmania?"

"For starters, it's the only location in the southern hemisphere, and the timing of the satellites is something like one thousandth of a second different from the birds orbiting the northern hemisphere. That's enough of a difference for me to rule it out, but I could be wrong. Because it's so unique, being the only one in the southern hemisphere, there's an off-the-wall chance that's our target."

I said, "I guess that means we're playing rock, paper, scissors with Mexico City, Georgetown, and Kuala Lumpur."

Chapter 24
What I Thought I Knew

I stood from the office chair—the one Clark called ergonomic—and stretched. "Apparently, *ergonomic* means more uncomfortable than sitting on a bear trap."

Clark recoiled. "Hey! That's a nice chair."

"It may be nice to look at, but that's where its nicety ends."

He frowned. "I'll bet you a hundred bucks that *nicety* isn't really a word."

I shook my head in disbelief. "A hundred bucks? Are you serious?"

His eyes turned cold. "Okay, if you're so confident, name the price. Pick any number you want, up to and including my net worth—which is considerably less than yours."

I paused, suddenly uncertain if *nicety* was truly a word. I believed I was right, but Clark's position sounded as if he'd already done the research and discovered the word missing from every dictionary he could find.

I said, "I think I'm out on the bet, but I want to know what makes you so confident."

He leaned back in his chair and laid his feet on the desk. "You're now guilty of the same sin twice in ten minutes."

"What sin?"

He crossed his ankles. "The sin of letting someone else talk you out of what you believe because they sounded more confident than you felt."

"Quit with the riddles, Master Yoda. What are you talking about?"

"I'm talking about Tasmania. You let Ginger talk you out of including someplace nobody's ever heard of from the most important list you've ever made. What was the name of that place?"

"Launceston. And you're right. I am guilty. So, we won't rule it out, but we'll keep it on the back burner for now."

Mongo said, "*Nicety* is a word, by the way."

Clark nodded. "Yep, it sure is. But I had our fearless leader questioning what he thought he knew."

Hunter looked like he was watching a tennis match, looking back and forth between Mongo and Clark. "Are you guys saying you think Tasmania is a target?"

Clark waved him off. "No, it's an outlier, at best, but the problem I have with the other three is that they're all likely to have . . . what was that phrase they kept using? Was it *electronic transactional calls*?"

I gave him a nod, and he continued.

"Mexico City is the financial hub of the country. Kuala Lumpur is a huge financial center in Malaysia. And Georgetown, Grand Cayman, has more international banks than any other city in the western hemisphere. Why couldn't the calls from those places qualify as those transactional call things?"

I tapped a finger to my temple. "You like to play dumb, but sometimes you let a little morsel of wisdom slip out that nobody expects."

"Yep, that's me . . . old morsel slipper. Seriously, though, don't let me or anyone else talk you out of your instincts."

I sighed. "I wish someone would've talked me out of hitting that house on Andros."

Hunter asked, "Does this mean we're abandoning The Bahamas?"

"Not yet," I said. "There's too much evidence pointing to the islands for us to walk away. I still think there's a Bahamian connection. Otherwise, Ambassador Woodford wouldn't have called us out there."

Clark looked up. "Unless Woodford's job was to point us toward the trap."

I groaned. "That's always a possibility. I think I'll ask him when we kick down his door."

"Now you're talking," Mongo said. "As much as I love the planning, I'll always prefer the knocking heads."

"I think you speak for all of us on that one," I said. "Well, maybe not Singer."

Our sniper let out a grunt. "It's a little different for me. You guys can knock heads without killing anybody, but when I do my job, bodies tend to pile up. Even *I'm* not good enough to shoot-to-wound with a fifty cal."

I let his somber revelation hang in the air for a few minutes, then I said, "Before we move on any of these potential targets, I think we should wait and see what the next call does to narrow down the search window."

Clark said, "I agree, but I'm still hoping for Tasmania. I want to see one of those devils like Bugs Bunny used to run into."

I shook my head. "You just lost all the wisdom points you earned ten minutes ago."

In a rare show of responsibility, Hunter said, "Focus, guys. We're ankle-deep in an ocean of unanswered questions. I don't know what the rest of the world is doing to find these terrorists, but I know for sure we're not making any progress by goofing off.

I say we get our heads and our butts back in the fight. If we don't, who will?"

I said, "That's an interesting question. Who else *is* in this fight?"

Clark dropped his feet from his desk. "The SEALs were in it, but now, I don't know. Surely the FBI is involved. We know the White House and Pentagon are players, but maybe Skipper can find out who else has their nose in the pie."

"Nose in the pie?" I asked. "I don't even know what that means, but Skipper told us DIA, State, Justice, and SOCOM were in the game early on. I think SOCOM's only job was running the SEALs, so they may be out."

Clark snapped his fingers. "Don't be so quick to count them out since they lost six SEALs. I'd say there's a better-than-good shot they're doubling down."

"That's something we're going to need to know," I said.

"Call your buddy, Dre."

I snatched up the sat-phone and thumbed the number.

His no-nonsense tone filled the earpiece. "Chief Lewis."

"Dre, it's Chase. I'm sorry to bother you. I know you have your hands full."

"Don't be ridiculous, Chase. I told you to call anytime. What can I do for you?"

"I need to know if you're still in the fight."

"What do you mean?"

"We're diving back in, and we don't want to butt heads with the other good guys on our way. I need to know who else is going after these guys."

"I see. Do you have a target package yet?"

"Not yet, but we're getting closer by the minute. We've got two crackpot analysts working around the clock, and we're narrowing in on them."

"Do you need us, Chase?"

"I don't know yet. Are you available if I do?"

"I looked you in the eye and told you we'd be there if you needed us. That's a promise a SEAL doesn't break. If the Navy won't authorize it, we'll take leave and come on our own dime."

"I couldn't ask you to do that, Dre, but it means a great deal to us that you'd offer. For now, we just need to know if SOCOM is tasking any action on the case."

"You're talking about classified stuff there, Cowboy, but what I can tell you is this. You're not going to bump heads with any SEALs in the next five days. If that changes, I'll let you know."

"Thanks, Dre. I appreciate you sticking your neck out."

He said, "No thanks are necessary. Keep your heads down and your powder dry. And don't lose my number. Got it?"

"Got it!" I hung up and turned to see Clark punching off his phone. "Who was that?"

He said, "I was talking with Skipper. She says we're the only boots on the ground right now. The FBI hostage rescue team is standing by, but without some coordinates, they're not going to move. What did Dre have to say?"

"They're standing down until we say we need them again. He said they'd take leave and jump on board if the Navy wouldn't authorize another deployment."

"Those guys are the real deal."

"So, I guess that means we're it until some solid, verifiable intel puts the terrorists someplace the HRT boys can hit."

"I think you're right," he said, "but I'm battling with a question."

"Let's hear it."

He took a long breath and let it out slowly. "When we get actionable intel from Skipper and Ginger, do we hit the target or surrender the intel to the feds?"

"Those are the decisions you make," I said. "That's way above my pay grade."

"It's not really up to me, either. I need to brief the Board."

I gestured toward his console. "Ring their phone."

"Speaking of phones . . ." Clark said. "Go in the main safe and get everybody a new phone. We're going to spend ten thousand bucks on sat-phone calls if we don't start using cell phones again."

He turned to his console while the rest of us headed for the safe. The electronic combination, along with my thumbprint, opened the vault door. A stack of new cellphones with each of our names on several boxes rested on the back wall. I pulled down one for each of us and passed them out. Minutes later, they were powered up and displaying an exact copy of what had been on the phones we destroyed in the lake on Andros.

Singer tossed his back to me. "My phone's fine. I didn't get to play in the mud with the rest of you."

He went back into the stack, and Hunter said, "I've never been in Clark's vault before. This is nice."

"It's my first time, too," I said. "He gave me the combo and set up my thumbprint last year, but I've never poked my head inside."

Hunter and Mongo perused the vault as if on an afternoon shopping trip.

"This isn't team gear," I said. "It's Clark's private stash."

"He's got good taste," Mongo said as he pulled a custom-built sniper rifle from the rack. "I never knew he was a sniper."

"Neither did I," Singer said.

I said, "There's a lot about Clark even I don't know, but if you can name a tactical school, you can bet he's been there and mastered the course."

Clark's voice boomed through the vault. "Hey! Get out of there, you bunch of looters. That's my stuff."

Mongo replaced the rifle. "We were just looking."

"No, *you* were touching. Everybody else was just looking."

We stepped from the vault, and I secured the heavy door behind us. "What did the Board say?"

He cleared his throat. "They said what I thought they'd say. If we get actionable intel, we are to report it directly to them and take necessary action. If they feel the intel should be forwarded to the appropriate agency, they would be the ones to make that happen."

"That means we're autonomous," I said.

"It sure does, College Boy, and I wouldn't have it any other way."

"Is that all they said?"

He shook his head. "They also said our tasking came directly from the president, so we had no obligation to coordinate with any other agency other than the Board."

"Does that mean we're sitting on our thumbs until Skipper and Ginger dig up something for us to sniff?"

"Not exactly. I gave them an abbreviated briefing on what we know and what we've done over the last two days. They acted like they already knew everything, but I surprised them with the Twin Otter that doesn't seem to exist."

I raised an eyebrow, "Oh, yeah? What did they have to say about that little jewel?"

"They ordered me to hide it in a hangar at Bonaventure until we can resolve the mystery of where and to whom it belongs."

"What did you tell them?"

He threw up a mock salute. "I told them aye-aye, sir."

I chuckled. "In that case, I guess we'd better head north."

The flight back to Largo in the Caravan was spent with everyone onboard sitting silently and pondering what the next operational order would be and when it would come. When my satphone rang on the tarmac at the Ocean Reef Club, that question —and a dozen more—were answered in no uncertain terms.

Chapter 25
Back in the Fight

Skipper's voice sounded dry and cold, as if in the previous minutes, she'd come to realize the world is a dark, dreadful place consumed by hatred and cruelty. "Chase, don't ask questions. I'm going to tell you everything I know. Another call came in. This time it went to NORAD at Cheyenne Mountain. The same electronically altered voice said, 'You clearly are not taking me seriously. Therefore, you have forced me to make you understand the severity of the situation into which you have placed yourselves. Beware junior sixteen and twenty-two and senior thirty-five.' I don't know what that means yet, but I'll figure it out."

She paused, apparently to compose herself, then said, "We have the timing, and Ginger is running the algorithm. Expect an answer in less than twenty minutes. Do you have anything for me?"

As I tried to digest the threat, I kept my response as short as possible. "We'll be home in three and a half hours. Sat-phone will remain hot."

Without another word, she disconnected, leaving me listening to dead air. I turned and briefed the team, trying to remember exactly what the terrorist had said. When I finished, I asked, "Does anyone have any ideas what that could mean?"

Mongo spoke barely above a whisper. "The first things I thought of were junior and senior senators from the sixteenth, twenty-second, and thirty-fifth states. I'm not a hundred percent on this, but I think those would be Tennessee, Alabama, and West Virginia."

Clark wasted no time in dialing a number from memory. When the line was answered, he spoke in a confident, commanding tone. "Credible threat! Evacuate all three Senate office buildings, immediately." As Clark listened intently, he aged before my eyes and whispered, "Godspeed." He slid the phone back into his pocket and slowly shook his head. "Mongo was right. Let's get home."

Clark and I climbed into the cockpit of the Twin Otter while Disco and the rest of the team mounted the Caravan. Other than cockpit commands and calls, my handler and I didn't speak until we leveled off at eleven thousand five hundred feet over the coastline of Florida. The anxiety of not knowing what Clark had heard on the telephone call left me yearning to hear what he knew.

Finally, he said, "I don't know how he does it, but Mongo's brain works on a different level than the rest of us."

"Who did you call, and what did they say?"

I called the Senate sergeant at arms to evacuate all three Senate office buildings, but someone beat me to it. They were already being evacuated, and there are already casualties."

"Casualties?" I asked. "What kind?"

"I don't know, but Skipper will know when we land. There's nothing we can do until we're back on the ground."

I felt as if a cannonball had just landed in my gut. "Who are these people, Clark?"

He sighed. "I don't know, but I think it's time to start listening to them, whoever they are."

Clark and the autopilot did most of the flying while I tried to keep my brain from exploding. We were six men who were exceptional in the practice of killing people and breaking things, and two women who were beyond masters of information management. We were well funded, but completely unsupported when additional manpower was required. The necessity to keep my team from knowing and interacting with the other American teams driven by the Board was paramount. Apparently, each of the teams had a particular set of skills that made them unique and solely capable. The SEALs were an option if the Navy would play along, but I couldn't stomach the thought of those brave men taking off their uniforms and signing out on leave to work alongside the six of us. The people behind the attack on America weren't going to stop until they either got what they wanted or somebody put bullets through their heads. My team was incapable of giving them the five billion dollars they demanded, but I had faith we could efficiently and effectively deliver the second option as soon as Ginger and Skipper had a set of GPS coordinates that would allow us to not-so-gently knock on the terrorists' door.

Clark let the Otter settle onto the runway with the touch of a seasoned aviator.

"Nicely done," I said. "How much time do you have in the Twin Otter?"

He checked his watch. "About three hours. I don't even have a multi-engine seaplane rating, but if we get to keep this one, we'll have to remedy that."

"I think we can handle that little technicality. In fact, if you'll give me your logbook, we'll call the past three hours prep for your check-ride."

He taxied to our main hangar and shut down. "I'm sure I have a logbook somewhere."

"Speaking of somewhere," I said, "let's hide this old girl down in hangar four. We can cover her up and let her sleep until somebody decides what to do with her."

"I'll drag it down there with the tug," he said.

With the Otter tucked away, the Caravan touched down on the numbers and taxied in just in time for the team to catch a ride to Bonaventure.

The double doors leading into the ops center were bolted and secure. My access code and thumbprint did nothing to budge either door. As I questioned my ability to memorize a six-digit access code, a disembodied voice filled the air. "Stand by, Chase."

Seconds later, Ginger—all four-feet-eight-inches of her—opened the door from inside, and her emerald-green eyes climbed Mongo's frame as if he were a tree she definitely wanted to climb. "You must be Mongo."

"And you must be Ginger," he said.

"I must be. We'll continue *this* later, but for now, you boys are going to want to hear what's happened while you were en route."

The six of us stepped inside the ops center, and Ginger re-secured the doors.

"Why didn't my code work?" I asked.

Skipper looked over her shoulder. "It's new security protocol I put in place. What's happening in here is far too sensitive for us not to have access control from this side of the door. It'll all make sense very soon. Sit down and listen."

We wasted no time claiming our seats around the conference table, and the analysts brought up what appeared to be live video from Washington D.C. Hundreds of people in chemical protective gear milled about as if dealing with nuclear fallout.

Without preamble, she began the briefing. "Eleven minutes after the call came into Cheyenne Mountain, a three-pronged attack occurred on all three Senate office buildings. What you're seeing here is the Russell Building, where the senators from Alabama have their offices. The office of the junior senator, Ted Thomlinson, was attacked by an aerosol that appears to be Sarin gas."

"Sarin?" I bellowed. "How is that possible?"

Skipper locked eyes with me. "I don't know, but I have a lot to brief. If I know any details, I'll include them in the briefing."

"I'm sorry."

She continued. "There are four dead in the senator's office . . . three aides and a courier. Three more were exposed and have been hospitalized and isolated. All three of them are expected to die within the hour. The senator appears to have been the target of the attack, but he was not in his office at the time. He's been moved to an undisclosed, secure location."

"The Greenbrier?" I asked.

She nodded. "Yes, he's most likely at the Greenbrier in West Virginia, but we don't know for sure."

She pressed a series of keys on her keyboard, and the video changed to a scene flooded with firetrucks, ambulances, and emergency vehicles of every description. "This is the Dirksen Building. Senator Melanie Tyler of Tennessee—the sixteenth state admitted to the union—was in her office when approximately ten gallons of a substance similar to napalm was released, engulfing the office in flames in seconds. The fire spread to several adjoining offices on the fourth floor. Senator Tyler and three staffers were burned beyond recognition in the blaze."

She looked up, obviously expecting questions, but none came. She hit a few more keys, and a third scene filled the screen. Workers clad in white hazmat suits scurried about with emergency vehicles, tents, and massive hanging drapes surrounding the building.

"This one is the Hart Building, and it is the most terrifying. The office of William Conroy, the senior senator from West Virginia, was targeted by what the DOD and EPA believe was a radiological dispersal device."

Clark almost yelled, "A dirty bomb?"

"Yes, a dirty bomb," Skipper said. "It's estimated that the initial explosion was similar to that of approximately one pound of C-Four. The dispersed radiological material is, most likely, stolen from a medical facility or animal irradiation plant. We have no details on exactly what element was released, but we know for sure it is radioactive."

Disco asked, "How many?"

Skipper bit her lip in an obvious effort to still herself. "This is the most severe of the three attacks. A meeting was being held in Senator Conroy's office. There were twenty-four people, including the senator, injured or killed in the initial explosion. We don't have solid numbers yet. Dozens more have likely been contaminated by the radioactive material. The Nuclear Regulatory Commission claims to have the radiation contained."

"How could this be possible?" I asked. "Who has the wherewithal to pull off something this big? It's starting to sound like state-sponsored terrorism to me."

Skipper pulled her glasses from her face and pawed at her tear-filled eyes. "I'm sorry, but this has me shaken up. I never expected to deal with anything like this."

Clark said, "Neither did we, but we all signed up for whatever the bad guys were throwing at us. What do you have on a location after the most recent call?"

Ginger said, "I'll take this one. The smuggler program came back with the one set of coordinates that was most improbable. The software says the calls are coming from Tasmania. The coordinates are slightly different than the previous set, but still well within tolerance."

"Does that mean you're certain that's where the calls are originating?" I asked.

She shook her head. "No. In fact, I think that's exactly where the calls are *not* originating."

"I'm not following."

She stood. "I know, but try to stick with me. The math is complex, so I'll break it down as much as possible. Do you remember the half-a-second anomaly I mentioned between the satellites in the northern hemisphere and the ones in the southern hemisphere?"

"Yes, I remember, but that didn't make any sense to me, either."

"It doesn't matter. What's important is that you know there *is* a small time anomaly between the two sets of satellites."

I nodded. "Okay, I've got that part."

She drew a circle on the whiteboard with a line from the center extending to the circle. "You're a pilot—and a good one from what I hear. If you're just one degree off on your heading, how far will you miss your target if you're flying sixty miles?"

"About one mile," I said.

"Good. Now, what if it was a six-hundred-mile flight?"

"That's pretty simple math. I'll be off approximately ten miles."

She tapped the board. "Exactly. The farther you fly, the more the error is magnified. Satellite communications work exactly the same way. No matter how high a satellite goes, the Earth is still going to produce a horizon the satellite can't see across. When this happens, it takes at least one additional satellite for two birds to talk with each other across that horizon. Are you still with me?"

"So far."

"This is the part that's going to get fuzzy. That error we talked about happens in millionths of a second when we're talking about satellite communications, but just like navigation, the time error is calculable and predictable. The interesting part about the time differential is that it isn't calculable to precision due to environmental factors. The closest we can accurately predict the differential is about nine ten-thousandths of a second. Are you still with me?"

I sat silently, shaking my head.

"Okay, it doesn't really matter if you're completely on board. Just know that we can get close, but we can never predict the differential to one-hundred-percent accuracy. When we pinpointed the coordinates, the calculation was precise, and I mean, like, spot-on perfect. It was too perfect—if such a thing exists. That made the computers happy, but it freaked me out, so I started digging."

She paused as if I was supposed to get involved, but all I could think about was summa cum baseball.

She huffed. "Don't you get it?"

"No, I don't get it at all," I said as I spun to face Mongo. "Do you get it?" He had the same glazed-over look as me, so I said, "Even *he* doesn't get it, so there's no hope of me understanding it."

"Ugh! It's simple. Okay, maybe not simple, but I figured it out. It's called projection modeling. We did it with the Star Wars system of space-based weaponry. Satellites are easy to find. I mean, like, really easy to find, so we came up with a way to make them behave as if they were somewhere else. The easiest somewhere else for a satellite to pretend to be is on the opposite side of the world. So, if you drilled a hole straight through the Earth, the satellite would appear to have fallen straight through the hole and popped out on the other side. That's what's happening here. The calls aren't coming from Tasmania. They're coming from the Azores . . . the exact opposite side of the planet."

Chapter 26
The Name

I sat in perplexed admiration, shaking my head. "I don't know how you two do it, but I'm thankful you're on our team."

Skipper pulled a pencil from behind her ear and gripped it between her thumb and the knuckle of her index finger like a pistol. "And we don't know how you guys step in front of terrorists with bombs and guns and beat them down every time. It takes all kinds, and Ginger and I are extremely glad you're on our team."

Clark knocked on the table. "That's enough ego-stroking. Does the Azores have an extradition treaty with us?"

Skipper slid her pencil back into place behind her ear. "The Azores belong to Portugal, and Portugal has an extradition treaty with the U.S."

Clark sighed. "Well, that doesn't make sense. Why would these guys go to the trouble of hiding someplace with an extradition treaty?"

Ginger said, "We don't know where these guys are hiding . . . yet. All we know is where the telephone is that made the threatening calls."

"What?" I said. "You've done all this, and none of it helps us find the terrorists? If that's the case, we've wasted a lot of time and resources and—"

Ginger held up a hand. "Calm down before you have an aneurism. We did all this work to find out where the calls originated from so we could then do the much simpler task of finding the source of the data that is transmitted from that telephone."

I furrowed my brow. "Data? We're not talking about data. We're talking about an altered human voice, aren't we?"

Ginger grinned. "Yes, we are, but to the phone line, there's no difference. It's all data, regardless of it being financial data or a human voice."

"So, have you done it yet?"

She and Skipper answered in unison. "We have."

I threw up my hands. "Let's have it, then. Where are these guys?"

"It's not that simple," Skipper began.

"Oh, for God's sake," I said. "Just give us the location."

Skipper huffed. "There are two locations. The first is a high-powered satellite phone on a remote island in The Bahamas called Rum Cay. Here are the precise coordinates for the antenna . . ." She slid a single sheet of paper across the table.

"Antenna? I thought you said it was a sat-phone."

"Yes, Chase, it's a high-powered sat-phone that is most likely connected to a power source other than a simple battery. A phone like that will have an external antenna. That's what we're capable of finding, so those are the coordinates for the antenna. The phone has to be close and physically connected to the antenna."

"Thank you. Please don't make it so complicated. We're grunts. Keep it simple, and point us toward the target."

Skipper showed me a patronizing grin. "You guys are far more than grunts, but I'll keep it simple. Rum Cay is target number one, and target number two is in Libreville, the capital of Gabon."

"Two targets?" Clark asked.

Skipper nodded. "Yeah, two targets. Two of the five calls have originated from Gabon, and the others came from Rum Cay."

I ran my hands through my hair. "That means we have to make a decision. As soon as we hit one target, the other will know, and they'll rabbit. We're going to have to call the SEALs back in."

Skipper raised a finger. "Wait a minute. There's a hitch."

"A hitch? What kind of hitch?"

"Maybe the lucky kind. During the most recent call, prior to the attacks on the senate buildings—that call came from Gabon, by the way—the phone they were using received a call while they were transmitting, and that call originated from a burner phone in Foggy Bottom, just across the Potomac from Arlington, Virginia."

My face landed in my palms, and I squeezed my eyelids closed as tightly as possible until flashes of light and floaters appeared in my vision. When I caught my breath, I said, "That means this isn't an uncoordinated attack from a foreign, state-sponsored source. That means somebody in D.C. is in on it."

Ginger grimaced. "Just because a call came from D.C. doesn't mean it was a call from someone in our government. It just means the person was in Foggy Bottom when they made the call. They could be a mole or a cell leader. This could still be an outsider attack."

I slowly shook my head. "No, it's an inside job. There's no question about it. The problem is, how inside, and who can we trust?"

Silence engulfed the ops center as every brain in the room processed the discovery. The big brains like Mongo's, Ginger's and Skipper's considered how they could pluck a name from the ones and zeros dancing inside the computer networks, but the rest of us knew the truth: The name wouldn't come floating out of a series of electrons drifting around inside some computer network someplace, no matter how much coaxing the analysts did. The name would tumble from the bloody lips of a terrified, tortured coconspirator taped to a chair, with one of us standing over him with a pair of bloodstained pliers and a nail gun.

I spun in my chair to face my handler. "Here's what I want to do. I want to surveil Rum Cay and count bodies, log shift changes, and plan a strike."

He nodded as he scratched at a notepad beneath his pen. "Keep going."

"Then I want to see Gabon. If we can get in, I believe that's where we'll find the white-collar crowd expecting a big paycheck at the end of this thing. That's who'll have the name we want."

He continued scribbling notes and didn't look up. "What about the hostages?"

"They're on Rum Cay. I'd bet my left leg on it."

Clark motioned toward the wall-mounted display. "Show us some aerials of Rum Cay, and make the first one big enough so we can see something we'll recognize."

Skipper's fingers flew across the keyboard, and in seconds, an aerial view of The Bahamas, from Cat Island to Crooked Island, with Rum Cay lying halfway between the two, appeared on the monitor.

"There it is," she said. "Do you know where you are, now?"

"We got it," I said. "Zoom in, and let's get the lay of the land on Rum Cay."

The picture changed to a composite satellite image layered with volumes of data.

"That's a little congested. Give us the topo first, and we'll add the rest of the information as we need it."

She stripped away everything except the bare satellite photo and the topographical lines. I leaned forward and studied the map as if there would be a test afterwards. In fact, there would be, but it wouldn't come in the controlled environment of a classroom. It would come on the ground in the form of resistance made of lead and racing through the air toward our heads.

"When was this shot taken?" I asked.

Skipper turned back to her computer and dug in. "It looks like it was taken yesterday at just after noon. The shadows are leaning slightly to the east, so that would confirm the time stamp."

"How big is it?"

"It's five miles long, east to west, and five miles wide at the eastern end. At the western shoreline, it's just under two miles wide, north to south."

Still focused on the photo, I asked, "Inhabitants?"

"There are fifty to seventy-five permanent residents, and all of them live in Port Nelson on the southeastern coastline of the island."

I scratched my head. "Everybody lives in Port Nelson?"

"As far as we know. There's a cave system on the north side of the island with some old Lucayan drawings and carvings. There's plenty of evidence of Arawak inhabitants a few hundred years ago, but outside of Port Nelson, it's pretty much deserted."

Hunter said, "That's exactly where I'd hide four high-value hostages if I had to pick a spot out there. Is there a source of fresh water?"

Ginger fielded that one. "Yes, there's a freshwater lake. I can only assume it's spring fed in addition to catching rainwater."

I squinted at the screen. "Zoom in. Is that . . . ?"

Both analysts grinned, and Skipper said, "Yes, sir, it is. That is an asphalt runway, forty-five hundred feet long, with an additional five hundred feet of overrun."

"It looks abandoned," I said.

Skipper shrugged. "It does look that way, but it's impossible to know for sure without putting eyes on it."

I leaned back in my chair. "Oh, we're definitely putting eyes and boots on it. Draw a great circle route from here to that airport, and give me the distance."

A gentle arc appeared on the aerial photo, and Skipper said, "Six hundred thirty miles."

I pointed to the screen. "That's Great Abaco, right?"

"Yes."

Finally, things were starting to look up.

"Give me a distance from here to Marsh Harbor on Abaco and then the rest of the route."

She tapped and said, "Four hundred miles to Marsh Harbor and two thirty to Rum Cay from there."

"That's well within range for the Caravan, even loaded with gear, provisions, humans, and parachutes."

Skipper croaked. "Parachutes?"

I gave her a nod. "Yep, parachutes and night vision."

"You're insane!"

Clark gave me a fist bump. "Nope, not insane. Just airborne!"

I bumped his fist and followed it up with an index finger pointed straight at his chest. "You're not going."

"What do you mean I'm not going? It's a night parachute insertion. Of course I'm going."

Instead of arguing with him, I pulled out my phone and dialed Maebelle. She was apparently in the kitchen at el Juez on South Beach, whipping up some type of culinary masterpiece, but her voice filled the speaker. "Hey, it's Maebelle. I'm sorry I can't take your call. Leave a message, and I'll call back as soon as I can."

I motioned toward the phone and eyed Clark. "Are you going to tell her, or am I?"

He growled and punched the end button on the phone. "Okay, fine. Maybe I'm not jumping in with you, but I'm at least driving."

Disco made a sound I couldn't recognize, and I turned to see his eyes the size of saucers. "What's wrong with you?"

"I'm, uh . . . I'm not qualified t o, u m . . . I c an't j ump i n. I don't know how."

Mongo threw a tree limb of an arm across the retired lieutenant colonel. "Relax, Air Force. I'll tie your butt to my rig and carry you down."

Disco's eyes darted between me and Mongo, fear still written all over his face.

I couldn't let the torture continue any longer. "Take it easy. You're not jumping in with us. You'll be up front while Clark plays jumpmaster and pushes us out the door."

Relief poured over him. "Whew, that was a close one. Why can't we just fly into the airport in the daylight instead of jumping in at night?"

A raucous round of laughter arose from the table, and Hunter said, "Because it's an excuse to make a night parachute insertion. Nobody—except old, broke-back Green Berets and retired Air Force pilots—turns down a chance at a nighttime HALO insertion."

That earned Hunter a special single-finger-salute from Clark.

Skipper said, "Excuse me, but what's a HALO insertion?"

Singer said, "It means high altitude, low opening, but with this bunch of heathens, we're going to need a legion of halo-wearing angels to keep us alive."

Skipper rolled her eyes. "Gotcha. What's the timetable?"

I surveyed the team with questioning eyes, and everyone returned the thumbs-up. I checked my watch. "We're wheels up as soon as we get the gear loaded."

Chapter 27
Geronimo!

With the mission parameters clearer than ever, we filed from the ops center and headed for the hangar. The next forty-eight hours of our lives promised to give us the best opportunity to stick our noses right into the business of our not-so-friendly neighborhood terrorists.

Hunter and Singer unlocked the airtight storage locker where we stored our parachutes and everything else a mouse might enjoy nibbling on. Disco and Clark towed the Caravan out, giving us more than enough room on the hangar floor to check our gear.

I handed out the instructions. "Pack your provisions, first. Plan on forty-eight hours. Don't go light on calories. We'll need all the energy we can muster. And even though the island has a fresh water source, we're packing all we'll need, plus twenty-five percent. Mongo tends to hit the ground pretty hard, so he bursts a lot of canteens."

The giant hefted a sandbag and launched it toward me. "Catch!"

I stepped aside and let it hit the floor. "Yep, that's pretty much how you hit the ground on these jumps."

"When was the last time you saw me jump?" he said.

I closed one eye and turned to stare at the ceiling. "I guess it was in Kazakhstan on the Russian border, and you hit the ground like a ton of bricks."

He planted both hands on his hips. "I had a hundred and thirty pounds of Russian SVR officer strapped to my chest. You'd hit the ground hard, too."

I said, "At least she was cute."

"Only on the outside." He turned away and barked. "Everybody check the dates on the reserves. If they've not been repacked in more than six months, let me know, and I'll repack them since I'm the only real rigger in this outfit."

"We're all riggers," Hunter said, "but we were smart enough not to get the license."

After close inspection, the gear was mission-ready, and Mongo didn't have to repack anything. With the gear and chutes aboard the Caravan, Hunter asked, "What are you carrying, Chase?"

"I'm taking my sixteen-inch, suppressed carbine."

"I like it," he said.

Well armed, well briefed, and well prepared, we climbed aboard the Caravan for the longest flight over water I'd ever made in the plane. To my surprise, Singer followed me aboard with a parachute pack draped across one shoulder and his cased .338 Lapua over the other.

"Where do you think you're going?" I asked.

"I'm deploying with my team. If Clark's doing the flying, somebody has to snipe for you, and I'm the only sniper you've got left."

I motioned toward the bandage on his arm. "The doc said nothing strenuous for eight weeks."

He scoffed. "Strenuous? This doesn't qualify. We're just jumping out of an airplane at ten thousand feet in the middle of the night with two hundred pounds of gear to land on an island we've never seen to spy on a group of terrorists bent on destroying what's left of our government. That's a piece of cake. Now, get out of my way so I can close the door."

Arguing with Singer would only result in him climbing aboard and jumping with us, so I didn't waste the energy. Secretly, it was comforting to know he'd be on the mission with a weapon he could thread a needle with at a mile and a half. Knowing Singer is on overwatch is almost like going into battle with God himself holding you in His hands.

Once at altitude, the Pratt and Whitney PT-6 turbine sang us to sleep as the sun fell below the western horizon. Warriors like my team have an innate sense of when their bodies need rest. Most people couldn't imagine sleeping on the flight to assault an island from the sky, but we allowed ourselves the temporary luxury of peaceful sleep until Clark waded through the minefield of sleeping bodies and announced, "Wake up, you bunch of lazy bums! We're thirty minutes out."

I yawned and stretched myself back to consciousness and watched every member of my team do the same. I grabbed Clark's sleeve. "Brief the jump."

He shook his head. "Thanks, College Boy. I wouldn't have known what to do next without you leading the way."

I gave him a playful shove. "Watch it, or I'll add you to the jump team, and we only brought four chutes."

He stretched the toe of his right foot beneath the pilot's seat and dragged an extra rig from its hiding place. "You didn't think I was going to stand in the door and shove you guys out without a parachute, did you? With you bunch of cowards, I wouldn't be surprised if you grabbed me for security on the way out the door."

"I *am* afraid of the dark, so it's possible."

He shoved me a little more aggressively than I'd initiated, but I probably deserved it.

He ordered, "Don and buddy-check your gear!"

We slithered into rucksacks on our chests and parachute rigs on our backs. Our rifle bags and tethers were attached to each of our right legs, and our helmets held our night vision nods.

Mongo waddled toward the rear door and let himself collapse to the floor. "I'll be lucky to get out the door with all this gear."

Clark said, "Don't worry. If you don't fit, I'll throw your gear out to you once you're outside."

"You're a real friend. You know that, Clark?"

"That's me."

With the responsibility of jumpmaster hanging from his neck, Clark walked through the four of us, checking every piece of gear. "Okay, it looks like most of you will survive the jump. The jump run will be at twelve thousand five hundred feet, so there's no chance of anyone on the ground hearing us. We'll run southwest to northeast. The wind is out of the east, zero-eight-zero at twelve, gusting to twenty. That's going to make for a wild ride. I'll put you out a mile east-north-east of the unlit airfield, so you'll find it on nods. The terrain around the airport rises to the north, so if you're going to miss, miss to the south or west. You'll have sixty-five to seventy-five seconds of freefall. I want all canopies fully open at two thousand feet. Keep your eyes on those altimeters. Depth perception on nods is terrible when you're falling at a hundred miles an hour. Any questions?"

None came, so he said, "Here's the order. Singer has more night jumps than the rest of us combined, so he's first out the door. Form up on him, and he'll point you toward the airport. After Singer, it's Hunter, Chase, then Mongo. If for some ungodly reason, you can't find Singer, aim for the big, long strip of asphalt, and you'll probably bump into him. Everybody is wearing an IR chemlight and IR reflective tape, so keep each other in sight. If you get separated, the rally point is the western end of the runway. Got it?"

"Got it," we echoed.

Disco looked over his shoulder from the cockpit and yelled, "Seven minutes!"

Clark gave one final check of our gear, patted each of us on the helmet, and ordered, "Move to the door!"

When he opened the door, the rush of cold wind caught me by surprise. It was eighty degrees on the ground two and a half miles beneath us, but not where we were.

Clark pulled down his nods, leaned out the door, and tossed an IR reflective streamer into the wind. While he was spotting and watching the streamer fall, Disco yelled, "Two minutes!"

Singer gave Clark's leg a tap and then held up two fingers.

Clark nodded and leaned back inside. "Five left, Disco!"

Disco gently rolled the airplane five degrees to the left, pulled the power back, raised the nose, and flattened the prop. "Thirty seconds!"

Clark yelled over the rush of the wind. "On your feet!" He stuck his head back out the door and pointed toward the ground. "There's the airport. Got it?"

Singer nodded. "Got it."

A mile east of the airport, Clark slapped Singer on the shoulder and yelled, "Go, go, go!"

We followed in close succession behind our sniper, making sure to kick away from the airplane as we went. Colliding with that huge pontoon would be disastrous at best. I arched my back and spread my arms and legs as my body accelerated through the night sky. What little moon there was shone low on the western horizon. From there, the glow could do little to highlight us as we fell, but it also provided almost no ground light.

Once stable in freefall, I rolled onto my back to make sure Mongo was out of the airplane. To my horror, I watched him twisting and clawing to exit the door. I rolled back over to spot

Singer and Hunter. They were precisely where I expected to find them, so I rolled back onto my back and breathed a sigh of relief as I saw the big man with his hands pinned at his sides and his boots pointed toward the sky. He was in an accelerating dive, heading straight at me. Trusting he'd seen us, I rolled back into a stable body position and flew myself to join Hunter and Singer in a side-by-side formation.

Seconds later, I felt Mongo's enormous hand on my left ankle, and I turned, signaling to ask if he was okay. He gave me the okay signal and maneuvered himself beside Singer, who was pointing at the runway. We all signaled that we had it in sight and focused our attention on our altimeters.

The air warmed as we descended, and the runway expanded as if a giant pair of fingers had pinched the Earth to zoom in. At thirty-five hundred feet, Singer waved us off, and we turned our bodies away from each other in a maneuver designed to allow our canopies to open without tangling with each other.

I glanced back and above to ensure I was clear and laced my thumb through the ripcord handle. Pulling straight away from my chest, the ripcord cleared its sheath, and the pilot chute leapt from my back and into the slipstream. The small parachute snatched the pin from the main and deployed the solid black nylon parachute from its container.

One one thousand . . .

Two one thousand . . .

Three one thousand . . .

And my feet swung beneath my body as the beautiful canopy bloomed over my head. I released the steering toggles and pumped the brakes once to make sure everything was open, clear, and operational. Once I knew I would float to the earth like a feather, I checked my surroundings to find two more perfectly shaped canopies a few hundred feet away, but two weren't enough. There should've been a third . . .

I yanked my left toggle, swinging through a tight arc to the left and scanning the sky beneath me through the turn, but nothing but island and ocean appeared beneath me. I yanked the right toggle as far as I could pull it, initiating a rapid turn to the right. The centrifugal force of the maneuver swung me from beneath my canopy, and I looked back into the inky sky, praying to spot a third chute, but it wasn't there. Panic filled my chest as I took inventory. Singer was two hundred feet in front of me, frantically searching for the other canopy, and Hunter appeared in my vision to the south, but Mongo's oversized parachute was nowhere in sight.

Chapter 28
Gravity and Gorillas

My descent toward the island below turned into an arduous, gravity-defying sinking into a dreadful pit of my own making. Six SEALs lost their lives under my command, and now Mongo, my friend and confidant, had struggled his way through the door of my airplane, plummeted to the ground on my orders, and most likely now lay in a sunken bed of debris some two thousand feet beneath me. Short of cutting away my parachute, there was nothing I could do to hasten my race to his side.

The necessity of silence as we drifted downward remained; however, every ounce of spirit I possessed cried out to yell to Hunter and Singer, praying one of them had seen Mongo's chute deploy. Doing so would endanger the three lives that remained in the fight and threaten the lives of the surviving hostages. I was left entrapped inside a prison of altitude and time, begging for the ground to pull harder and the wind beneath my parachute to release its unrelenting grasp on my nylon jailer twenty feet above my head.

At one hundred feet above the ground, I pulled the line holding my rifle bag to my leg and let the weapon fall beneath me, stopping at the limit of the fifteen-foot tether designed to allow the rifle bag to touch down two seconds before my boots hit the sand.

A bad landing with three feet of inflexible rifle strapped to a leg is the perfect recipe for a broken leg—and worse. The bag touched down, and I dragged it across the surface for a few seconds before I flared from my fall and stepped back to the ground, turning to collapse and collect my parachute.

Recover my rifle, kneel or lay prone, study the terrain, analyze potential threats, and spot my fellow paratroopers would've been the logical, time-proven series of events that should've immediately followed my landing in a hostile environment, but anxiety, terror, and reckless abandon refused to allow me anything approaching logic or reason. Instead, I shucked off my parachute pack and rucksack, abandoning them in place, and ran toward the western end of the runway. The sound of thundering booted feet accompanied my hastened breath as both Hunter and Singer approached in the same sprint.

Winded and still scared, I begged, "Did either of you see a fourth chute?"

Hunter shook his head, and Singer pointed to his right. "I may have seen a reserve chute for an instant about a mile to the north."

The next question sickened me, but it had to be asked. "Did either of you hear contact?"

Both warriors shook their heads.

"Neither did I, so that's a positive in our favor. We likely would've heard him prang in if he went in without either chute opening." Fear was replaced with responsibility, and I ordered, "Hide your chutes, recover your weapons, and sling your gear. We're going to find him. Be back here in three minutes."

The three of us turned, sprinted back to our gear, and returned well inside the allotted time. I pulled the radio from my ruck and keyed the mic. "Four, this is one . . . over." I waited for a radioed reply, but none came, so I sent the call again.

Still, no reply.

I glanced into the sky, hoping to catch a glimpse of either the Caravan circling or Mongo drifting silently toward the ground under a parachute that had opened far too early. I was rewarded with neither, so I keyed up again. "Five, One, over."

Clark's voice filled my earpiece. "Go for Five."

"We're three safe on deck, but we lost Mongo. Did you see a fourth chute?"

"Negative, One. We saw only three."

"Roger," I said, gagging on the word.

He said, "We're headed to Stella Maris, twenty-five miles to the west for fuel. I taped the jump with the IR filter on the camera. I'll review the video and report back."

The turmoil in my gut raged until I took a knee and deposited the contents of my stomach onto the sandy ground.

Hunter knelt at my side. "Are you okay, brother?"

I wiped my mouth on my sleeve and stood. "I will be when we find Mongo." Composing myself, I said, "Form up fifteen feet abreast, and let's walk toward the spot where Singer thought he saw the reserve."

We lined up and started our walk to the north with Singer praying in a whisper and all three of us scanning the ground, trees, and shrubs for any sign of a parachute or a body.

What would we do when we found him? Would we scrap the mission and carry what remained of his body back to the airport? Losing six men I barely knew was the worst pain I'd ever endured as a team leader, but believing my brother had given his life trying to save others felt like the weight of a thousand worlds bearing down against my flesh.

We searched for most of an hour, and I made radio calls every ten minutes, hoping against hope I'd hear Mongo answer, but I was left wanting.

Singer yanked me from my misery when he said, "There's a broken branch in a tree at two o'clock and fifty meters."

The three of us abandoned our orderly, meticulous walk and sprinted for the tree. Under the night vision nods, the broken limbs were clearly visible, their white fleshy interior almost glowing where they broke from the trunk of the tree. The scene beneath the tree left my stomach convulsing and my mind melting inside my head. Tactical gear was spread across a twenty-foot radius from a depression only a few feet from the base of the tree.

Seeing Mongo's gear spread across the ground, broken and useless, left me with the familiar feeling of longing to have been the one who was lost. It should've been me who hit the ground at a hundred miles per hour, not the gentle, caring man beneath the gruff exterior of a giant.

It should've been me.

Singer reached down and lifted what remained of Mongo's rucksack and held it in front of him. "This is definitely Mongo's gear, but there's no blood . . . no body . . . no Mongo. He wasn't wearing this pack when it hit the tree. He's not here."

Relief and hope flooded over me as I lunged toward our sniper. He was right. There was no evidence of a body of any size, let alone three hundred pounds of flesh and bone. Mongo's pack had plummeted to the ground, but where was its owner?

I grabbed Singer's arm. "This is a good sign, right?"

He flipped up his nods and blinked, trying to adjust to the darkness. "Maybe, but if his pack came off, his parachute could've followed. You have to make the call. Are we continuing the mission or searching for Mongo?"

There was no hesitation and no decision to be made. "We find Mongo before anything else. If he's alive, he's likely hurt, and we'll have to get him out of here. The mission can wait."

Singer pulled a compass from his gear and spun around beneath the tree. He studied the compass, terrain, and sky. "If his pack came off before his chute opened, he has to be between here and the airport. If his chute didn't open, or if it came off before he opened it, his body will be off to the east. What's the call?"

The answer to that question didn't come so easily. I studied the options. "You and Hunter head back toward the airport. I'll search to the east. Radio checks every ten minutes. If we get out of radio range, we'll backtrack to reestablish coms."

"Sounds good," he said. "Clark and Disco should be airborne again soon. If they establish a high orbit, they can relay radio calls."

I gave him a nod and turned for the east. With every step, I feared the next footfall would place me in sight of Mongo's crushed corpse. Ten minutes into the walk, I'd seen nothing, and I lifted my radio to my lips to answer Singer's radio check. "Loud and clear. How me?"

"I have you the same. Nothing yet," he said.

The same routine continued for twenty more minutes until Clark's voice came through my earpiece. "One, this is Five airborne . . . over."

I keyed up. "Go for One."

"I've got some bad news, Chase. I checked the video while Disco was refueling, and it shows three full canopy deployments and one streamer. The camera never saw a reserve chute."

Trying, but failing to remain hopeful, I asked, "Where was the streamer?"

"It was half a mile east of the airport."

"Roger. We'll keep looking."

"Roger. We'll establish a high orbit until the sun comes up."

I looked back in the direction I'd come and spoke into the mic. "Two, One . . . over."

"Two's up," came Singer's reply.

"Did you copy Clark's call?"

"Affirmative, and we're moving east of the airport. There was no sign of him between his gear and the airfield."

"Roger," I said. "We'll rendezvous east of the airport."

Twenty more minutes of walking over the rugged terrain under my nods delivered me due east of the airport, so I turned west, expecting to find Hunter and Singer making their way east, but instead, I heard motion like a pair of monkeys fighting in a tree. I took a knee and raised my rifle with its infrared beam of light visible only through night vision devices. Through my nods, the world in front of me lit up, and the monkeys I'd expected to see weren't there.

I lowered my rifle and sprinted toward the commotion. Arriving beneath the tree, I looked up to see something more closely resembling a gorilla than a pair of fighting monkeys. Dangling thirty feet above my head was our beloved Mongo without his rucksack, helmet, or rifle. He was kicking furiously and pulling on the risers of his reserve parachute, trying to swing close enough to another limb to free himself and climb down.

Without shouting, I grinned up at him. "Need a hand, paratrooper?"

Suspended in the darkness, he squinted down at me. "Is that you, Chase?"

"Yeah, big man. It's me. Just relax. We'll get you down."

I called Singer and Hunter on the radio. "Walk toward my IR beam. I found our boy playing in a tree about a quarter mile east of the runway."

Thundering hoofbeats echoed from the west, and soon my team was whole again. But getting a gorilla out of a tree proved more difficult than I'd expected.

Hunter scampered up the tree and tossed a line across a massive limb above Mongo and let it fall to within a foot of the suspended giant. "Tie yourself off to that line, and cut your risers. We'll either lower you like a piano, or you'll catapult the three of us out of sight."

Hunter returned to the ground, and the three of us held the line as we watched Mongo cut himself free of his parachute. Thankfully, the three of us combined outweighed Mongo by an adequate margin, allowing us to ease him to the ground without dropping the big lug.

He picked himself up and dusted off his pants. "I knew I could count on you guys to let me down."

"That's what we do," I said, "continually let you down. How did you manage to hit the only tree within a mile?"

He looked up at his reserve chute and lines still hanging in the branches. "I don't know, but Singer's prayer must've had something to do with it. I got stuck in the door trying to exit the plane, and Clark had to give me a shove. My rucksack got torn away in the tussle, and I guess something must've gone wrong with the main chute, as well."

He paused to wipe the sweat from his brow. "When I pulled, the drogue came out, but the chute was just a streamer. I cut it away and waited for the reserve to come out, but it was hung up. The Earth sure started looking pretty big and rushing at me faster than I wanted, so I reached behind me and wrestled with my reserve until it finally hopped off my back. I got part of a canopy before I hit this tree. It's the tree that saved my life. The canopy never fully opened, so if I'd hit the ground, I would've been the world's biggest, messiest pancake. The reserve getting caught up in the tree is all that saved me."

Chapter 29
Concerned Citizens

With the team reunited, I gave our air asset a call. "Five, One . . . over."

"Go ahead, One."

"We're continuing mission."

Clark said, "Roger, One. We'll relay to the ops center. They've been a little worried."

I tucked the radio away and headed north.

Mongo said, "Did any of you guys happen to see a helmet, a rifle, or half a dozen water bladders?"

Singer shook his head. "Nope. It looks like you're going to be completely dependent on the rest of us for your survival over the next two days."

Mongo laughed. "I have faith in you."

We continued at a cautious pace through the early morning darkness. As we came close enough to hear the surf on the north shore of the island, I said, "Hold up. Let's see if we can spot our cave."

We knelt in the low brush and scanned the terrain.

Of course, it was Singer who spoke up first. "I've got it. Two o'clock and three hundred meters."

"It must be nice to be able to see in the dark," Mongo said.

I scolded him. "You're the one who lost his nods."

Singer pulled off his helmet and handed it to Mongo. "Here. I can see through my scope."

The sniper raised his rifle and took in the world through the highest-quality night vision scope that had ever been built, and Mongo perched Singer's helmet on his head and pulled down the nods. "Oh, yeah. I've got it now. Are we sure that's the only cave?"

Singer focused his scope. "It may not be the only cave on the island, but there's a path worn in front of it and a black antenna ten or twelve feet tall, just up the slope from the mouth of the cave."

We held our position, silently watching the mouth of the cave for twenty minutes.

I glanced at my watch. "The sun will be up in just over an hour. Are we going to hit them now or watch them all day and hit them tonight?"

Singer whispered, "You're the boss, but I can take out that antenna right now."

"Let's not do that just yet," I said. "It may come in handy. I'm concerned about not knowing how many fighters we're facing, but I'm leaning toward hitting them now."

Hunter said, "I'm not sure it matters how many we're facing. We have the advantage of extreme surprise. There's no way they know we're here, and there's no way they're ready for a ground attack. I'm with you. I think we should hit 'em now. God only knows what they'll do with another twelve hours."

Mongo weighed in. "I don't have a rifle, but I've still got my sidearm, and now I've got Singer's nods. I say we go for it."

My decision was made. "Singer, you're on overwatch. Are you happy with this position?"

"Sure. I don't see a better perch. This'll work just fine."

"All right. Dig in, and you'll manage coms with Clark."

He settled into the prone position with his rifle resting on his bag. "Oh, sure . . . Make *me* tell Daddy we're abandoning the plan."

Hunter and I dropped our packs beside our sniper, and Mongo would've done the same if he hadn't dropped his from two miles high.

"Form up on me. I have the lead. Hunter's on my heels, and Mongo's bringing up the rear with his cute little pistol."

We crouched and moved only at a pace that would leave us silent during our approach. We'd spring the trap soon enough, but the element of surprise had far too much value to throw away.

It took half an hour for us to cover the ground between our sniper's nest and the entrance to the cave. The eastern sky was beginning to show signs of the coming daylight, but the sun's position wouldn't matter once we were inside.

Reaching the cave entrance, we stood on bent knees and moved in our three-man room-clearing posture. Our ability to anticipate each other's moves made us a deadly trio in almost any environment. A cave with only one entrance and exit was little more than a tomb for the terrorists inside.

As I led the team into the inner darkness of the cave, I held out a hand and motioned toward the ground. Hunter and Mongo focused on the tripwire I discovered, and they stepped over the hazard. Mongo turned once across the wire and disarmed the trap, pocketing the hand grenade attached to one end of the wire.

Around a pair of sharp bends in the cave, light began to filter out of the bowels of the tunnel. Using the walls as cover and concealment, we pressed forward, ever closer to the source of the dim light. Around the final bend in the wall, the tunnel opened into a room perhaps twelve to fifteen feet square with four cots lined against the back wall and three to the left. Chains dangled from above each of the four cots and ran to the ankles of four prisoners. The swollen midsection of the victim on the far right rose and fell in rhythmic breaths, and my suspicions about the validity of the beheading video were confirmed. Congressman Jimmy Paige was alive and still in one piece.

Two men with rifles leaning against the wall beside them sat on short folding stools, drinking coffee from metal cups. To their left stood a wooden table with a radio of some design I didn't recognize and a small console containing a keypad. A headset rested on the table, and wiring protruded from beneath, leading deeper into the cave system.

I gave the signal for Hunter and Mongo to hold position, and then I eased forward to provide a slightly improved assessment of the room. The new position rewarded me with a view of three more sleeping forms. Raising three fingers into the air over my left shoulder, I relayed the new headcount to my partners.

I slipped backward silently and rejoined my team. "Ready?"

Both men nodded.

I motioned into the opening and shouldered my suppressed MP5. Hunter stepped beside me, and we moved forward in practiced synchronization until the tips of our suppressors penetrated the light. Instinctually, I checked the ground for another tripwire but found only boots ready for battle.

With the slightest of nudges from my left elbow, Hunter and I moved forward in locked step, and Mongo stepped into the light and turned left to manage the three sleeping terrorists who'd soon be awake, confused, and terrified.

Our concealment of darkness was behind us, and the gig was up. Showtime had arrived.

The coffee-drinking men looked up simultaneously and dropped their cups in surprise. Each of them lunged for their weapons, sealing their fate. The hiss of Hunter's round leaving the muzzle of the suppressor sounded only milliseconds before mine. The back of the first man's head exploded, spraying blood and gray matter onto the rock wall behind him. My rounds impacted high on the second man's chest, and my T-box shot missed low, sending a round straight through his clenched teeth.

Hunter spun left, and I turned to the right, scanning the room for additional threats. By the time we surveyed the space, two of the three remaining terrorists were sitting up on their cots with eyes like beach balls. Hunter stepped forward and yanked the cover from the first man at the same instant Mongo kicked over the cot of the third man who'd managed to sleep through the melee.

The man tumbled to the ground and looked up in shock. "What the . . ."

Mongo placed a size fourteen boot against his head and pinned him to the ground, facedown, while driving the butt of his pistol into the face of the second man still fighting to escape. The blow left him wilting to the floor beside his pinned-down comrade.

Hunter stepped into the one remaining man who'd backed himself against the wall in fear. The former Air Force combat controller turned world-class bad-ass stuck the end of his suppressor against the guy's forehead and hissed, "Do you want to live?"

Unable to nod, the man let out a groan.

My partner said, "I'll take that as a yes. Now, get on your knees."

He followed Hunter's order and melted to the ground.

While Mongo wrapped the wrists of his victim in flex-cuffs, Hunter did the same with his compliant prisoner. They left both men bound hand and foot, with their ankles flex-cuffed to their wrists, rendering them motionless.

The commotion brought the four hostages from their slumber, and their chains rattled like ghosts of Christmas past. The initial fear on their faces was soon replaced by relief when the realization of what had just occurred fell upon them. Tears of relief came, but there was no time for emotion.

I stood in front of them with my rifle still trained on the unconscious man lying between Hunter and Mongo. "The two behind me are dead, and these three are under control. How many more are there?"

The man I recognized as Supreme Court Justice Mathew Caputo said, "That's all of them. There was another one, but she killed him."

I turned to face Governor Laura Holcombe. "Nicely done, ma'am. Are you injured?"

She shook her head and held up her cuffed wrists. "No, but I'd like to get out of these."

I glanced to ensure my partners had our prisoners under control and pulled my handcuff key from my pocket. In seconds, I had all four free of their bindings. "Are any of you hurt? Can all of you walk?"

Governor Holcombe pointed her chin toward Congressman Jimmy Paige. "He's diabetic and hasn't had insulin in days. I doubt he can walk far."

"No problem. I can carry him," came Mongo's baritone from behind me.

Congressman David Solomon eyed Mongo. "You look like you could carry all of us . . . at the same time. Who are you guys? You're not SEALs, are you?"

"No, sir," I said. "We're just concerned citizens, and I bet you'd like to get a ride home."

"Yeah, we'd like that a lot."

I motioned toward our prisoners. "Get those three outside, and put Singer on them. Then come back, and we'll get these four out of here."

Hunter knelt beside the man he'd trussed up like a rodeo calf. "I can tie a rope around your neck and drag you and your buddy out of here, or I can cut your ankles free and you can walk out. It's up to you, but keep in mind, if you run, you'll die with a bullet in the back of your head."

"We'll walk," he said in a submissive voice.

Mongo slung the unconscious man across his shoulder and headed for the mouth of the cave with Hunter and the two ambulatory prisoners at gunpoint behind him.

Governor Holcombe stood from her cot. "Give me a pistol, and I'll go with them. I can guard them while you get everyone else out."

I gave her a smile. "You've already killed your quota of bad guys on this little outing, so I think it'd be best if you stay here with me. We've got a sniper outside who'll watch over them until our ride gets here."

She said, "I'd still feel better if you'd let me hold that pistol on your hip until this is over."

I looked down at my sidearm and back at the governor, then I drew my pistol. "Don't kill anybody unless they're trying to kill me. Deal?"

She winked and took the Glock from my gloved hand. "You've got a deal, Mr. Concerned Citizen."

Chapter 30
Nobodies from Nowhere

Mongo and Hunter returned to the room inside the cave where I waited with the newly armed governor from South Carolina, the Supreme Court justice, a pair of congressmen, and two dead bad guys.

Hunter laid a pair of body bags beside the dearly departed and rolled the bodies into the plastic envelopes.

Mongo extended a hand toward Congressman Jimmy Paige. "Can you stand up, sir?"

Without a word, the frail lawmaker forced himself to his feet, leaning heavily on Mongo. The exerted energy left the man barely conscious and incapable of standing without support.

Mongo helped him back onto his cot. "I've got a better idea. Cots make great litters. Hunter, you get his feet, and I'll take his head. We'll come back for the good terrorists."

Hunter lifted the foot of Paige's cot and headed for the cave entrance with Mongo trailing and holding the head of the cot a foot higher than Hunter's end.

The justice, the governor, and the remaining congressman climbed to their feet, each rubbing their wrists from days spent cuffed and immobile.

"What did your partner mean by 'good terrorists'?" the justice asked.

I said, "It's not politically correct, sir, but the only good terrorists are the ones in body bags, and those two qualify."

As Hunter and Mongo disappeared down the corridor with Paige, I said, "Follow me, single file, and keep a hand on the person in front of you. It's dark in the passage, but only for about a hundred feet. The only light I have is infrared, so you can't see it with your naked eyes. Let's go."

Like a row of ducklings following their mother, we moved slowly from the interior of the cave and into the first light of dawn. The liberated hostages squinted against the morning sun as it bloomed across the horizon.

Mongo knelt beside Congressman Paige's cot and started an IV. With fluids flowing, he checked the congressman's blood sugar and injected the required insulin into his arm.

"How long has it been since all of you have eaten?" I asked.

Governor Holcombe said, "They fed us once a day, but not much. We'd gladly take you up on an All-Star breakfast if you can find a Waffle House."

"We can do better than that," Hunter said as he passed out MREs in brown plastic bags. "We've got combat cuisine, but nothing scattered, covered, and chunked."

"Go back and get the body bags. Singer and I will stay out here and wait for the Caravan. I assume Disco and Clark are on their way."

Hunter and Mongo vanished back into the cave, and Singer said, "They'll be on the beach in minutes. I called them as soon as the boys brought these guys out."

I sat down beside Congressman David Solomon as he stared at the MRE pouch. "Would you like for me to open that for you, Congressman?"

He stared at me for a long moment and then back at the pouch without a word.

"Are you okay, sir?"

He nodded slowly. "Just a bit overwhelmed."

I lifted the MRE from his hands and sliced into it. "Here you go. Getting some calories into your body will help."

Singer tossed me a canteen of water, and I propped it against the congressman's leg. "Drink some water, too. The plane will be here any minute."

He squeezed a thin line of peanut butter onto a single cracker and touched it to his lips. "A plane? There's no place to land a plane out here."

"Just enjoy your crackers, sir. We'll take care of everything else."

I stood and dusted myself off just as Hunter laid a body bag on the sandy ground and motioned for me to join him.

When I stepped to his side, he turned away from everyone and whispered, "What are we going to do with these guys?"

I looked down at the unmarked body bags. "I don't know, but we can't leave them here."

"I'm not just talking about the dead guys. I mean everybody."

I looked across our collection of American elites and enemies of the state all sitting within feet of each other, the tables turned, the cuffs on new wrists and ankles, and freedom and liberation worn on the faces of the previously imprisoned. "We'll rely on Clark and the Board for that decision. It was our job to find them, free them, and capture or kill their captors. There's hours of de-briefing to be done with the good guys, and even more awaiting the unlucky trio we didn't shoot in the face."

"Speaking of Clark," Hunter said. "I think I hear him now."

I turned my attention skyward to see the Caravan less than three hundred feet overhead and descending. Her pontoons glided onto the gently rolling morning ocean before turning back for the beach. With Disco at the controls, Clark stood on the starboard pontoon with an anchor and line. As the bows of the pontoons brushed against the narrow, sandy shoreline, Clark leapt to the ground and buried the anchor several feet up the beach, securing the seaplane in place for the short time she'd spend on the surface.

Clark galloped up the gentle slope and took in the scene we'd created at the mouth of the cave. "It looks like you guys have been busy. Oh, and congratulations, Mongo, for still being alive when we all thought you'd pranged in."

The big man offered a mock salute, and Clark took over as the incident commander. "All right. Somebody tell me about casualties. It looks like the two in the bags speak for themselves, but how's everybody else?"

Every eye turned to me, so I said, "Congressman Paige is non-ambulatory and in partial diabetic shock. He's on his second bag of fluids, and insulin was administered. Governor Holcombe, Congressman Solomon, and Justice Caputo suffered no major injuries. Like you said, the guys in the bags are becoming room temperature after going for their rifles when we politely introduced ourselves."

Clark chuckled. "Yes, I'm sure that's exactly how it happened. What about those three?"

"They initially refused to cooperate, but with a little encouragement, they came around to our way of thinking. The guy in the middle has at least a broken nose, à la Mongo, and the other two are trussed up for the sake of discomfort. I mean . . . security."

Clark slid the toe of his boot beneath the unconscious man's face and lifted his chin. "Well done, Mongo."

Our bruiser almost blushed. "Gee, thanks. It's what I do."

Governor Holcombe sat in disbelief at the scene playing out in front of her. "Are you sure you guys aren't SEALs?"

I shook my head. "Oh, no, ma'am. We're afraid of the water, and we hate violence. We'd never make it through BUDS training. We're the sensitive type."

Before the governor and I could extend our interaction, Clark said, "Let's get 'em on the plane. Sick guy, first, then the healthy ones, followed by tying the bad guys to the pontoons. If they fall off along the way, that means less work for us."

Mongo and Hunter loaded Congressman Paige aboard first and positioned him in one of the Caravan's plush reclining seats. Clark and Singer escorted the former hostages down the hill and onto the plane, where they found seats of their own.

Hunter said, "Why don't we just kick these guys down the hill and let 'em roll to the water?"

Unconscious guy rolled like a log, but the other two didn't enjoy the descent down the short slope. Hunter and I shouldered the body bags and followed the terrorists down to the water's edge. The bagged corpses fit nicely into the storage bins of the pontoons, and as much as I wanted to tie the others to the floats, I didn't have the heart. They found themselves cuffed to the cargo tie-downs in the floor of the Caravan.

I counted heads to double-check that we had everyone on board. "The gang's all here, but we need to run back into the cave and secure the equipment."

"Get some pictures before you dismantle anything," Clark said. "The shots might come in handy if these guys live long enough to go to trial."

Mongo, Hunter, and I made short work of disassembling the communications gear from inside the cave. In fewer than ten minutes, we were loaded up and taxiing away from the beach.

"Wait a minute!" I yelled. "Governor, what did you do with the body of the guy you killed?"

"You'll never find him," she said through a broad grin. "The animals ate what was left of him after I carved him up with his own knife."

"I like you more every time you open your mouth, ma'am. If you ever get tired of politics, I think we could use you on our little team."

"How's the pay?" she asked.

In unison, three voices said, "Lousy!"

She chuckled. "Sounds like my kind of work. Where are you taking us, by the way?"

Clark gestured toward the cuffed terrorists. "We're going to drop these folks off with some friends of ours a couple hundred miles south of here in a little place you may have heard of—Guantanamo Bay, I think it's called."

Congressman Solomon smiled for the first time. "Can we stay and watch?"

Clark shrugged. "You can do whatever you want, sir. You're a congressman. But my orders are to deliver you to the Naval Air Station in Key West."

He nodded. "I guess NAS Key West does sound better than an interrogation cell at Gitmo."

Disco added power and put the nose in the wind. Ten minutes later, we were cruising southbound for the southeastern coast of Cuba.

Clark said, "See what you can get out of those guys before we hand them off to the trained professionals with power drills and electric probes."

The previously unconscious terrorist came around after ten seconds of smelling salts beneath his demolished nose.

"Welcome back," I said. "We missed you, and you almost missed the excitement."

The man shook his head furiously and tugged at his restraints.

"Calm down. I wouldn't want you to hurt yourself. That's my job."

I reached for my pistol and found only an empty holster. I looked toward the front of the plane. "Hey, Governor, do you want to have a little fun?"

"I thought you'd never ask," she said as she unbuckled and climbed from her seat.

She joined me on the floor beside terrorist number one.

"Start with his right kneecap," I said.

She slipped my Glock from her waistband and pressed the muzzle to the man's knee.

I leaned in close. "You will answer my questions, or I'm turning her loose on you."

He growled, "You won't let her shoot me inside the airplane. The bullet will tear the plane apart."

I ignored him. "Who's paying you?"

He narrowed his eyes. "Go ahead. Let her shoot me."

I turned to the governor. "Don't pull the trigger yet. Just apply a little more pressure."

She leaned forward, driving the muzzle into the man's kneecap until he groaned.

"See there?" I said. "We don't have to shoot you to make it hurt. Now, tell me who's paying you."

He winced against the pain and cursed.

"Oh, we've got a tough one here." I pulled off my armored plate carrier and held it in front of his face. "Do you know what this is?" I didn't give him time to answer before I yanked his leg off the floor and shoved the vest beneath his knee. "It's a bulletproof vest, and it'll work just fine to protect my airplane from her bullet leaving the back of what'll be left of your knee. Now, tell me who's paying you."

"You won't do it," he hissed. "You're not allowed to torture me. It's a violation of the Geneva Convention."

I raised a finger. "Ah, you may have a point there. Let's consult our legal department."

I turned to Justice Caputo. "I'm sorry to bother you, Judge, but our guest has brought up a perplexing legal question, and I wonder if you could give us an opinion."

He spun in his seat. "I'd be glad to help. What's the question?"

"It concerns the application of the Geneva Convention. Is this man an armed enemy combatant?"

"It's possible he could be considered such," Justice Caputo said.

"And how about me? To your knowledge, am I an agent of the United States government or a member of the uniformed armed services?"

The justice shook his head. "Clearly, you are not. Therefore, in my opinion, this scenario is not covered under the Geneva Convention, so please, carry on."

Instead of turning back to my questioning, I stared into the governor's eyes. "How badly do you want to shoot this man?"

She grinned. "So badly."

"Good. That's what I thought. I'm going to ask him the question once more. If he doesn't answer in, oh, let's say three seconds, you have my permission to put as many holes in him as you'd like."

As it turned out, I didn't have to ask the question again. He chose to become compliant almost instantly.

"Dussault! That's all I know. I don't know his first name, I swear. Just Dussault."

The governor thrust all her weight onto the Glock pressed against his knee, and the man screamed in agony, jerking and bucking against the assault.

"Damn it!" she said. "I really wanted to shoot him."

I reached for the pistol and pulled it from her hand. "Don't worry, ma'am. You'll have another chance before all of this is over."

I stepped away from our prisoners and pulled out my sat-phone. "Hey, Skipper. Run the name Dussault. One of our guests just volunteered to cooperate and gave up that name as the man who's paying them."

I pocketed the phone, and the governor grabbed my shirt. "Tell me who you people are. Are you CIA?"

I gently pulled her hands from my shirt. "We're nobodies from nowhere, ma'am, and that's exactly who and what we'll continue to be."

Chapter 31
Gitmo Get Gone

Allowing a communist country to exist less than a hundred miles from the shores of the United States never made sense to me, and having an American military base inside that communist nation made even less sense. Clearly, politics are *not* for me.

There are few things more enjoyable for me than landing on the water. The exhilaration of exchanging aerodynamic lift for nautical buoyancy is, somehow, magical, but my fascination doesn't end there. The stacks of manuals, codified law, and instructional material it would take for a mere mortal to understand both aeronautical and nautical law would sink a battleship, but that is what's required of a seaplane pilot. Until the floats touch the water, he is bound by every silly rule the Federal Aviation Administration could dream up, but the instant the keel of the plane's floats touches the surface of the water, the flying machine and its captain are enshrouded by nautical law and COLREGs—the International Regulations for Preventing Collisions at Sea—published by the International Maritime Organization. Both Clark and Disco were well-qualified seaplane pilots with a thorough understanding of the applicable law, but the task that lay ahead of us on that day wasn't covered in any book, pamphlet, or regulation. We were truly flying—and splashing down—entirely by the seat of our pants.

The elongated island of communist Cuba stretched some seven hundred miles through the northwestern Caribbean, separating the Florida Keys from the Cayman Islands and Jamaica. We skirted the eastern tip of the island by fifteen miles, leaving a nice buffer between our pristine Caravan and the government who would love to shoot it down. We wouldn't be able to maintain the buffer and complete our mission, though. At some point, we had to turn our propeller toward the mysterious and foreboding island.

We made that fearful turn seventy miles southwest of the eastern tip of Cuba and started bleeding off altitude. We had no interest in telling anyone who or where we were. Our mission on that picture-postcard-perfect morning was anything but authorized and appreciated by Castro and his socialist regime.

Flying at one hundred feet above the water was not an assignment the Caravan's autopilot would accept, so Disco flew the approach by hand as the Cuban shoreline drew ominously closer by the minute. Patrol boats weren't likely, especially with a thousand well-armed, itchy-fingered United States Marines guarding the Guantanamo Bay Naval Base. Our destination technically fell microscopically inside U.S. territory, but Cuban security forces have never been particularly good at recognizing invisible lines on contested maps. I had no way to know how many Marines would make up our welcoming party just east of Kittery Beach, but my limited experience with Marines, regardless of their quantity, told me the only thing they loved more than drinking and chasing women was killing communists, so knowing they were on our team and waiting patiently for our arrival made me feel all warm and fuzzy.

The wind from the northeast left the sea placid and inviting off the coast, and Disco made the landing look easy. His post-landing, step-taxiing maneuver left me more than a little baffled, but he put us on the beach as gently as possible. A pair of Marines approached, giving the propeller a wide berth, and Clark tossed them the anchor and line. Once the anchor was firmly seated in the sand, Disco shut down the turbine and gave the okay to open the doors.

The same two Marines who'd anchored us waded into the knee-deep water and looked up at me as they steadied themselves against the portside pontoon. "Permission to come aboard, sir?"

"Come aboard," I said to the Marines as I watched a man in cargo shorts, combat boots, and a black Van Halen T-shirt step onto the bow of the pontoon. Whoever the man was, he lacked the Marines' nautical courtesy and asked no one for permission to board.

The two Marines lifted the first prisoner by his armpits and knees and placed him in the door with his legs dangling down the ladder. Van Halen drew a set of flex-cuffs from his waistband and slapped them around the man's already bound ankles, and I wondered why he didn't trust my cuffs. He placed a boot on the prisoner's ankle and yanked the flex-cuffs tighter than they were ever intended to be pulled. Then, he shoved the man's knees aside and leaned into the cabin of the Caravan. The flex-cuff routine was repeated on his wrists, even though the man was already bound. With his personal flex-cuffs on the terrorist, the man slid a hand inside the waist of the prisoner's pants and yanked him from the doorway. The prisoner's feet hit the pontoon, but his momentum drove him forward and sent him splashing facedown into the shallow water.

Ignoring the man in the water, Van Halen motioned toward the prisoner with the bloody, broken nose, and tossed a pair of flex-cuffs into the plane. "Give me that one next."

The Marines re-cuffed the man and duck-walked him to the door. Before they could set him down, the mysterious man bounded up the boarding ladder, grabbed the prisoner's shirt, and leaned within inches of him. "What happened to your face?"

The bound man opened his mouth to answer, but Van Halen pulled him through the door and face-first into the sea. I stepped to the window to see the two men thrashing and twisting wildly in the shallow blue water.

"Don't worry, kid. They'll float when they stop panicking," Van Halen said as the Marines delivered his next victim to the doorway. He looked up at the terrorist and widened his eyes. "You look like a sensible man of distinction who deserves some respect. Here, let me hold your arm as you hop down the ladder. Be careful. I wouldn't want you to get hurt."

The cuffed man eyed Van Halen with trepidation and slid his feet onto the top rung of the ladder. The Marine steadied him and helped him ease his feet from the first rung to the second. The instant his feet landed on the rung, Van Halen delivered a powerful kick to the man's shins, driving his bound ankles through the rungs of the boarding ladder. As his body folded at the waist, he face-planted on the deck of the pontoon.

Van Halen grabbed a handful of the man's hair, yanked his head up, and inspected the injury. "Good. Now you look like your buddy. Get in the water!" He yanked the man from the ladder and deposited him into the sea.

The two original Marines were joined by a dozen more, and they fished the terrorists out of the sea and tossed them onto the coarse sand of the narrow beach.

Van Halen shot a thumb toward the remaining occupants of the plane. "Are they the hostages?"

"Not anymore," I said.

He climbed aboard and pushed past me, his wet boots dripping salt water all over the interior of the Caravan.

He spun and sat on the floor, facing the former hostages, and began his interrogation. I listened intently but didn't interrupt. His questioning lasted fifteen minutes, and he climbed back to his feet.

"How about the two bodies?"

I pointed out the door. "They're bagged and stowed in the pontoons."

He gave me a nod and leapt from the plane to the deck of the pontoon, ignoring the ladder. He showed no more respect to the dead than he had the living and threw the body bags into the light surf. Incapable of panicking, the corpses floated just as Van Halen said they would.

With the bizarre encounter behind us, I checked the pontoons for water and pumped out what little there was while Clark recovered the anchor and shoved us off the beach.

Disco let the gentle breeze blow us offshore, using the water rudders as well as the aerodynamic rudders to sail the big airplane backward. His mastery of the technique left me wondering if there was anything in the aeronautical realm he couldn't do.

We took off and turned to the west for our three-minute flight to the Guantanamo Bay Airport, just west of the mouth of the bay. Our passengers disembarked for bathrooms and snacks. Even Congressman Paige was feeling well enough to walk under his own power. I stayed with them and escorted the four who would typically step off an airplane and onto a red carpet at any U.S. military facility, but in the interest of my continued mission, I definitely didn't need them being recognized.

A lineman refueled the Caravan, and everyone was back aboard in less than half an hour.

Before we took off, I knelt beside Disco in the captain's seat. "I need to ask you something, if you don't mind."

He closed his checklist and turned in the seat. "Sure, what is it?"

I pointed toward the east. "When we landed out there, you kept us on a high-speed step taxi a lot longer than I would have. What was that about?"

"That's because it wasn't my first time beaching on that particular strip of sand. There's a reef about a foot under the water at low tide. I tore the water rudders off an old PBY Catalina on that reef a dozen years ago, and I didn't want a repeat performance today."

I chuckled. "I should've known. Experience is one of the few things you can't buy but you have to earn."

"You're right about that," he said. "Once I realized we were at high-tide, I felt comfortable sailing off the beach without giving the reef another thought. Take a look on our way out. You'll be able to see the reef. It's impossible to miss . . . Just ask the PBY crew chief."

I stood and laid a hand on his shoulder. "I won't question you again."

"You can question me all you want. It's your airplane, your team, and your operation. I'm just the hired help."

I pulled my sunglasses down my nose and glared at him across the rims. "Get those thoughts out of your head, Colonel. It's our airplane, our team, and our op. All for one, and one for all."

"All right. Just like the Three Musketeers, right?"

"Exactly. And I'll buy your dinner if you can name all three of them."

He closed one eye and thought back to freshman world literature class. "Athos, Porthos, and Aramis, but you always buy dinner anyway."

I gave him the thumbs-up. "Get back to work. We're still a long way from home."

The shortest distance between two points is a terrible plan when those two points are Key West and Gitmo. We flew the low-level, circuitous route back around the eastern end of the island and due north from there until we were well clear of Cuban airspace. If we were intercepted, the Cubans would have questions I had no intention of answering.

I sat on the arm of one of the few remaining seats in the Caravan. "How's everybody feeling?"

Nods came, and Governor Holcombe asked, "Who was that guy who questioned us?"

I motioned toward Clark. "According to that guy up there in the right seat, he was a CIA interrogator."

"So, you and he work for the same organization?"

"Yes, ma'am. The American people."

The answer seemed to satisfy her at least temporarily, so I asked, "Does anyone need or want anything? We don't have many luxuries aboard. This is a working airplane and not a first-class ticket, but we'll do anything we can to make you more comfortable."

Justice Caputo laid a hand on my arm. "Son, whatever your name is, and whoever you work for, you've made the four of us more comfortable than we ever thought we'd feel again. I'm not ashamed to admit I was getting things right with God in that cave because I never thought I'd see the sunlight again. We owe you a debt we'll never be able to repay, but I, for one, want to make sure you and this team of yours have my direct number if there's ever anything I can do for you."

An echo of agreement came from the remaining three.

"Thank you," I said. "That means a great deal to me and the team. However, it's highly unlikely you'll ever hear from or see us again. We don't exactly run in the same circles as politicians and judges. Besides, we're camera shy, and we hate newspaper reporters."

Just under four hours later, thanks to the northeast wind, we touched down on Boca Chica Key at Naval Air Station Key West to an entirely different kind of reception than we'd received in Cuba.

Three U.S. Navy ambulances, four armored vehicles, six fire trucks, and a staff car met us on the ramp at the base of the tower. My team made no effort to get involved with the grip-and-grin formality of the moment. Instead, we pulled our hats down low, kept our sunglasses on, and drifted to the opposite side of the airplane.

In the distance sat a camouflaged pickup truck with a man sitting on the open tailgate.

I gave Clark an elbow. "Is that who I think it is?"

He squinted through the late afternoon sun and put on his crooked grin. "I think it is. Let's go find out."

Six civilians wandering around on a Naval Air Station would usually get a lot of negative attention, but the commotion around the congressmen, governor, and Supreme Court justice had every eye trained on the reception and not the ragged-looking commandos strolling across the ramp.

When we drew within fifty feet of the beat-up pickup truck, Master Chief Dre Lewis stood with a wooden box under one arm. He gave us a half-hearted salute and held out the box. "I don't have anything to drink, boys, but I brought the cigars. Even though you're only half finished with this one, you've got to celebrate the victories."

We each accepted a fine cigar grown and rolled on the same island we'd left only four hours before.

Dre patted the tailgate. "Hop in. I know a spot where the beer is cold and they don't frown on cigar smoke."

We piled into the back of his truck, and when we came to a stop, we found ourselves in the gravel parking lot of the Boca Chica Marina. It didn't take long for six knuckle-draggers and a

SEAL to commandeer a pair of tables on the deck and fire up our Cubans. We told the story of the assault on Rum Cay, the feisty female governor from South Carolina, and the CIA interrogator from Gitmo.

Dre said, "I hate I missed it. That sounds like a grand ol' time."

"It wasn't bad," I said. "It's always nice to chalk up another one in the win column."

He raised his bottle. "Here's to winning!"

We raised our bottles and drank the toast.

Dre finished his beer and waved for another. When it arrived, he wiped the top and inspected the amber lager inside the bottle. "So, I guess that C-Five on the ramp is for you guys, huh?"

Every eye turned to Clark, and he pulled off his sunglasses and let out a long breath. "Yep, I guess it is. You want to come with us?"

Dre tapped the rim of his bottle to Clark's. "I wouldn't miss it for the world."

Chapter 32
The Cake Eaters

Disco, Hunter, Mongo, and Singer turned to me as if I'd shown up at their birthday party without a gift, so I turned to Clark. "Care to let me in on the C-Five, or were you planning to spring it on us after we'd had a few cocktails?"

"Take it easy. I wasn't hiding anything from you. We've just been a little too busy to brief phase two."

I scanned the deck. "It looks like we're the only ones here, so now is as good a time as any."

Clark checked for himself, including walking to the ice machine and peeking around the corner. "First, I'll give you what we know. Then, I'll give you what we think." He paused and took a sip. "No, on second thought, first, I'll say this. Nicely done on Rum Cay. Excellent decision-making, perfect execution. Well done all around. Dre is right. We have to celebrate all the victories along the way. The Board is pleased, I'm pleased, and you bet your tails those four people you pulled out of that cave are pleased. I guess the only folks who aren't happy about it are the bodies and the guests at Chez Gitmo. You guys deserve a long vacation for what you did down on that island. But you're not getting one."

We laughed even though we didn't want to.

He continued. "Here's what we know. The primary calls are definitely being routed through the Azores, but there's no reason for us to go all the way out there. I'll let our naval contingent fill you in on that little tidbit." He gestured toward the SEAL.

Dre said, "I'll try to keep this from sounding like a military briefing. Based on your analyst's intel, a team of SEALs just *happened* to be in the neighborhood of the Azores, so they were tasked with the enviable job of having a look. They found a bank of computers and nothing else. Thanks to the tech they had with them, we now know every thought that computer has before it thinks it, and we'll be gleaning intel from that baby like there's no tomorrow. And that's pretty much all I've got. So it's all yours, Clark."

"Our next target is . . ." As if paranoia had him wrapped around its little finger, Clark checked over both shoulders and leaned in. "We're headed for Gabon. Skipper and Ginger have a solid fix on the transmitter, but it's mobile, so we still don't know if it's a satellite phone, a cell phone, or some sort of base station like they had in the cave, but we're leaning toward sat-phone at the moment. Any questions so far?"

I raised a finger.

"Yeah, go ahead, Chase."

"Is the electronic alteration of the voice being done by the computers on the Azores, or from the original source in"—I leaned in for show and whispered—"Gabon?"

"Go ahead and laugh it up, hotshot. Your day will come. To answer your question, we don't know yet, but we think it's happening at the source."

"Who's we?" I asked.

Clark scowled. "What?"

"You said *we* think it's happening at the source. Who is *we*?"

"I misspoke, Mr. Perfectionist. Skipper and Ginger think it's being done at the source. I was using the royal we."

I said, "It doesn't make a lot of sense that the station would be mobile if it was also producing the altered voice. That sounds like something that would be done from a computer."

Clark looked down the table. "Mongo, got any ideas?"

"It could be a laptop with a satellite or cellular modem. If that's not it, I'm stumped."

"I'll buy that," I said. "I'm sorry to have interrupted."

Clark said, "Another thing we know for sure is that the Rum Cay site was run entirely by hired thugs. None of the guys you picked up were connected with anyone high-level. They were just worker bees. As much as it meant to recover the hostages safely, that's never been the primary mission. With the attacks in D.C., we're clearly dealing with international terrorists, and we're going to take them down. That starts—and maybe ends—in Gabon. We're going to put you guys on the ground and surveil the location of the transmitter. Unlike Rum Cay, when you called an audible, we're running this one by the book. First, we watch, catalog, and memorize every move they make. Then, after we know everything we can find out about their schedule and routine, we hit them hard. But we're taking prisoners . . . no more dead bodies. These guys are too valuable to send them to Saint Peter right away. We're going to extract every morsel we can from their brains before we turn them over to the authorities."

"Is that what the C-Five is for?" I asked. "To get us to Gabon?"

"It is, but it probably won't get you all the way. It'll get you as far as Ramstein Air Base in Germany, but you'll probably do the rest of the trip on a Herc."

I sat my beer down. "You've got to be kidding me. Are you serious? A three-thousand-mile trip on a C-One-Thirty?"

"It's actually a little farther than that, but you won't be doing the whole thing in the Herc. We'll probably do a ground insertion into Libreville."

I shook my head. "Oh, this keeps getting better and better. Why aren't the SEALs doing this one? They're bigger, stronger, and faster than us. They've got the tools and the training to do exactly this kind of thing. I don't get it. Why is this one ours?"

Clark turned to the SEAL. "Dre, do you want to take this one?"

"Sure. That's an easy answer. This one is in your lap and not the SEALs' for exactly two reasons. First, the military has a very strict set of rules they have to follow—especially in countries with no status of forces agreement, like Gabon."

I said, "So, we're going because we can break the rules?"

Clark shook his head. "No, you're going because for you guys, there are no rules."

"I think it's coming together for me now. This is one of those missions when we say, 'Here, hold my dignity. I'm about to do some sketchy stuff.'"

"You got it, College Boy."

"Fine, I can swallow that, but Dre said there were exactly two reasons. What's the other one?"

Clark grinned. "Because the president said so."

I faced my team. "Anybody want out?"

No one flinched.

"Anybody think this is a terrible plan?"

Everyone raised their hands.

"Anybody got a better plan?"

The hands went down.

I turned back to my handler. "You've been throwing around the word 'we' quite a bit. Are you coming with us?"

"Nope. This is a direct-action mission. I'll weigh you down if and when push comes to shove."

"So, we're an unsupported, five-man tactical team six thousand miles from home on the wrong side of the planet that isn't allowed to kill anybody. Is that about right?"

"Nope, you're not a five-man team." He motioned toward Dre. "You're a six-man team."

"I thought you said the SEALs couldn't run this one because of the 'rules.'"

Dre raised an eyebrow. "Actually, I'm the one who said that, and it's still true. The SEALs aren't going."

"But you're a SEAL," I said.

"Not anymore. The Navy hung the thing in The Bahamas on me and said I had one of two options. Take a demotion and a desk job or retire. Guess which one I picked."

I grimaced. "I'm sorry, Dre. I had no idea that would happen, and it's my fault. I made the calls. Listen, we've got some friends— one in particular who nobody outranks. I'll pick up the phone, and we can have this fixed in a matter of minutes."

He lifted his bottle and pointed the rim toward mine. "Relax, Chase. Drink your beer and chill out. Every call you made on the island was the same one I would've made. The outcome would've been the same no matter which one of us was calling the shots. It's already settled. My retirement packet is in, and I'm on terminal leave."

"You've had a brilliant career, though. To have it end with the Navy looking down on you just isn't right."

"Look at me, Chase. Do I look like the kind of man who gives a rip about what some admiral thinks of me? What I care about is the same thing you care about, and that was having my men know they could always rely on me. There's never been a SEAL who walked beside me into a fight who would question my ability, my loyalty, or my devotion to him. I was—and still am—a rock-solid team leader. That's what I'm carrying away from the Navy. Who cares what the Pentagon thinks? Just like you, I'm a warfighter, not a bureaucrat. So, drink up, my brother. To hell with the cake eaters."

There was nothing about retired Master Chief Dre Lewis I disliked or distrusted, but something in my gut didn't like the way Clark dropped him in our laps only hours before an assignment halfway around the world.

Whether it was truly his bladder or his keen sense of team dynamics that sent Dre to his feet, I'll never know, but he said, "Excuse me, gentlemen. I need to make a head call."

When he disappeared inside the mirror-glass door, I gave Clark a look. "It's nothing against Dre. He's as solid as they come, but I don't know how I feel about you throwing him in bed with us right now."

Clark raised a hand. "Slow down, there. I didn't throw him in your lap. He's offering to go, and that's all so far. There's no way I'd ever throw somebody onto *your* team."

I turned to four of the finest men I'd ever known. "As I've said before, this isn't a democracy, but your opinions matter, so let's hear them."

Never shy when it came time for expressing an opinion, Hunter said, "He's as solid as they come, and we could probably learn a lot from him, but we don't know him well enough to follow him through a darkened door. I've got nothing against him deploying with us as long as he knows he's not in charge."

"Anybody else?" I asked.

Mongo spoke up. "I'm with Hunter. Dre's a good dude, but we still haven't been in a gunfight with him. If he comes, I want him in the back."

"How about you, Singer?"

The quiet killer said, "If you say he's one of us, he's one of us, and I'll put a bullet through anybody who tries to hurt him."

I looked up at our chief pilot. "Disco?"

He threw up both hands. "I'm the new guy. What I say means less than the cigar ashes on the ground."

"That's not true," I said. "You're a full partner. Every one of us feels the same about you. Just because you did your fighting from a cockpit doesn't mean you're not a door kicker like the rest of us. Tell me what you think."

He took another draw from his cigar and let the smoke obscure his face. "To tell the truth, he said something I didn't like out on Andros."

My ears perked up. "Do tell."

"This isn't a direct quote. I'm paraphrasing. But when we were planning the mission, he told you that you could be in charge until you did something stupid, and then it became his operation. He may have earned that right on the Teams, but not on *this* team . . . yet."

Singer, Hunter, and Mongo nodded in unison.

Hunter said, "Yeah, I'm glad you brought that up, Disco. He's got to know he's low man, regardless of how many stripes he wore in the Navy."

We sat, drank, and smoked in silence for several minutes before Dre returned.

When he reached the table, he said, "Let me guess. Everybody said I could come along for the ride, but I needed to know my place was at the bottom of the totem pole until I prove myself. Was I close?"

I motioned toward his empty chair. "Sit down, and finish your beer. We've got an op to run, new guy."

Chapter 33
The French Connection

I wouldn't consider climbing aboard the C-5, America's largest transport airplane, before speaking with the two most important women in my life. My first ring sounded in the ops center at Bonaventure Plantation. Skipper had two ways of answering the phone: she either made me feel like I was the most important person in the world, or that I was a misbehaving five-year-old. That day, it was the better of the two.

"Hey, Chase! Welcome back to the States. Nice job on Rum Cay! You earned a lot of atta-boy points from a lot of places with that one. Is everybody okay?"

"Yeah, we're all fine. Singer's back in the fight, so that's a relief. I guess you heard about Mongo wandering off."

"Yeah, Clark told me about it. I was terrified, but I'm so glad it worked out. Anyway, what's up?"

"We're ready to head for Africa, but I didn't want to get on the plane without catching up with you. We're taking Dre, the SEAL, with us. I guess you know that story, too."

"I know a little about it, and it's sad. I did some initial vetting, and he's squeaky clean. Is he coming on full-time?"

"I don't know yet. I've got too many other things to think about right now. We'll see how he does on the ground and what the team thinks. For now, let's consider him a temp."

"Got it. Now, let's talk about Henri Dussault. I climbed down his throat, and he's definitely not one of the good guys. How much do you want to hear?"

"Just give me the crucial elements for now."

"Sure, I can do that. He's obviously French, but his mother was Russian. He was educated at Oxford and ended up in finance. Of course, I haven't had time to research every detail of his career, but suffice it to say, his clients aren't opening savings accounts. From what I found, he's spent his life funneling money to and from anybody who needs to keep it quiet. That's not the best part, though . . ."

"Before we move on," I said, "are you talking about funding terrorism?"

"I couldn't find any glaring evidence of him directly facilitating Islamic terrorism, but he seems to flip-flop quite a bit when it comes to whose side he's on in the never-ending warlord games in Africa."

I tucked that tidbit away. "Let's hear the best part."

She shuffled some papers. "He's quasi-married to Tiffany Gallagher. You know who she is, right?"

"Yes, I know about her. She's former Ambassador Michael Gallagher's ex-wife, but what do you mean by quasi-married?"

"They're living like they're married, and she uses his last name, but I can't find any evidence of them ever being pronounced man and wife."

I considered the intel. "That's interesting, but I'm not sure it really matters. Do you know where they are right now?"

"I know where *he* is, but she's a little slippery. It's possible she's with him in Libreville, but we've not spotted her yet."

"We? Do we have somebody on him?"

"The deputy chief of station is on him, and we've flagged his passport."

"Does the COS know we're coming?"

Skipper said, "The chief of station is on prolonged leave, so the deputy is acting chief. It's a small station, but yes, they know you're coming."

"Send me the contact info for the DCOS so I can touch base when we hit the ground."

"It's already done. I just sent it to your phone."

I ran the whole thing through my head for a moment. "I think that covers everything I need right now, but do you have anything else?"

She laughed. "I've got about a million other things to tell you, but they can wait. Check in from your first stop, and I'll update you on anything that happens between now and then."

"Will do. Hey, Skipper . . ."

"Yeah?"

"Get some rest. I need you at your best when we hit the ground in Gabon, and to be your best, you have to be well rested."

She groaned. "There's so much to do. I can sleep when all of this is over."

"It wasn't a request. I'm putting myself and five men on the ground against international terrorists who've proven they can stay a dozen steps ahead of everybody else. The team and I need you sharp, clearheaded, and fresh off a good night's sleep."

Ignoring me, she said, "Call your wife," and hung up.

The order in which I called Skipper and Penny bore no semblance to the order in which I value them. Personally, no one was more important in my life than Penny, and professionally, no one was more important to my safety in the field than Skipper.

"Chase! I'm so glad you called. Are you okay? Is everyone okay? Are you home? What's going on? Tell me."

I couldn't suppress the smile. "That's my girl . . . always full of energy and questions. I'm fine. The team's fine. I can't discuss everything on the phone, but my little project is going well. We're at the halfway point and headed for the plane to start phase two now."

"Oh! I wish I could be there to give you a huge hug and, well, I'll let you use your imagination for the rest."

"I have a fantastic imagination."

She giggled. "I know you do. Do you have time for me to tell you what's going on out here?"

"Sure. I've always got time for you."

She huffed. "Liar. But I love you for saying so. Anyway, I got an offer from the studio to become a staff writer."

"What does that mean?"

"I'm not really sure yet, but I talked with Graham Lightner, my agent, about it, and he said to turn it down. He says they're trying to lock me down on the cheap and that I'll make a lot more money freelancing. I guess that means he thinks he can keep selling my screenplays. What do you think?"

"Do I need to shoot somebody or blow something up?"

"What? No! Why would you say that?"

I laughed. "Because that's what I do. I know nothing about that Hollywood business, but if you need something blown up, I'm your guy."

"You're always my guy, no matter what I need. I guess I have to trust Graham. He's the one who got me this far."

"No. *You* got you this far. He just knocked on a door for you. Your writing did the rest. I'll support any decision you make, but remember to let me know if you want to watch something explode."

I could almost see her perfect smile when she said, "Go to work, silly boy. I'll be home when you get back. I love you!"

"Hopefully, we'll be home in a few days. If I can't check in with you, Skipper will keep you posted. I love you, too."

* * *

Clark called a huddle at the base of the loading ramp. "This is the part when I'm supposed to say something inspirational and send you on your way, but I'm no good at speeches, so go get the bad guys and shake 'em 'til the answers we need fall out of them. I'll fly the Caravan home and be in the ops center with Skipper and Ginger if you need me."

I shook his hand. "We're a little short on clean underwear and bullets. Do you think you might be able to scare us up a care package before we get to Africa?"

He slapped me on the back. "Oh, ye of little faith. Get on the plane. Santa Claus knows where to find you."

The cavernous interior of the Air Force C-5 Galaxy made it hard to believe something that size could get off the ground under its own power. My concerns about not having the gear we'd need for the deployment flew out the window as soon as the loadmaster cocked his head toward a massive container strapped to the deck of the airplane. "Anything you need should be in there."

I swung the locking bar on the container door and pulled it open. Inside was a veritable tactical toy store. The team wasted no time pushing past me. Weaponry, clothes, cameras, ammunition, and every imaginable gadget we could need lined the walls. I was pleased that Santa had come down the chimney with everything we wanted for Christmas, but the journey ahead didn't include the C-5.

"How are we going to get this stuff to Libreville?" I asked no one in particular, but the loadmaster must've thought I was addressing him.

"I don't know, sir. That's not my problem. It's my job to tie it down inside this airplane. What you do with it after that is up to you."

From deep inside the container, Mongo held up a pair of boots. "They've got my size!"

"Take what we need, guys, but remember, this ride only takes us to Germany. After that, gear gets heavy."

Everyone, including me, built the kit they needed and left the rest.

I found the loadmaster and read from his uniform. "Staff Sergeant Warren."

He looked up. "Yes, sir."

"Do I need to sign for the gear?"

He chuckled. "Not hardly. None of that stuff is inventoried. It's all yours if you want it."

I said, "We've got what we need. You can have the rest."

"No, thank you, sir. What you don't take is going to the bottom of the Atlantic before we touch down at Ramstein."

"The bottom of the ocean?" I asked.

"Yes, sir. I've already drilled the holes in the container. We'll slow down and dump the whole thing out the back over the North Atlantic."

I said, "Do me a favor, will you? Before you shove it out, come upstairs and get us. I'm sure we'd love to see that thing hit the water."

"Whatever you say, sir."

"You can cut the *sir* business. We're just regular dudes."

"You may be dudes, sir, but I don't think there's anything regular about you guys. Get settled in upstairs, and we'll be airborne before you know it."

We climbed the stairs to the passenger area of the monstrous plane and settled into airline seats facing backward.

Disco said, "Before you bunch of boots ask, the seats are turned backward because the Air Force believes you're more likely to survive a crash facing backward. I was an A-Ten driver, so I never flew heavy iron, but my guess would be nobody's surviving a crash in this thing, no matter which way he's facing."

Chapter 34
Shift Change

The nine-hour, five-thousand-mile flight to Ramstein Air Force Base afforded us plenty of time to catch up on the sleep we'd missed.

When the lights came on, we yawned and stretched to life.

"What time is it?" somebody's sleepy voice asked.

I checked my watch and did the math. "It's almost noon in Germany, but our bodies still think it's four a.m."

The loadmaster came bounding up the stairs as if he had no need for sleep. "We're descending into Ramstein now, and we'll be on the ground in twenty minutes or so. Does anyone need anything?"

I checked my team and turned back to Sergeant Warren. "Have you seen Dre?"

Warren held out his hand as if measuring someone's height. "Black guy, shaved head, about this tall?"

"That's him."

"Oh, yeah. He told me to tell you he got scared over Iceland and jumped out."

I wasn't convinced Warren was kidding until he burst into laughter. "I'm just messing with you, sir. He's downstairs doing pullups. That dude's hardcore."

"Yeah, you could say that. You wouldn't happen to have any coffee on board, would you?"

"I thought you might ask, so I've got a pot brewing right now." He motioned to a stainless-steel commercial coffee maker at the front of the passenger area. "Help yourselves."

We mainlined the caffeine until we touched down at Ramstein and walked down the loading ramp into another world. Piles of snow lined the airport, and mists of fog rose from our noses on every exhalation.

Hunter hugged himself. "Nope! Not digging this. How soon can we head south?"

Warren caught the question. "I forgot to tell you, but we got word en route that you and the airplane will continue with a new crew."

"How soon?" Hunter asked.

Warren checked his watch. "It'll take a couple of hours to refuel and brief the new crew, but you'll be headed back toward the sun before you know it."

Hunter scurried back up the ramp. "Wake me up when we get to the equator."

I said, "Hey, Warren. I thought you told me you were going to let us watch you throw that box into the ocean last night."

He shrugged. "I did, but we got orders to leave the gear on the plane and let you guys sleep."

I shook his hand. "Thanks for the ride, Sergeant Warren."

He shot a glance at the container and then back at me. "Whoever you guys are, and wherever you're going, be safe, okay?"

"Safe isn't what we do, Warren, but I'll bring everybody home when the smoke clears."

He gave me a final nod and trotted across the ramp. Almost all of my team and I made our way back to the airline seats and seventy-degree air upstairs. Dre showed up half an hour later.

"Where've you been?"

He wiped sweat from his brow. "I went for a little run. I got four miles in, but my pace was a little off. It's probably the cold air."

Eyes set on me, and I pulled Dre to the back of the compartment. "What would you have done if the newest guy on your team disappeared for half an hour on his first deployment with you?"

He grunted. "I'm sorry, Chase. You're right. I've got to get my head around being the new guy. It won't happen again."

"No worries. I can't afford to lose you."

"I hear you," he said. "If you don't mind, I'm going to run into base ops and get a shower before we go."

"Go, but we need you back here in twenty."

"You got it, boss." He disappeared down the stairs.

Mongo said, "Were you getting the new guy's mind right?"

I said, "It's a big transition for him coming from being the leader of a SEAL team to being low man with us. It'll take him a few days to adjust."

"Just as long as he's in the fight when the fight comes, it's all good with me."

"He will be," I said. "They've got some chow in base ops if you're hungry."

That bit of news sent my team back into Sergeant Warren's goody box downstairs for sweatshirts and gloves.

Lunch was cafeteria-style and hit the spot.

Dre joined us at the table, but before he sat down, he said, "Hey, guys. I'm sorry about disappearing this morning. It won't happen again."

Singer pointed toward an empty chair. "Sit down and eat, High-Speed. You're making the rest of us look bad. If you run away again, I'll wait until you're two miles away before I start shooting . . . just to give you a sporting chance."

We laughed and ate like a big happy family until an Air Force lieutenant colonel in a flight suit walked in and leaned down to whisper something to Dre. Almost instantly, the SEAL shook his head and pointed at me.

The colonel motioned for me to follow him, so I wiped my mouth and said, "I'll be right back."

He led me through a pair of double doors and down a long corridor until we stopped in front of a door with a cipher lock. He thumbed in the code and pushed through the door. After flipping on the lights, he turned and stuck out his hand. "I'm Lieutenant Colonel Waters."

I shook his offered hand. "It's nice to meet you, Colonel."

He huffed. "All you special ops guys are just alike. How 'bout I just call you Mr. Bond?"

"You can call me Chase, Colonel."

"Is that your name or what you do?"

"It's my name. What I do is catch."

He pulled a small notepad from one of the seven thousand pockets on his flight suit. "From what they tell me about this mission, it's not going to be catch and release. I need to know what you need from me."

"No, we eat what we catch, but I'm afraid you have me at a bit of a disadvantage. What are you offering to do for us?"

He looked perplexed. "I was briefed to provide heavy airlift support for a covert operation to equatorial Africa. That means the airplane and an augmented crew made up of five pilots, including the aircraft commander—that's me—three engineers, three loadmasters, two crew chiefs, a pararescueman, a French-speaking translator, and six security police officers."

"That's a lot of people to fly the six of us into Africa."

He still wore the confounded expression. "Pardon me for asking, but is this your first deployment, Chase?"

"It's my first one with two hundred million dollars worth of Air Force hardware and personnel. We usually operate in small-unit tactics—not out of one of the world's biggest airplanes."

He chewed on my admission for a moment. "I've flown with Master Chief Lewis on a couple of missions. He knows the gig."

"Wait here," I said. "I'll be right back."

I returned to the small room with five of the world's most capable warriors in tow. "All right, Colonel. The gang's all here, so we can carry on." I turned to my team. "This is Colonel Waters. He's the aircraft commander of an augmented crew who are here to support our mission. The colonel wants to know what we need from him."

"Let's start with ingress and egress," the colonel said.

Dre raised a finger, and I was thankful for the help. He asked, "How long are you and your crew prepared to be on the ground?"

"We're on indefinite orders for the duration of the operation, Master Chief."

"Just Dre," he said. "No more Master Chief."

"I see. Well, as I said, we're yours until the operation is complete. We're here to provide whatever you need and take you wherever you need to go."

I cleared my throat, silently in awe of the support the president had delivered. "In that case, Colonel, we need you to put us on the ground in Libreville, Gabon, and remain ready to fly at a moment's notice with an unknown number of detainees. Keep a flight plan open to Guantanamo Bay. And I want to see you and the highest-ranking security police officer before we depart."

The colonel offered a stern-faced nod. "Consider it done. Anything else?"

I turned to my team. "Did I miss anything?" I wanted everyone's answer, but I looked first to the most experienced man in the room, and the SEAL shook his head.

Singer raised his head. "I have a question. How badly is a C-Five going to stick out at the airport in Libreville? I've never been there, so I don't know anything about what comes, goes, and stays on that airport."

He appeared to direct the question at me, so I turned to Colonel Waters.

Waters said, "C-Fives aren't rare in Libreville. We often deliver the diplomatic pouches and embassy personnel. They're dependable airplanes, but like all machines, they break down from time to time. The Air Force has a long history of conveniently breaking down in places the crew wouldn't mind being stranded. I'm not sure Gabon qualifies, but it won't be hard to sell the story that we're waiting for parts to repair a fictional problem."

The answer seemed to satisfy Singer, so I said, "That's all. Let's mount up. Colonel, you and I can meet with the ranking security officer on the plane."

Motivating a team like mine required little more than pointing toward a target. They never hesitated, and that day was no exception. We'd clearly been on the frozen ground of Ramstein Air Force Base long enough.

Back aboard the aircraft, the cargo area had been converted into a bivouac site: hanging hammocks, inflatable mattresses, four pallets of netted gear, and one additional pallet that had my undivided attention.

"What's under that tarp?"

Dre threw an arm over my shoulder. "Surely you've learned by now that SEALs never leave home without a boat." He untied the tarp and pulled it away, exposing a shiny new rigid hull inflatable boat with more than enough room for a full team of six and all the prisoners we could want. The pair of oversized engines looked powerful enough to push the RHIB far faster than I'd be willing to risk.

"I'm starting to think we may keep you, Master Chief."

"I'm not pretty, but I can swim, and I can fight."

Colonel Waters stood by the forward stairs leading to the passenger area with a tall, lean, uniformed man to his left. He pointed at the man and then up the stairs.

I gave him the thumbs-up. "Let's get upstairs and brief the security chief."

Dre said, "I'll grab the rest of the team."

"Gentlemen, this is Master Sergeant Titus Macmillan. He's the ranking security policeman on the team." The colonel pointed me out. "And this is Chase. He's the team commander. You'll report directly to him. His orders are my orders."

I shook his hand and slid onto the edge of a seat. "We don't spend a lot of time calling each other by rank, so do you mind if I call you Titus?"

"You're in charge, sir. Call me whatever you want. The colonel said you wanted to brief me on the mission."

"Actually," I said, "*we* want to brief you on the mission. It's a team concept with us. May I assume you have a TS security clearance and a signed non-disclosure agreement?"

"You may."

"Good. Here's what I plan to do when we hit the deck in Libreville. We're going to spend at least twenty-four hours doing nothing more than watching and listening. If we see and hear what I expect, we'll take prisoners—"

Titus held up a finger. "If I may, sir, I'd like to recommend we refer to them as *detainees*. The legal distinction becomes important when you start encouraging them to talk."

I shot Hunter a look and pointed back toward Titus. "I like this guy already."

Hunter gave me a wink.

"Thank you, Titus. I'll keep that in mind. When we deliver these *detainees*, you and your team will be responsible for making sure they don't change their mind about sticking around."

"I get it," he said. "We'll be sure to show them all the hospitality they deserve. I assume one of you will be handling the interrogations."

"Yes, that'll fall to us. That's all for now. I wanted to chat with you so we'd all be singing from the same sheet of music."

Master Sergeant Titus Macmillan said, "This isn't my first time in the choir, sir."

Chapter 35
Political Plausible Deniability

The flight was uneventful and gave us a little more time to let our bodies align with our new time zone. No matter how much I rested, or how many times I told myself it was going to work out, I couldn't get the thought of a C-5 Galaxy being on the ramp of a civilian airport in Africa and not attracting unwanted attention.

Whoever Colonel Waters placed at the controls of the massive airplane that afternoon clearly took a great deal of pride in his ability to put such a beast back on the ground with the finesse of a surgeon. We rolled out nearly the full length of the runway, but instead of turning onto a taxiway, the pilots spun the airplane around on the runway and back-taxied to midfield. Nothing about the maneuver made sense until we turned left instead of right. The right turn would've taken us to the commercial and airline ramp with passenger gates, baggage handlers, fuel trucks, and thousands of prying eyes, but the left turn took us someplace much more appropriate for our mission. When we came to a stop, we were well clear of the airport proper and tucked nicely into a forest of trees almost tall enough to hide the tail of the C-5.

We took the stairs four and five at a time, abandoning the comfort of the passenger cabin for the cargo area. The colonel's crew was already hard at work converting the belly of the beast from a traveling circus into a ground-based tactical operation center.

The colonel waded through the fiasco and pulled me aside. "Come find me after you've checked in with your people."

I gave him a wordless nod and called home. To my surprise, it was Ginger's voice in my ear.

"Ops Center."

"Good evening, Ginger. It's Chase. How are things back home?"

"For starters, it's not evening here. It's just after two p.m."

"It's evening here in the jungle. If I tracked the time zones correctly, it's around nine."

"The jungle? That must mean you're on-site."

"We are," I said, "Whatever you and Skipper did to score us this ride was a job well done."

"I'd love to take the credit, but that was a gift from a high-ranking friends of yours . . . one in particular."

"I thought that might be the case. Before we get into what's new, did you and Skipper get some rest?"

"We did. In fact, she's on a chow-run now. We each got about six solid hours, and we feel like new women."

"If you're telling the truth, I'm happy to hear it."

"No, seriously . . . We slept in shifts so someone would be at the helm all the time. We both needed the rest. Thank you for insisting."

"Can you give us the update, or should we wait for Skipper?"

She giggled. "We're pretty much interchangeable now. She's turned into the second-finest analyst I know, and she might even be tied for first."

"I don't know what we'd do without her," I said. "Since you're interchangeable, let's hear it."

She cleared her throat. "First, we've narrowed down the source of the calls a little tighter, and I have a theory. Every call originating from that source has happened near the edge of the water, except for one. It originated about half a mile offshore. I initially wrote it off as an anomaly, but with a fresh head after the rest you ordered, I believe at least the antenna is on a boat."

"Why do you say at least the antenna?"

"It's possible the whole station is on a boat—or a ship—but something about that doesn't smell right. It's just a hunch, but I think it's a base station on shore transmitting via a low-power network to an amplifier and transmitter on a boat of some kind."

She read off the coordinates, and I jotted them down.

"We'll put eyes on it tonight and get a better look in the morning. Santa brought us an early Christmas present. We just happen to have a boat of our own."

"I know. I've got a list of every piece of hardware on that airplane. I know more about your load-out than you do."

"Speaking of knowing more than me, do you have dossiers on the crew?"

She shuffled some files. "I do, and you have nothing to worry about. Everybody is as clean as a whistle. I've got . . . Well, actually, Skipper's got a theory on Tiffany Gallagher. She thinks she's still in Libreville and probably behind this whole ordeal."

"What makes her think that?"

"She can't sell me on it yet because it's still just a hunch, but she's convinced. I mean, some of it makes sense. She leaves the ambassador and hooks up with this Henri Dussault guy, who's some kind of money-funneling machine, plus one of the demands was to unseat the judge who screwed her over so badly in the divorce. The fact that she's so hard to track down now makes her even more spooky."

"Spooky? Is that some kind of analyst code for something sinister?"

She laughed. "Yeah, you could say that. I just mean she's hard to locate, almost impossible to track, and there's that whole woman-scorned thing."

"Yeah, I know that thing, but I'm afraid I'll have to see something a little more substantial than *spooky* before I'm ready to convict poor little Tiffany."

"I'll let you take that up with Skipper, but just don't rule her out . . . yet."

"Okay, I'll keep her in the maybe category. What else do you have?"

"Oh, I almost forgot, but you'll love this. Believe it or not, we've been able to keep the rescue of the hostages out of the headlines. I don't know how much longer we'll be able to do it, but for now, it's likely the team in Gabon doesn't know their little buddies in The Bahamas are now enjoying the hospitality of Gitmo."

"You're right. That's hard to believe, but the longer we can keep it that way, the better. We'll likely move on the target here tomorrow night after some good, solid recon, so if you can give us thirty-six more hours of the same, we may be able to piece this thing together and have some answers before all the mice get scared and scatter to the wind."

"We don't have a lot of control over what leaks, but we'll keep our fingers crossed."

"What about the other prisoners on the release demand list?"

"Francis Jerome Donaldson, the guy the president pardoned from Victorville, died this morning, so he's a non-factor now. The others are still locked up, but we're working a scheme with some media outlets to falsely report their release to buy a little more time for you."

"I like that plan. Keep at it. Is there anything else?"

"That's it for now," she said. "We're here if you need us."

"Thanks, Ginger. And tell Skipper I said thank you for getting some rest."

"I will. Bye, Chase. Be safe."

My team was huddled around but only heard my side of the briefing.

"Nothing major except for one detail," I said. "Ginger thinks the transmitter and antenna for the comms from here are on a boat of some kind. She sent the coordinates."

Hunter cocked his head. "Why would they put the transmitter on a boat instead of staying with it? That adds a layer of complexity to an already sketchy operation. I'm not buying it. I mean, the transmitter may be on a boat, but if it is, I'll wager the bad guys are on the boat with it."

"We'll know soon enough. Let's find a way to get Dre's RHIB into the water."

The SEAL threw up his hands. "It's not mine. It's ours. And I know exactly how to get it into the water."

"You guys get the boat ready to launch. I have to talk with Colonel Waters before we head out."

I found Waters upstairs with the other officers.

"Ah, there you are, Chase. We didn't get to make introductions before we took off, but I want you to meet—"

"I'm sorry, but we don't have time for this right now. We're hitting the ground, but you said you wanted to talk after I checked in."

He led me away from the group. "You understand the concept of compartmentalization and plausible deniability, right?"

I slapped a hand on his back. "Don't worry, Colonel. I promise not to screw up your shot at full-bird colonel, but I'm probably going to do some sketchy stuff in the next thirty-six hours. On top of all that, I'm not very good at politics, so I recommend you find something else to manage if you don't want any of this to drip onto your personnel file."

He huffed. "I don't want you getting ideas that you can run off and do whatever you want over here. We've all got someone to answer to, and I'm not going to let a bunch of cowboys—"

"Actually, Colonel, that's exactly what you're going to do, and if you're under the delusion that you're in charge, I'm sure you know the number to the White House switchboard. Feel free to give them a call and have the president explain how you don't fall anywhere on my team's chain of command. Have a good night. I've got some bad guys to catch."

Dre was right. As it turned out, his plan to launch the RHIB was flawless. When I found my team, they were connecting the boat's trailer to the hitch of a Toyota Land Cruiser inside the cargo bay.

"Where'd you find this?" I asked.

Disco looked up from the driver's seat. "You don't want to know. Just get in."

Ten minutes later, the RHIB was floating in the mouth of the Gabon Estuary on the edge of the Atlantic Ocean, and our SEAL was at the helm.

Chapter 36
Nautical Hide-and-Seek

Disco hid the Land Cruiser and trailer, I can only assume to prevent someone else from claiming the truck just like we'd done. With the vehicle secure, Disco slithered over the tube and aboard the RHIB as Dre fired up the engines.

He idled away from the shoreline and turned straight out to sea before bringing the boat up on plane. It ran beautifully and maneuvered like a sports car.

Once well offshore, Dre turned to the southeast into the estuary and tapped on the GPS. "This thing finally figured out we weren't in Kansas anymore. Plug in the coordinates you got from the analyst."

I pulled my note from my pocket and typed in the figures as we cut across the smooth surface of the ever-shallowing waterway. Soon, a magenta line appeared, indicating a direct route to our target, but direct routes are rarely our preferred course of travel.

Under night vision, we continued our trek farther into the African waterway. The lights of Libreville soon gave way to the absolute black of the jungle, just past Pointe Owendo, a small commercial port on a peninsula jutting into the estuary. Dre brought the boat off plane and cut the engines, allowing us to drift aground on the pebbled beach of an island in the perfect position to surveil the port.

With Mongo's help, Singer built his nest in an uprooted tree leaning against several more trees. From his perch fifteen feet above the beach, his Starlight scope gave him a perfect view of the port.

The sounds of the jungle reminded me of days spent watching *Tarzan* as a child, and I couldn't stop hearing Tarzan say, "Ung, bull Mangani," every time Mongo moved.

Singer made his first report from his lofty nest. "I've got four vessels. Two are disabled, and one is a hundred-year-old harbor tug. The remaining boat looks to be around a hundred-footer. I think she's a pumper, like the fire department boats in New York City."

"How about antennas?" I asked.

"I've never seen a boat without antennas, but this one seems to have more than her share. There's one above the bridge that looks a lot like the one we found on Rum Cay. I can take it out if you want."

"No, don't shoot it, but I'd like to get a closer look."

Singer said, "I've got movement on the deck."

"How many?"

"Three. Two men, and likely a woman. Two of them are having a smoke, and the other appears to be on a cell phone."

Telling Singer to keep watching would be like asking ice to melt in the sun. It was going to happen, and nothing could stop it.

I dialed the ops center, and Skipper answered. "Ops."

"It's Chase. I need you to listen for a call from Gabon. Someone's making a call from the deck of a suspect boat."

"I'm on it," she said.

Singer said, "He's off the phone, and smoke break seems to be over. They're heading back inside."

"The call ended, Skipper."

She grunted. "Nothing. There's an extremely short delay between call initiation and detection, but it's less than a second, so whoever he was calling, he wasn't using the line we're monitoring."

"Thanks for trying. We'll get 'em next time."

Singer said, "One of the smokers went back up to the bridge, and the second man and the woman are walking off the boat."

"Watch the walkers," I said.

"They're getting into an SUV of some kind, but I can't ID it."

I turned to Dre. "Put eyes on that boat, and give me your best guess how many crew are aboard right now."

He scampered up the leaning tree and lay beside Singer. Peering through the scope, he said, "Singer was definitely right. It's a fireboat, and I make out one body in the bridge, but a crew complement would be a guess."

"You're the SEAL. Your guesses carry a little more weight than most others when it comes to boats."

He lay silent for a while, staring through the scope. When he'd seen all he needed, down from the nest he came. "There will be at least one engineer on board, plus the guy in the wheelhouse standing anchor watch. That thing is big enough to have crew quarters, so there could be as many as ten or twelve, but there's at least two."

"That's not much help," I said.

"The big question I would want answered is this . . . Are the two who left in the SUV on a beer run, or are they gone for the night? The number of bodies on board isn't as important as the number of non-sleeping bodies."

Dre was right. We needed a lot more information, so I grabbed Dre's collar and called an audible. "Take Hunter, and get back to the plane. We need three DPVs, waterproof comms, and rebreathers."

Dre leapt aboard the RHIB, and Hunter shoved the boat from the sand. They were gone in an instant, and the remainder of the team took up positions and set in for a long night of surveillance. But I had no intention of spending my night warm, dry, and staring through binoculars.

It took Hunter and Dre just over an hour to make it back to our cozy little island. We moved everyone beneath Singer's position so he could hear the plan.

I said, "As much as I love this little island, I don't like the idea of being stranded on it. We're moving to the tree line on the mainland to the north. That'll shorten our swim without leaving the surveillance team stranded. Dre, Hunter, and I are going to board the boat and get a closer look. Any questions?"

With Singer's arm still less than 100 percent, Mongo helped him down from the nest. We idled across the open water between the island and mainland. Engine noise above an idle could catch the attention of the anchor watch on the bridge. The crossing took twenty minutes at that pace, but the man in the wheelhouse never looked our way.

We crept along the shoreline in five feet of water with only one engine putting along. When we came within three quarters of a mile of the boat, I motioned toward the beach, and Dre stuck the bow on the coarse sand. We stepped from the boat, and Mongo heaved it farther up the beach. A dilapidated concrete structure stood just inside the tree line, offering a field of fire across the open water as well as onto the boat. Singer made the structure his temporary home while the three of us donned full facemasks with comms, fins, and rebreathers.

Before I slipped into the water, I said, "Mongo, it's your mission. You call the shots. We'll check comms as soon as we're submerged."

He nodded, and we silently let our bodies slip into the water. I was pleased to feel the warm water envelop me, but even in the mid-eighties, the water was cold enough to kill us if we spent too much time without the protection of a wetsuit.

With our heads submerged, I spoke first. "Comm-check. Report."

Hunter said, "Two's up. Loud and clear."

The remainder of the team reported the same, and we reemerged to take a compass bearing on the boat. I gave Dre the hand signal to lead, and he sank into the black water like a leviathan of the deep. Hunter and I followed, keeping Dre's fins between us as the diver propulsion vehicles pulled us toward our target. We covered the fourteen hundred yards in twelve minutes and drifted to a stop.

Dre motioned for us to look upward, and we obeyed. To our delight, the hull and twin screws of the fireboat sat six feet above our heads.

"You SEALs are pretty good at this underwater navigation stuff."

Dre shrugged. "We all get lucky sometimes. Let's tie our DPVs to the bottom and have a look."

We followed Dre to the muddy bottom and tied our gear to a small rock outcropping. Knowing where our DPVs, masks, and fins would be when we left the boat was a handy bit of knowledge to possess.

While still on the bottom, I said, "We're staying together on the boat and away from the lights. That means we'll ingress over the stern and make our way forward along the starboard side. We'll penetrate the interior at the first opportunity. Remember, we're window shopping only. No gunfire, no sounds, and no prisoners on this run."

Hunter asked, "What are the rules of engagement if we get ambushed?"

"Don't get ambushed. Let's go."

We each took one long, final breath from our rebreathers and pulled off our masks. Dre led the way to the surface with one hand over his head to feel for the hull. We surfaced only inches behind the vessel and climbed across the stern in silence.

I was thankful to see there was no stern watch, and we slipped around the railing to the starboard side.

I spoke into the whisper-comms, "We're safe on board."

Mongo's voice filled my earpiece. "Roger. Sitrep unchanged."

"Roger," I whispered.

We moved forward along the starboard rail at a snail's pace until we reached a hatch. It was dogged shut, so Dre gripped the wheel and leaned against it. The first two inches of the turn sounded like a screaming child, so he stepped back from the hatch and shook his head. I motioned forward, and we continued our slow, steady movement toward the bow.

The second hatch we found was pinned open, likely to allow some air circulation inside the boat. The hatch lay approximately amidships, making Singer's guess of a one-hundred-foot boat accurate.

Inside the structure of the boat, a ladder leading upward lay to our right, while a second ladder leading down into the engine room lay on our left. I motioned to my eyes and then down the ladder before pointing toward Dre.

He knelt at the top of the ladder and rolled onto his back with each hand gripping the handrail. He eased himself downward, inch-by-inch, leading with his head. Being able to see into the engine room without being seen or heard was crucial. Hunter and I each grabbed one of Dre's ankles and took some of the stress from his wrists. When he could see into the space, he rolled his boot against my wrist, and we held him firmly in place.

He spent thirty seconds in the awkward position before tapping my wrist twice. We hauled him up slowly until he was back on the deck. He held up one finger and then simulated a pillow with two hands, laying his face against it. I silently thanked God for the sleeping engineer.

Four more short paces into the interior, a corridor opened up toward the stern, and we stepped into the opening. Four hatches were closed with no light protruding around any of them. I stepped in front of the first hatch and pressed my left ear to the metallic door. Only the sounds of the generator running in the engine room came through. We checked each of the four hatches with the same results. I turned the latch on the door to the last cabin on the port side. It rotated easily without a sound, and I pressed inward. The compartment held an empty bunk, a small desk, and a wall locker. We made our way forward, checking the three remaining compartments. Each revealed the same absence of sleeping crew. Things were finally going my way.

We returned to the forward ladder and climbed the treads with our soaked boots pinned to the extreme edges to avoid our weight causing the treads to creak. So far, the only sounds we'd made were the pings of the drops of water falling from our clothes and onto the metal deck.

The ladder deposited us on the upper deck with the hatch to the wheelhouse just ahead and left. The hatch was hanging open less than an inch, allowing the sounds of soft music to escape. The music made for excellent cover for our movement.

We stepped through the open hatch to the catwalk outside the wheelhouse, and I held up the okay signal for Singer. The single click of his tongue against his teeth through my earpiece gave me the comfort of knowing one press of Singer's trigger could solve most problems we could encounter in the coming minutes. However, that trigger-press would also set off an avalanche none of us wanted or needed.

The three of us crouched on the catwalk, and I raised my head into the corner of the aftmost wheelhouse window. My view was limited, but what I saw terrified me. The man inside on anchor-watch duty jumped to his feet and lifted a phone to his ear. He reached across a console and thumbed the volume knob of the radio, eliminating our covering noise. I couldn't hear him through the heavy glass, so I turned and signaled for Hunter to move back inside the passageway and listen to the conversation.

He crawled into position and activated his mic, broadcasting one side of the conversation across our net. My heart sank when I heard the man speaking French. I couldn't understand anything he said, but if Mongo was listening, his steel-trap mind wasn't missing a syllable.

The man slammed down the phone and drove his thumb into a switch on the console. This time, in native English, he said, "Bring the main engines online, and make ready for sea!"

With that order, Hunter backed from the corridor and looked up at me from the hatch, awaiting instructions. I paused long enough to hear the man's heightened tone.

"Ricco! Are you there?" He repeated the questions into the intercom twice more before swearing and running from the wheelhouse.

When I saw the man bolt for the door, I gestured for Hunter to move. With no time to spare, Hunter propelled himself forward and through the railing, catching the edge of the catwalk with his fingertips and leaving his body dangling from the grate.

I moved forward and raised my head far enough to see the man exit the wheelhouse. From my vantage point, I could see the hatch and Hunter's ever-whitening grip on the catwalk.

As soon as the man was clear of the corridor and bounding down the ladder, I lunged for my partner and grabbed his wrist. Dre moved into position and grabbed the other. We soon had Hunter back on the catwalk, but with the man roaming the boat, most likely on his way to wake the sleeping engineer, we were pinned on the highest and smallest deck of the vessel.

"We've got to move," I ordered. "Stay on the starboard side, and make your way down the exterior."

Hunter shook his hands, hoping to restore feeling and circulation to his fingertips.

Dre was the first over the rail, and he scampered down the exterior of the boat like a cat. Hunter was next, and I followed him across the railing. Neither of us moved with the speed and agility of the SEAL, but we found ourselves on a ledge, clinging to the boat as if our lives depended on it.

Singer's voice sounded in my ear. "There's a protrusion three or four feet aft and maybe four feet below. It's only large enough for one of you at a time, but it will get you back to the main deck."

Dre made the leap and bounded off the protrusion, landing on the balls of his feet almost silently below. Hunter leaped but missed the protrusion with his left foot, striking it with his right and sending him tumbling backward toward the water.

Back into the water was an option, but not the best one. Dre looked up to see Hunter falling backward, and he threw himself forward, reaching upward with both hands. The two collided, and Dre pressed him against the steel bulkhead, allowing him to slide to the deck at Dre's feet.

Hoping to emulate Dre's descent and not Hunter's, I stepped toward the protrusion and continued downward onto the deck below. My descent was far from silent, but I was unhurt and still on my feet.

I turned to my partner and stuck out a hand. "Are you hurt?"

He grabbed my offered hand. "Not bad. Let's move."

With the three of us upright, we moved for the aft deck. We reached the stern deck in seconds. In ten more feet, we'd be back in the water and descending toward our dive gear.

I replayed the commands the man issued from the bridge. *Bring the main engines online, and make ready for sea.*

With the command to stop only milliseconds away from escaping my lips, the aft deck of the boat turned into the surface of the sun. Every light they had seemed to be trying to burn a hole through the deck.

Dre froze, and Hunter pinned himself to the bulkhead. I knelt and crept forward, hoping to get a glimpse of what was happening on the stern deck. I tapped Hunter, and he tapped Dre. Both men looked down at me, and I motioned to move inside the vessel. We backtracked forward to the open hatch and bounded through. Dre hit the lever on the first compartment and forced the door inward. We followed him through the door and sealed it behind us.

Praying my comms would penetrate the steel hull of the fireboat, I said, "We're pinned inside. The anchor watch ordered engines online and make ready for sea."

Mongo answered, "I was afraid of that. He was speaking French when you patched him through your comms. I couldn't make out everything, but someone's returning to the boat outside of their plan. He was obviously frightened."

Singer said, "Do you have cover?"

"We do," I said. "We're inside an interior compartment. How many men do you see on deck?"

"Just two," he said. "The anchor watch is casting off lines, and someone came from the interior onto the stern deck to secure the lines."

"That's probably the engineer. Are the stacks making smoke?"

"Affirmative."

"It looks like we're going for a ride. Stay with us in the RHIB if you can. It's time for the three of us to play a little game I like to call nautical hide-and-seek."

Chapter 37
My Coffin

With the main engines running, the vibration inside the boat was enough to allow normal conversation without the risk of being heard outside the compartment.

"What's the plan?" Dre asked.

I said, "I'm still working on it, but we're definitely going to sea.

Mongo, get a call to Colonel Waters and let him know what's happening, then call Skipper. We may need some satellite coverage if she can get it."

"Roger."

I closed my eyes and worked through the likely scenarios. When I'd untangled the reality from the shock of being pinned down, I said, "It's likely they've been spooked by learning the hostages are free. It was only a matter of time before word leaked out, and then every news outlet in the world would report it."

Hunter said, "You're probably right, but what do you think these guys are going to do?"

"They're probably going to make another threatening call and then run."

"Run?" he asked. "Where are they going to run on a boat that might make fifteen knots at full steam?"

"I don't know. Dre, what do you know about the west coast of Africa?"

"I know there's a big island about two hundred miles west of here called São Tomé and Príncipe. It probably has an airport, but I don't know anything about it. If my memory is correct, I think Portugal owns the islands."

Mongo called. "It looks like we've got a crew coming on board. I see three men heading toward the boat, and the SUV from earlier just pulled up."

"Are the woman and man both in the SUV?" I asked.

"They were," he said. "Now they're jogging toward the boat. You've still got time to get off if you go now."

"As much as I'd like that, we can't abandon ship. This may be our only chance to catch these guys before they scatter in the wind."

"Roger. Colonel Waters is standing by, and Skipper is working on tasking a satellite. What else do you need?"

I asked Dre, "What's the endurance on the RHIB?"

He looked at the overhead for a few seconds. "I'd say six to eight hours at the speed this tub will run, but maybe two at full throttle."

I keyed up. "I need you to stay with us as long as you can. Dre thinks the RHIB has six hours of endurance matching our speed, but that's just an educated guess."

He said, "We'll follow you to Singapore, even if we have to throw a line and ski behind you."

Dre asked, "What's the range and battery life on these comms?"

"Line of sight and about four hours."

"I recommend we shut mine and Hunter's down, and keep yours hot. When yours dies, we can bring one of ours online."

"Good thinking," I said. "But I hope this thing is over long before we need fresh batteries."

Dre said, "We can end this thing anytime we want. Disabling this tug takes about ten seconds, and she'll be dead in the water. You give the word, and I'll make it happen."

"I'll keep that in my pocket for now, but it may come in handy before this is over. How many people can that lifeboat out back carry?"

Dre said, "I'm ashamed to admit I didn't get a good enough look, but it'd have to be big enough for a full crew. I'd say the full complement for this thing is ten or twelve."

"That means we've got a capable boat, even after we disable this one."

Dre nodded, and Hunter said, "If they're just going offshore to make another call and run, how are we supposed to know when they're doing either?"

I keyed up. "Mongo. Make sure Skipper is listening for a call from this boat. If one is made, we need to know, ASAP."

"Roger."

"There, we've solved that problem," I said. "All that remains is to wait and see what happens next."

The look on Dre's face told me he didn't like my plan.

I asked, "The rest of the guys know this, but everyone's opinion counts, so what's on your mind?"

He sighed. "I'm not good at waiting—especially clumped together. If *I* were calling the shots, we'd split up and hide separately. That way, if they find one of us, there's two more to fight. With us pinned down in here, if they find one of us, they've got us all."

I considered his recommendation. "I agree. Let's split up. I'll make my way toward the bridge so I can hear commands. Dre, you get to the engine room in case we need to shut this thing down. And Hunter, unless you've got a better idea, I want you to stay here."

Both men nodded.

"And I'm sure you know the rules have changed now. If we get discovered, we fight our way out. Understood?"

Again, both nodded.

I pressed an ear to the door and listened for footfalls. The noise of the engines made the task impossible, but I had to go through the motions just in case I got lucky.

Before we moved out, I called Mongo. "Is everyone on board?"

"Negative. Two are still on the dock. The guy I think is the engineer is on the aft deck with a hammer and torch."

"Is the bridge manned?" I asked.

"Not that I can see. Stand by."

Singer's voice came. "The bridge is still empty, Chase."

"Roger . . . Hunter, Dre, now's our chance. They've got some drama on the aft deck, so we should be able to get into position without being detected. Keep your comms on."

I pulled the door inward and peered in both directions. There was nobody in the corridor, so I stepped through and hustled to the forward ladder. I felt Dre come through the door behind me, but I never saw him in the darkness of the corridors.

Seeing the hatch of the bridge standing open, I slowly progressed in an arcing pattern through the opening as if I were cutting the pie to clear a room of combatants. The only difference was the absence of a weapon in my hands. With the bridge empty, I took in the space, memorizing as much of it as possible—especially the base station communication panel near the starboard side console. I'd been completely blind to the console when I was on the outside catwalk, looking in, prior to our hurried escape attempt.

I found a wall locker near the back of the wheelhouse and crammed my two hundred thirty pounds inside. Nothing about the space was comfortable, but it gave me the perfect vantage point from which to hear everything being said on the navigation bridge.

Once in position, I keyed my mic. "Dre, are you in position?"

His reply came amidst a howl of mechanical noises, but I picked out his voice from deep within the sounds. "Affirmative."

As the psychology of being enclosed in a box shorter than my own height set in, it became a constant struggle to remain calm when everything inside me wanted to burst through the door and put an end to the whole madness.

That wasn't my first time in such a predicament. When I endured the equivalent of the Army's SERE school at The Ranch during my training, I was taught how to survive, evade, resist, and escape. The portion of the course that left the most indelible stain on my psyche was the ability to endure pain and discomfort for hour upon torturous hour. Keeping my mind and body quiet while uncomfortable and frozen in place was the only option I had for the foreseeable future.

Mongo spoke through my earpiece. "They're casting off the final lines, and we're moving to the RHIB."

It was my turn to click in response, and the sound of my tongue falling against my teeth sounded like thunder inside my vertical coffin.

Footfalls entering the bridge sounded over the hum of the engines, and soon, the feeling of motion told me we'd maneuvered free of the dock and were moving into deeper water. I focused on the direction of the turns, trying to piece together an overlay of the boat's motion, but from within the confines of the locker, the task was an exercise in confusion and frustration.

The absence of voices in the wheelhouse left me believing there was only one other person in the room with me. If it became necessary to overpower one person to take command of the vessel, I had no doubt that I was capable. Knowing the boat could be under my command in seconds left my mind questioning why I would continue to imprison my body inside the locker.

Time passed at an immeasurable rate. Rustling inside the locker to hopefully see my watch was unthinkable, so I was left with no concept of time, direction, or speed, leaving me to be little more than a captive to a world of confusion.

An increase in both engine noise and oscillation of the boat made me believe we'd left the protection of the estuary and entered the Gulf of Guinea and the South Atlantic. A one-hundred-foot vessel is formidable in enclosed waters, but upon the open ocean, she's but a speck on an endless expanse of unforgiving water.

It may have been thirty minutes, or perhaps three hours—I was incapable of discerning between the two inside my tomb. But I was thankful beyond imagination to hear Mongo's voice.

"We're thirty miles offshore in six-to-eight-foot swells. This is well beyond the limits of the RHIB, and the sun will be up in less than an hour."

Unable to reply, I willed Hunter or Dre to respond, until finally, the mechanical roar of the engine room filled my earpiece, and Dre's voice cut through the thunder. "I can stop us in under a minute."

Mongo gave the command. "Do it!"

Once the engine's roar fell to a deafening silence, our game of hide-and-seek would be over, and the fight would be on. I waited an eternity for the vibration to stop and the forward motion of the vessel to give way to helpless bobbing on the swells. When it came, I heard the voice of the man at the helm for the first time since I'd folded myself into the locker.

"What's happening down there?"

He pounded on the console and yelled even louder into the intercom. "What's going on? What happened to the engines?"

A gruff voice blasted through the speaker. "We're under attack! There's a man . . ."

I waited and listened as the man drove what must've been his fists into the console, cursed, and yelled into the intercom. "Abandon ship! Abandon ship!"

The instant I heard his foot hit the deck beyond my locker, I sprang from my entrapment and lunged toward him. My feet and legs protested from their time spent immobile, but I labored on, stumbling toward the fleeing man who had no idea I was behind him. When his foot left the deck to descend the ladder, I wanted to lace an arm beneath his chin and drag him back into the wheelhouse on his way to unconsciousness, but the leap was beyond my power with my knees and ankles crying out with every stride. As a last resort, I planted a numb foot on the deck and exploded forward with my other boot high in the air. My momentum carried me into the man's back with my boot landing firmly between his shoulder blades. Maintaining his hold on the railing was an impossibility as he collapsed forward, striking his forehead on the overhead and sending blood in every direction. He was falling, but so was I. I would either collide with the overhead and suffer a similar fate as my victim, or I would curl my body into a ball and careen down the free space. I chose option number two, and I came to rest on top of the helmsman—perhaps the captain—in a crushing collision of bone, muscle, and flesh at the foot of the ladder. The sound of the man's spine cracking beneath my weight sent shudders through my head, but there was nothing to be done. The life had been taken, and there was one less man left in the fight.

Chapter 38
How It Ends

I stood on trembling knees as the feeling slowly returned. The corpse of the man I'd killed lay in a helpless heap at my feet. I pulled his body from its place and wedged him behind the ladder.

As I stumbled toward the corridor, Hunter burst from the small compartment in which he'd been waiting and raised his pistol into my face. I took a staggering stride backward and threw my hands into the air, relying on Hunter's instinct to not shoot a surrendering man.

Recognition flamed in his eyes as he lowered the weapon. "Are you hurt?"

I shook him off. "No, I'm okay, but we've got to get to the aft deck. They're abandoning ship."

The adrenaline that carried me the first few strides down the darkened corridor behind my partner failed the instant we reached the hatch, and I collapsed to the deck.

Feeling me fall against him, Hunter spun and knelt beside me. "What happened? Are you all right?"

He yanked a waterproof light from his pocket and shone the beam down on my right foot that was pointing in a direction no one's foot should ever point.

"Oh, boy. This is bad," he hissed as he reached for my foot.

I remember hoping he'd turn it the right direction, fearing it would separate from my leg if he turned it the wrong way. Logic is often the first psychological sense to fail when extreme trauma unleashes unimaginable pain on the human body. I'd, no doubt, broken the ankle in my eight-foot fall on the man at the base of the ladder, but the pain was yet to come.

Hunter dug into the pockets of his cargo pants and pulled out a roll of duct tape. He wrapped the foot that clearly belonged to someone else in increasingly tighter layers and around the lower leg that belonged to me. With his supply of tape exhausted, he yanked my tourniquet from my belt and laced it around my leg, just below the knee.

With the foot secured and the bleeding under control, my partner took my face in his hands. "Listen to me, Chase. Pull your pistol and kill anybody who approaches you, unless you hear your name. Got it?"

I stared down at my foot, worthless and dying at the end of my leg.

He shook me. "Chase! Draw your sidearm! Do it now!"

In slow motion, I followed his command and drew my Glock from behind my right hipbone. When I looked back up at him, he slapped me twice, harder than I'd ever been slapped.

"Do not pass out! You got me? Do not go to sleep! If anybody shows up without yelling your name, you pull that trigger until it clicks. Do you understand?" I nodded, and he wedged me against the hatch. "I'll be back for you. Wait right here. I'll be back!"

With one final shake, he stood and moved out of the corridor. The pain wasn't coming yet, but the confusion and shock were slowly creeping into my mind like an inescapable rising shadow. I threw my hand against the bulkhead, hoping to feel the pain, and thankfully, it came. My hand throbbed as I returned it to my pistol. Something made sense, and I could build on that. If I could feel my hand, I could keep myself conscious and in the fight.

Voices filled my ear—the voices of my partner and Mongo.

"They're in the lifeboat and heading north. Don't let them get away!"

"We're on them! As soon as I can get Singer close enough, he'll stop them with his rifle, and we'll come back for you."

The sounds of waves crashing into the hull of the ship offered to sing me to sleep, but I resisted, biting the inside of my jaw until my mouth filled with my own blood. Anything to stay awake . . . Sleep wasn't an option.

Suddenly, the sounds of the waves slapping at the ship parted and gave way to the sounds of bodies colliding and striking the deck. I heard Hunter's groans and blow after blow of fists on flesh pouring through the open corridor. Unfamiliar voices and pain-filled cries came from the aft deck. At least three voices . . . Maybe four.

Fearing my partner was in the fight of his life, I forced my body forward and onto my one remaining foot. Hauling myself upward by the rail, I stood with stars circling my head. I had to get to Hunter. I had to get back in the fight. The tourniquet ached, but I pushed back the pain and cranked the windlass arm another turn before tucking it beneath its plastic keeper. I might lose the foot, but I would not lose Hunter. I had to get to him, no matter the cost.

Light filtered through the intersecting corridor, and I hopped in short leaps toward the light. The sounds of blow after blow continued from outside, and the world moved in slow motion as I forced myself ever forward, pistol in hand, and hopping, jumping, lunging until light from the aft deck flooded my eyes.

I threw myself to the deck and squinted against the light as I raised my Glock. Bodies rolled and fell, only to climb back onto wavering legs and to be sent crashing, again and again, back to the deck. Three bodies—maybe four—waged war against each other before my eyes, but the blinding light left me incapable of discerning Hunter from his attackers. I aimed time after time, only to be tossed back and forth in the hatch opening.

I filled my lungs with air and yelled, "Hunter! Get down!"

One man dived to the deck, and I had to believe it was my partner. I double-tapped each man, pulling the trigger a total of six times, each explosion sending another projectile through the waiting flesh of Hunter's tormentors until no more bodies stood and the echoing report of my weapon was silent.

I heard my brother say, "Good shootin', partner." He pulled himself to me, and I lowered my pistol. He threw a hand behind my head and looked into my eyes. "How're you doing?"

I tried to smile. "I'm not getting the crap kicked out of me by three deckhands."

He almost laughed. "Yeah, thanks to you, neither am I . . . now."

We lay on the deck, me barely conscious from blood loss and shock, and Hunter beaten and battered beyond what any mortal human could withstand.

"Where's our SEAL?" he breathed.

"Engine room, maybe."

"Where's your radio?"

"I don't know."

He patted my face twice and pulled himself to his feet. Stepping over me, he forced himself down the corridor and around the corner to the engine room ladder. "Dre! Dre! Are you down there?"

I heard a voice as if a thousand miles away, but I couldn't make out what it was saying, so I holstered my pistol and dragged myself toward the ladder. As I grew closer, I saw Hunter sitting on the top step, his face bloody and torn. "Master Chief! Are you down there?"

The weak voice rang out again. "Is that you, Hunter?"

"Yeah, Dre, it's me. Are you hurt?"

"You might say that. I took a shotgun blast to the thigh. Pretty sure my femur's gone, but I shoved the shotgun up the engineer's ass and settled the score. From the looks of things down here, I think I won on a split decision."

Hunter spat, sending blood flying from his lips. "I think everybody's dead. Chase lost a foot, and if I had my druthers, I'd probably trade with him. Ribs, jaw, maybe a wrist or two . . . That's all I broke, but I'm alive."

At that moment, a sharp sound like a hundred firecrackers cooking off simultaneously rang through the air.

Hunter tried to yell. "What was that?"

Dre's voice echoed up the ladder. "That was a blasting cap without any C-Four. Get off the boat! Get Chase off the boat!"

"I'm coming down to get you," Hunter yelled, but Dre screamed, "Get off the boat! It's rigged to blow! Get off, now!"

I reached up for the rail and dragged myself upright as Hunter threw an arm around my back. I hopped as he tugged me through the hatch and onto the aft deck.

When we reached the rail, he spun me around and laid a bloody hand against my chest. "Get in the water, Chase. I'm going back for Dre."

I watched him plant a foot before shoving me backward over the rail, so I wrapped both arms around his wrist and forearm and lifted my one remaining foot. His energy and my weight sent both of us cascading over the rail and into the water.

When we resurfaced, both spitting and clawing for breath, I said, "Swim me far enough away, and I'll let you go back."

He rolled me onto my back and dragged me through the water with adrenaline-charged strokes, and I kicked and stroked, trying to add distance and speed to our escape. A hundred yards from the vessel, I tugged at his belt, and he stopped stroking. We drifted to a stop, and he turned to see the progress we'd made.

"Can you stay afloat?" he asked through heaving breaths.

Knowing I would fall victim to shock or the sharks before he could return, I wrapped him in my arms and whispered, "Yeah, I can stay on the surface. Go get our SEAL."

Our eyes met as I pushed away, and I saw the horrible decision racing behind his eyes. His bruised and broken face, the blood now washed away, peered back and forth between me and the doomed ship with our teammate still in its bowels.

I looked away and shoved my partner as hard as I could. The force sent my body beneath the swells for an instant, and when I resurfaced, the boat erupted in black and orange billows of fire and smoke, and the air filled with flying debris.

I watched Hunter inhale an enormous breath, and I did the same. He kicked with a mighty stroke and landed both hands on top of my head, driving me under. I reached for his belt and dug both hands around the webbing as we exhaled together, determined to keep our bodies beneath the surface as long as possible. We'd survived the blast, but the flying debris would be ten thousand missiles filling the sky.

My lungs burned and yearned to fill with cool, clean air, but the surface above us echoed with falling pieces of every part of the boat until we'd held ourselves under as long as either of us could do. We looked skyward, and our bodies followed until our lungs were rewarded with smoke and cinder. We gagged and coughed as we stared into the sinking remains of the boat a hundred yards distant. The surface was littered with objects floating, some still burning, all twisted beyond recognition.

We clung to floating debris and rode the swells as they rose and fell, our eyes cast to the north, where our only hope for survival raced away in maddening pursuit of a lifeboat holding three of the world's most ruthless terrorists.

Unable to tear our eyes from the northern horizon, Hunter said, "They either saw the explosion and they'll come back, or this is how it ends."

Chapter 39
Don't Drink the Water

Being injured is bearable. Being cold is bearable. Being wet is bear-able. And being deserted is bearable. But combining two, three, or all four of those conditions complicates the situation exponen-tially. Our injuries limited our abilities to exert physical effort to aid in our own rescue. Although the eighty-five-degree water felt warm for the first hour of submersion, in time, the water would deplete our bodies' abilities to keep themselves warm enough to survive. The constant state of being wet made it impossible to stay warm. The thirst associated with the physical and psychological stress of being submerged, injured, and cold was miserable enough on its own, but coupled with the abundance of salt water that would be lethal if we'd allowed ourselves to drink it, was a con-stant reminder of how dire and deadly our situation had become. The reality of our desertion compounded the severity of one of the worst situations in which we could've found ourselves.

Having spent more time in the water than anyone on our team, Hunter was, by far, the subject-matter expert on water survival. "Remember the rule of twos," he said. "You can survive for two minutes without air, two days without water, and two weeks with-out food. Even injured, we're in better shape than the average fisherman who falls overboard. That means we're up in the threes, at least."

"Is that supposed to make me feel better?" I asked as I continued harvesting anything that would float.

"Take off your belt," he said.

"My belt? Why?"

"Because I'm going to tie us together. Sooner or later, one or both of us is going to fall asleep, and drifting apart is the last thing we need."

I unbuckled and removed my belt. Hunter fashioned a tether from the two belts and lashed us together. Aside from the practical element of the small task, there was something reassuring and hopeful about the effort.

In the early days of my career, Clark Johnson taught me more about staying alive than anyone else in my life. I'd been pinned down by gunfire and outnumbered beyond my ability to count, but Clark taught me how to fight my way out. I'd been dunked in the Moscow River within sight of the Kremlin and would've frozen to death had Clark not kept me alive. Clark held a place in my heart no one would ever replace, but there was something unspoken, something wordlessly devotional about Hunter tying us together. We may not survive the coming hours or days, but neither of us would die alone.

"Chase! Chase! Look at me!"

I opened my eyes to see terror in Hunter's face. "Where did you go, man? You've got to keep your eyes open. Stay with me."

"Sorry. I was just . . ."

"It doesn't matter," he said. "We'll both get delusional before this is over, but we have to focus in the early hours to get as much done as possible while we still have calories to burn and the wits to make good decisions."

"Yeah, I get it. What now?"

"Pull off your shirt, and cut it into strips about an inch or two wide. We're making rope. Tie the ends together, and make it as long as possible."

I didn't understand why we were making rope, but I followed his instructions, and soon, we had three dozen feet or more of cotton rope.

"Now, we're building a raft. Gather everything you can as close as you can, and we're going to tie it together. We have to get our bodies out of the water as much as possible."

We spent the next hour fabricating our floating home for what might be the rest of our lives. Our life raft made of trash and torn cotton shirts was incapable of keeping us dry, but it got us out of the water. The swells that had felt like six-to-eight-footers from the security of the fireboat now felt like tsunamis and threatened to knock us from our raft every few seconds.

"Should we tie ourselves to the raft?"

He shook his head. "No. If it capsizes, we'd be trapped underneath it. If the waves don't subside, our homemade island isn't going to stay together long enough to get us anywhere. But if we get lucky, with this wind, we may come within sight of land in twenty-four hours."

"They'll come back for us," I said.

"Yeah, but coming back for us and finding us are two different animals. We have to assume we're on our own, even if they're searching for us."

As we perched on our lifeboat, no bigger than a door, he said, "I need to look at your foot."

I'd all but forgotten my foot was little more than ground beef. "Okay, go ahead." I pulled my leg around my body and positioned it so he could inspect what was left of it.

He sighed deeply. "I'm going to move the tourniquet down, and it's going to hurt."

"Why are you moving it?"

"Our situation has changed. When I put it on the first time, I thought we'd be in the hands of a good surgeon in a few hours. He could've saved the foot, but now we have to focus on saving as much of the leg as possible. I'm moving the tourniquet down as far as I can. We have to keep the bleeding at bay, but I don't want to risk losing the whole leg below the knee. Just hold on, and yell if you have to. It's going to hurt like Hell itself when I cut it loose."

Stone Hunter had never been more correct in his life. When the tourniquet came off, the edges of my vision closed in until I was looking for light through a drinking straw. A branding iron would've hurt less, but it had to be done. The animalistic bellow that came from my throat was like no sound I'd ever made before that instant, and I prayed I'd never make it again.

Hunter resituated the strap barely above my wound and cranked the windlass until the blood stopped oozing from what would become my stump.

Losing my foot was way down the list of priorities, but somehow, that's all my brain would think about. Sharks, hypothermia, dehydration, starvation, and hysteria all fell above losing the foot, but my brain didn't care. It had chosen its focal point and refused to stray.

Would Penny leave me for an actor or a producer with an even number of feet? Would I still be able to fly? What if my house catches on fire again? Would I be able to run to safety? Is this how Anya felt when I shot off her toe in Saint Thomas? Would Clark stop calling me College Boy and come up with some moniker related to my odd number of feet? Would I—

"Chase!"

I shook off my stupor.

"You did it again. Are you okay?"

His question struck me as funny in the moment. I'd never been less okay, but Hunter's perspective of what qualified as "okay" left me feeling reassured. "Sorry. I let myself drift inside my head . . . again."

The west wind howled, and the swells continued to build, and for a moment, I forgot about my foot and tried to remember the three factors in wave height.

Are wind speed and direction two separate things or just one thing? If they are two, then there would be four elements involved, but what are the other two? Duration—how long the wind had been blowing. That has to be one of them. So, that's three . . . But I know there's another.

"It's *fetch*, Hop Along College Boy. You know *fetch* . . . the distance over water the wind travels."

The voice was Clark's, but he wasn't here. It had to be Hunter.

"What?" I asked.

Hunter said, "What do you mean, what? I don't know what you're talking about."

"Fetch."

"Fetch?" He grabbed my neck with one hand. "Chase, I need you to stay with me, buddy. This thing's going to get a lot worse before it gets better, and you're losing it. I need you to stay with me. What's your favorite song?"

Is he right? Am I losing it? Is he even real?

Hunter scooped water with his cupped hands and threw it into my face. "Song, Chase! What's your favorite song? We're going to sing a song together."

"I don't know. 'Jesus Loves Me' is a pretty good song."

"Yes, yes, it is, but I don't think I know all the words. Teach it to me. Teach me the song, Chase."

Two minutes—or perhaps two days—into singing lessons, the world around me came into stark focus. My leg felt like it was on fire, and my stomach growled. "I lost a lot of blood, Hunter. I'm not sure what we've been doing. It's a little blurry, but I feel okay right now."

"Yeah, you did lose a lot of blood, buddy, but you're not going to lose any more."

"How long?" I asked.

"We're not counting the hours. That will drive us both out of our minds, and I'm afraid one of us is almost there already. We'll count sunrises and sunsets. That's our clock until we get rescued."

I stared into the perfect blue sky. "Have you ever thought about quitting?"

"Quitting what?"

"This."

"Oh, yeah. I'm ready to quit this shipwrecked gig right now."

I let my upper body lean against his. "I don't have much left, man. I'm—"

He said, "This isn't the part where you tell me it's okay for me to eat you if you die first, is it? 'Cause trust me, if you die, I don't need your permission."

It was funny, and I thought I was laughing, but it came out as hacks and gagging coughs.

Hunter lifted my chin. "Did you drink the water?"

"What water?"

"Any water."

The world that had been clear and bright turned gray and soft. "No, I don't think so."

"That's good. Don't drink it."

Time passed in shadows moving eastward. One moment I would stare into the sun and see a black abyss, and other moments, I saw a thousand suns burning from every direction. I felt my soul pressing against my flesh in desperate attempts to abandon what remained of my body, and at precisely the right moments, when I was ready to surrender my immortal soul to the heavens and waters and wind, Hunter would shake me from my surrender.

"I'm hungry," I moaned.

He looked at me in utter confusion. "You can't be hungry. We just ate. I had the cheeseburger, and you had the grouper basket."

"Okay."

Darkness fell on me. Perhaps it fell on both of us, but I couldn't be sure. I remember feeling Hunter shiver as we sat back to back on the raft. It was cold. I was cold, and Hunter was cold, and the sun had abandoned us.

Everything was real, and everything was a hallucination.

"Lights," I whispered.

"Those are stars," he said.

"So, they're real?"

Through chattering teeth, he said, "They're real. Some people believe they burned out a billion years ago and that what we see is the light from a star that no longer exists."

"That's silly, but they're pretty no matter how old they are."

He turned his head to the sky. "They sure are."

"Not those lights," I said. "I know those are stars. I meant those lights."

He spun to follow my outstretched finger. "Where?"

"There, down low. Wait for the water to fall."

He rearranged our belts still holding us together and stumbled to his feet, his knees bent as they absorbed the motion of the water. I remember thinking he looked like Bambi, the baby deer, trying to stand on the ice. He fell twice and stood again, holding my shoulder for support. Perhaps the support was for him, but I'll always believe he did it so I'd know he was still there.

"See them?" I asked in a hoarse, croaking tone.

"Not yet. Are you sure you saw them in that direction?"

"I'm sure," I said. "Stars don't move."

He balanced and stumbled, raised his head as high as he could, and collapsed beside me. His breath came in raspy, jerking hiccups. "You must've been right."

"Right about what?"

"Right about Jesus loving you. Those *are* lights, you one-footed, crazy-headed, double naught spy."

"I'm not a spy. Is it Mongo?"

"There's no way to know, but who else would be out here shining a light around like he's looking for his lost keys in the tall grass?"

"Grass would be nice," I said.

I don't think he was talking to me when he said, "I'd give a million dollars for a flare gun," but I answered anyway.

"I've got a Glock."

"A Glock?" he almost yelled. "You've still got your pistol?"

"Yeah, it's in my pocket. I had to put it somewhere when you made me give you my belt."

He grabbed my face with both hands and planted a dehydrated, sunburnt kiss right in the middle of my forehead. I fumbled with the button on my cargo pants pocket until Hunter lost the patience to watch me continue to lose the battle with a little plastic button. He grabbed the flap of my pocket and ripped it from my pants, thrusting his hand into the now permanently open pocket. He leapt back to his feet and fired off the nine remaining rounds in the magazine.

I'll never know if it was the thunder of the pistol's report or the orange flame belching from the muzzle that caught the attention of the crew of the boat, but I'll never care.

Chapter 40
Anything Resembling a Saw

"Where's Hunter?"

Those may not have been the first words I spoke when I opened my eyes to see the Air Force pararescueman starting what turned out to be my second IV of the night.

"He's right over there, sir."

I squinted against the thundering headache. "Right over where?"

"I'm right here, Chase. We're back aboard the airplane, and we're safe."

"What about Clark?"

"What about him?" Hunter asked. "He's in the ops center at Bonaventure with Skipper and Ginger."

"Are you sure?"

"Yeah, I'm sure. We talked to him five minutes ago."

I blinked, hoping to clear the spiderwebs from my head. "Are you sure he wasn't in the water with us?"

Hunter materialized beside the makeshift gurney I was lying on. "I'm sure. Clark is just fine."

Hunter blocked the glaring light, and soon his battered features came into focus.

"You don't look so good."

He waved me off. "You ought to see the other guys." I reached up, and he grabbed my hand. "We made it, buddy."

My head swam, and I suddenly felt warm for the first time. "Mongo?"

The giant stepped into the light, casting an enormous shadow across my body. "I'm here. We're all here."

I fought off the fog as my head continued to drift. "I feel . . ."

The pararescueman said, "That's the morphine. Just relax and let it do its job."

"I can't. I need to . . ." As the haze deepened, I reached for Mongo. "Did you catch them?"

I lost my battle with the narcotics before I could register Mongo's answer, but I only slept for a few seconds.

When I woke again, I'd been moved, and my foot felt like it was being crushed beneath a steamroller. I was sitting up, mostly, but the morphine continued casting its shadowy spell over me. The headache was gone, but the pain in my foot was excruciating. I tried adjusting my position, but an unfamiliar voice and a foreign hand stopped me. "Hey. Easy there, sir. How are you feeling?"

I looked up into his face. "Who are you?"

"I'm the PJ—the pararescueman on your mission, sir."

"Stop calling me sir, and can you do something about the pain in my foot?"

He swallowed hard, stuck a stethoscope into his ears, and moved the bell down my leg.

"What are you doing? My heart is up here."

He covered his lips with one finger and focused intently on what he was hearing . . . or perhaps not hearing.

He pulled the scope from his ears and draped it around his neck. "I was listening for a pulse in your leg. We had no choice. The foot had to be amputated."

It sounded as if he were talking to someone else—some poor guy with only half the number of feet he was born with. Thankfully, my foot was still attached; otherwise, it wouldn't feel like someone was stabbing it with a red-hot fireplace poker.

He kept talking, and I felt sorry for his patient. "The pain you feel is called phantom pain, sir. Your brain doesn't understand why it's not receiving sensory input from the amputated foot, so it's taking a guess at how it should feel."

My God! He's talking to me!

I leaned forward and stared down where my right foot should've been. Instead of a bandaged, badly injured foot, there was . . . nothing. At that moment, my brain did something even more difficult to explain. It screamed, *Now I'll never be able to catch for the Braves.*

I prayed the words hadn't actually left my mouth, and I grabbed the PJ's arm. "Did *you* cut it off?"

He pulled away. "No, sir. The doctor from the embassy amputated the foot last night. We insisted on bringing you back to the airplane so we could get you back to the States as soon as possible."

"Where's Mongo?" I demanded.

"I assume Mongo is the big one, right?"

"Yeah."

"I'll get him, sir. Just try to relax. If necessary, I can give you some more pain meds, but you're probably going to want to be awake."

"Just get Mongo."

He returned seconds later, and Mongo took a knee beside my reclining seat.

I grabbed a handful of his shirt and pulled. "Tell me you caught them!"

"We caught them. Do you want to hear the story?"

"Other than getting my foot back, there's nothing I want more."

He ignored the foot comment. "You should've seen Singer. It was some of the best shooting I've ever seen. We had the speed to catch them, but just barely. They ran north for ten miles and then turned west. I still think they were headed for that big island. We were running twenty knots or so with Disco at the wheel. I was spotting because I was the tallest thing on the boat."

"You're the tallest thing on every boat."

"It wasn't much advantage at the time, but we kept them in sight. Singer spent three hours lying on the starboard tube at the bow. He had his right leg and right arm wrapped in the lines so tight it looked like a tourniquet. I don't think he ever took his eye out of that scope, even when the waves crashed over the bow every few seconds."

"Did he make the shot?" I asked, my impatience growing by the second.

"I'm getting there. Keep your pants on. A little more than three hours into the chase, he yelled at me to have Disco speed up. I relayed the command, and he kept calling out speed changes for ten minutes or more. I didn't know what he was doing at first, but when we got in sync with the swells and the boat they were running in, everything became perfectly clear. We topped the swells at the same instant the other boat did. We stayed in that cycle for maybe a minute, and Singer pulled the trigger. One shot—that's all it took. One shot, and they were dead in the water. He said he was gunning for the engine, but he hit the transmission instead. They tried to fight us off with a couple of flare guns, but that didn't go so well. We boarded anyway and rolled 'em up."

"I hate I missed the excitement. Where are they now?"

"That's the best part," he said. "The Air Police have them pinned up like goats downstairs."

"I've got one more question."

"Let's hear it."

"Is my right foot really gone?"

Instinctually, he looked down and nodded. "It's gone. But you're alive, and now that you're awake, we can head back to the States."

"What about the SEAL?"

Mongo hung his head. "The news isn't so good for him, I'm afraid."

I squeezed my eyes closed as I added Master Chief DeAndre Lewis to the catalog I'd never lay down, the scroll bearing the names of the men I'd failed, the men who gave their lives under my command.

Mongo said, "It looks like he's going to lose his whole leg."

"What?"

"Yeah, it's a shame. His door-kicking days are probably over. We put him on an L-One-hundred flight this morning for Cairo."

"You mean he's alive?"

Mongo furrowed his brow. "Yeah, he's alive. In fact, he's the reason we found you. Unlike a couple grunts I know, he apparently had the presence of mind to keep his radio and a lifejacket with him when he dragged himself up the stairs from the engine room and bailed overboard. He got burnt up a little from the explosion, but not too bad. He was a lot closer to the boat than you when it cooked off. It was the shotgun blast to the leg that took him out of the fight, but not before he put the engineer down with his own gun. The PJ says they'll probably take the whole leg, so compared to him . . ."

He didn't finish the sentence, but he was right. My injuries could've been much worse. I don't think I'll ever consider myself lucky, but I know I'll never kick a guy down a ladder after being cramped up in a wooden box for two hours again.

"Who are they?"

Mongo smiled. "I thought you'd never ask. We've got Henri Dussault, a woman who refuses to identify herself, and for the cherry on top, we've got former Ambassador John Woodford."

I smiled. "You don't say."

"Since you left me in charge while you were out playing in the water, I decided to let them sit on ice until you could sit in on the interrogation. I've even got a tactical baptismal setup down there that would make Clark proud."

"This team could do a lot worse than having you in charge. You know that?"

He shook his head. "Perish the thought. You're the boss, and that's the way it's going to stay. Now, come on. Let's get you downstairs and have a little fun."

I looked up at the PJ. "Do you have anything that looks like a crutch?"

"I just happen to have a pair of things that look exactly like crutches, but that leg is going to scream at you when you stand up."

I accepted the pair of aluminum crutches he offered. "As long as it's the leg and not the phantom foot, I think I can take it."

The PJ knew what he was talking about. My stump didn't like being the lowest point on my body, and the pain made me want another dose of the PJ's morphine.

"Are you all right, sir?"

"I'm fine. Just give me a minute to catch my breath."

He said, "Me and the big guy can carry you down the steps if you want."

"There's an unnecessary element in that equation, PJ. Mongo doesn't need your help."

The last time I'd been taken for a piggyback ride, I must've been a preschooler. I can't say it was fun, but the laugh it got from the rest of the crew in the cargo area of the C-5 was worth the embarrassment.

Mongo put me down, and I thwarted attempts at sympathy by saying, "Let's see them."

Titus, the senior security police officer, said, "Follow me," and we waded through the gear and personal items scattered about the deck. When we came to a black curtain strung up on a wireframe, he jerked back a panel, bathing the interior of the space with fluorescent light. The three detainees inside the shroud squinted against the glaring assault, and I stepped inside their temporary darkened quarters.

I stared down at the three most recent international terrorists sitting on the metal deck of the airplane. They looked like frightened children with their wrists and ankles bound and gags in their mouths. I peered into their souls through the horror in their eyes. When I came to the woman, I narrowed my gaze and lifted one crutch from the floor. I placed the rubber foot of the crutch in the center of the woman's forehead and pressed hard enough for her to realize I was serious. "Have you ever seen anyone undergo waterboarding?"

She glared up at me. "You can't torture us. We have rights."

I shoved my crutch, leaving her sprawling on her back like an overturned turtle, and I turned to face Titus. "Tell the pilots to get us in the air. And I need a few things . . ."

"Name it, sir."

"I need plenty of towels, anything that'll soak up blood, and some rope."

"Is there anything else?"

I gave the trio one more look. "Yeah, bring me anything you've got resembling a saw. The bigger, the better."

"Yes, sir," he said, and turned away.

When he was well out of earshot, I leaned toward the detainees and hissed, "Please resist. I've got a lot of scores to settle."

I hobbled my way back outside the shroud and found Hunter. "Are you up for this? It's going to get messy."

"How messy?"

"Sarin gas, dirty nuke, and napalm in the Senate office buildings, six dead SEALs, one missing leg, an amputated foot, and one former combat controller beaten to a pulp kind of messy."

He stood and cracked his knuckles. "Since Clark's not here, I call dibs on waterboarding."

The massive plane began to move beneath us, and soon we were climbing away from Africa and out over the wide Atlantic Ocean.

When the plane leveled off, I said, "It's time to have some fun. I want everybody upstairs, except my team, Titus, and the PJ."

The crowd of curious onlookers reluctantly climbed the stairs, and I said to Mongo, "Find me a stack of phonebooks or some lumber—anything that'll stop a nine-millimeter."

Titus jerked the curtain away, and I grabbed former Ambassador Woodford by the hair and dragged him across the deck and just outside the tent. Mongo hefted him into the air and deposited him on a makeshift inclined bench with Woodford's feet at least twenty-four inches above his head.

Loud enough for the two remaining terrorists to hear, I asked, "Hey, Titus. How far offshore are we?"

"A little over a hundred miles," came his practiced reply.

"Good! That makes us a ship at sea—well outside any legal jurisdiction on the planet. He's all yours, Hunter."

My partner wrapped Woodford's head in a thin towel and stuck his knee into his solar plexus, forcing the air from his lungs. Next, Hunter poured a five-gallon bucket of water slowly over Woodford's shrouded face. His diaphragm convulsed trying to refill his lungs with the air Hunter had forced from his chest. Instead of air, though, his lungs found only gallon after gallon of cold water.

When the bucket was empty, Mongo ripped the towel from Woodford's head and yanked him upright. The man gagged and coughed, blood pouring from his nose and mouth. Hunter landed a punch in the center of the man's chest, expelling what air remained in his lungs.

When he caught his breath, the tears came, and the begging began. "What do you want to know? I'll tell you anything!"

Hunter said, "Nope, not yet. I'm not convinced you're scared enough to tell the truth. Wrap him back up. We're going again."

Mongo swirled the soaked towel back around his head and forced him, once again, onto his back. His muffled cries escaped the sodden cloth. "Please, I'll do whatev—"

This time, Hunter hit him with a flood of water so strong it nearly knocked the man from the bench. He bucked and riled, coughing and gagging with every attempted breath, each one shorter and more labored than the one before.

"Get him up!" I roared.

Mongo yanked him upright and jerked the towel from his head. Defeated and terrified, Woodford begged in gasping, tear-filled breaths. "Please . . . I'll . . . do . . . anything."

Hunter slid a third five-gallon bucket of water against the side of the bench and looked up at me.

I said, "Dunk him."

Mongo lifted the man by his ankles and stuck his head into the bucket while Hunter sent punch after torturous punch to the man's gut. After thirty seconds, I nudged Mongo with my crutch, and he lifted the man from the bucket, depositing him on the cold metal deck.

Water, blood, and vomit puddled around his head, and the whimpering came. "I'll tell you everything. I will."

Hunter knelt beside him, rolled his face upward, and stuck the muzzle of his Glock between Woodford's eyes. I yanked back the curtain, giving Dussault and the woman a full view of their coconspirator lying in a puddle of his own filth.

I growled, "You don't get it, Woodford. We're not doing this to make *you* talk. We're doing this to make *them* talk."

Mongo hefted Woodford by his belt and threw him onto the deck beside the two remaining detainees. I crutch-walked back into the tent to find the two still-dry terrorists staring down at their partner, drenched by both water and his own fluids from both ends of his body.

"Who's next?" I asked.

Neither detainee could look away from Woodford's pitiful form still sobbing on the deck beside them.

I placed a crutch against the woman's shoulder and gave her a shove. "What's your name?"

A quick glance between Woodford and me, and she turned to stone.

"That's fine with me. Two of my partners out there still believe in chivalry, but not me. This is my favorite part."

I hobbled backward and cocked my head toward her. "Bring the woman out. This one will be quick."

Mongo lifted her by her armpits as she thrashed and struggled against his strength.

"Spread out the towels," I ordered. Hunter and Disco spread two layers of towels on the deck, and I said, "Put her on the towels!"

Mongo made an audible performance of depositing the woman on the pile. Continuing the charade for Dussault's benefit, I commanded, "Give me the pistol, and hold her down."

Hunter racked the slide on his Glock, in spite of a round already being chambered. The psychological effect of a racking slide is powerful. He slapped the pistol into my hand and threw down a pair of Kevlar body armor vests between her knees.

I yelled at the woman. "This is over for you after one question. Answer me, and you get to live. Lie to me or refuse to answer, and I put two in your skull. What is your name?"

I gave Mongo the nod, and he laced his massive arms around the woman's head and neck, locking his right hand inside his left elbow and stopping the flow of blood to her brain. She wilted in his arms.

"Tell me your name!"

Two seconds later, I pressed the trigger twice, sending two nine-millimeter hollow-points harmlessly into the body armor.

"Wrap her up, and get her out of here," I demanded. "And give me the saw!"

Titus provided the ultimate psychological weapon—a length of flexible sawblade with a finger ring at each end. The tool was designed to cut small tree limbs in a survival situation by wrapping the blade around the limb, inserting a finger in each end, and sawing back and forth until the limb fell free.

Mongo and Hunter followed me behind the curtain, where Dussault sat, trembling in fear beside Woodford, who'd fallen unconscious from the stress of having been waterboarded.

"Hold him down," I ordered, and I clumsily threw myself down at his feet.

Mongo grabbed the Frenchman's torso, and Hunter pinned his foot to the deck as I wrapped the saw blade around his ankle.

"Look at me, Dussault. Do I look like the kind of man who makes idle threats? Your friend there is barely alive and still has two lungs half full of water. Your woman chose to assert her Fifth Amendment right to remain silent, so I silenced her forever. Now, it's your turn. Because of you, I lost a foot, and I think I remember reading in the Bible something about an eye for an eye. Do you think a foot for a foot is the same thing?"

He jerked and chewed through his bottom lip before the teeth of the saw scratched his flesh. He flushed pale, and his pupils dilated to three times their normal size.

I gave the blade a pair of quick pulls, tearing through the material of his pants and socks. "Is this whole thing your scheme? Did you dream it up?" I jerked twice more, allowing the teeth to penetrate flesh.

He began to quiver in convulsive jerks and twitches.

"Are you ready to talk, Dussault?"

His lips flashed blue as if deprived of oxygen, and his tongue stuck to his teeth as he spoke in trembling syllables. "It . . . was . . . her. I . . . swear it. Please!"

One more pull sent the blade an eighth of an inch deeper into white flesh, and his eyes rolled back in his head.

"Wake him up," I demanded.

Mongo slapped him back to consciousness.

When he focused on the blade again, I leaned in. "It was *who*, Dussault? Who is behind all of this? Who is the mastermind?"

What fell from his mouth next took me completely by surprise.

"Her . . . sister!"

"Who's sister, Henri? What are you talking about?"

I didn't draw the blade, but I pulled it snug against his torn flesh.

He screamed, "Tiffany's sister! Simone!"

"Simone who?"

He choked on the name. "Simone Tolliver."

I shook my head in utter disbelief. "Simone Tolliver, the undersecretary of state, Simone Tolliver?"

He melted down, tears pouring from his face and his body shuddering uncontrollably.

I turned to Disco behind me. "Find a way to get me on the phone with Clark. Now!"

Epilogue

Agents from the Federal Bureau of Investigation's Joint Terrorism Task Force arrested Undersecretary Simone Tolliver at her home in Foggy Bottom only minutes after Clark Johnson made the call to the attorney general.

The C-5 commanded by Lieutenant Colonel Waters landed safely at Guantanamo Bay, where all three of our detainees were transferred into the custody of the same man wearing the same black Van Halen T-shirt. Our terrorists, no doubt, would soon beg for release back into my custody, for the hospitality I showed them was five-star compared to the treatment Van Halen would dole out. Henri Dussault would require little encouragement. His life spent hiding behind international account numbers hadn't prepared him for the harsh reality of the world around which he'd danced for decades, passing billions of dollars from the purses of true supporters and into the hands of true believers.

The governor, and Supreme Court justice, and congressmen were released into the loving arms of their families, uninjured, but scarred more deeply than anyone who loved them would ever know. They'd stared into the face of pure, greed-driven evil in their captors, but also into the eyes of freedom-loving warriors whose compassion and sacrifice would never be equaled nor forgotten. Every vote on Capitol Hill, every decision made within the hallowed halls of the highest court in the Free World, and every order sent down to the South Carolina National Guard would, for the rest of their lives, be tempered by the bravery, kindness, and immovability they'd seen in my team, my men, my warriors.

Six weeks post-deployment, I sat in one of my favorite spots in all the world: the gazebo at Bonaventure Plantation, housing the eighteenth-century cannon that had fired its final thundering round during the War of 1812 on the gun deck of a British warship. Beside me sat the woman who'd proven to me what boundless love can do to a man's soul. Penny Fulton held an unopened envelope with the seal of the United States Air Force embossed on its cover.

"Aren't you going to open it?" she asked.

"Nothing in that envelope could make this night better, so I don't care what's inside. You open it."

Unhesitant, she slid a fingernail beneath the flap and removed a single sheet from inside. I ignored the envelope, its contents, and the look on her face.

She held the page beneath the light. "It says you're cordially invited to attend the promotion ceremony of somebody named Gary D. Waters, who's being promoted to the rank of colonel."

"Let me see," I said, reaching for the paper. Two seconds with it above the flame of the cigar lighter answered Penny's next question.

We wouldn't be in attendance.

The deck cannon wasn't the only old dog of war inside the gazebo that night. To my right sat Master Chief DeAndre Lewis, U.S. Navy, Retired. From time to time, just to hear him laugh, I reached across the space with my prosthetic foot and kicked the hell out of his newly fitted prosthetic leg attached at the hip. The SEAL had fought, bled, and won in every corner of the globe for two decades, leaving him hardened and sharpened like the cutting edge of a warrior's blade, but his laugh was that of an innocent child and one of the greatest sounds I'd ever heard.

"You know, Chase, I don't think I'm cut out for this civilian covert ops thing. I'm afraid if I keep going to war with you bunch of maniacs, pretty soon, I won't have a leg to stand on."

I raised my glass, and he raised his. "To old frogmen who never die . . . They just smell that way."

My perfect wife and Hollywood's favorite new screenwriter ran her bare toes across my carbon-fiber foot. "You know what I think, Mr. Spy Man?"

"I'm not a spy, but tell me what you think."

She laid her chin on my shoulder, nibbled at my ear, and whispered, "Dre's not the only one who should retire."

Author's Note

Before I crawl into the confessional and bare my soul, asking for absolution from you, I must first express my sincerest gratitude for giving me the most fascinating, rewarding, and downright fun job anyone could ever have. Being your private storyteller is my dream come true, and I love every minute of it. I've done a lot of things in my life that most people never get to experience, and for those things, I'm grateful. They make fantastic tales of fiction, but getting to sit down every day and write about my imaginary friends for you is nothing short of too good to be true. I treasure the gift you've given me, and it will never be taken for granted.

Now, into the confessional we go . . .

Forgive me, reader, for I have made it all up. All of it. Well, most of it. We'll start with Andros Island, the largest island of The Bahamas. It and the interior lake I describe in this novel exist. I didn't make it up, but I made it taller than it really is. The rising terrain I described during the assault on the booby-trapped house doesn't exist. Although there is some elevation change on the island, nothing like I described exists. And for stretching the truth, I am deeply not sorry.

Next is Rum Cay. What a magnificent, awe-inspiring island Rum Cay is. It does exist, and there are caves on the north side of the island, but I doubt anyone has ever used any of them for such a sinister purpose as I described. The HALO (high altitude, low opening) is an insertion technique that has been used by covert operators for decades. The parachute malfunction Mongo suffered is possible. Sometimes chutes come out of their bag, waving like a flag, refusing to open, and doing nothing to arrest the descent rate of their wearer. The cutaway procedure and deployment of the reserve chute is purely fictional. The care with which reserve parachutes are manufactured, packed, and stowed is almost bulletproof. There is little that could've been done to Mongo's rig, as Clark shoved him through the door of the Caravan, that could've created such a deployment delay in the reserve. I greatly exaggerated the fallibility of Mongo's reserve, and I'm not sorry for that one, either.

I suppose we should talk about Guantanamo Bay. Ah, let's not. It's more fun that way. Who knows what goes on down there? Maybe I made it up. Or maybe not.

The country of Gabon, and specifically, the city of Libreville, are quite real, and their citizens do speak French. My dear friend, on whom the character of Clark Johnson is based, spent a portion of his professional life assigned to the U.S. Embassy in Gabon. His adventures, memories, and unique perception of the equatorial nation were the inspiration for the climactic closing scene in this novel. I found no history of terrorism being perpetrated from the Western African nation, nor by its people. I have nothing against the French, but it's fun to give a bad guy a foreign accent. Henri Dussault probably doesn't exist, but if he does, I hope he's a crooked banker. Do I feel bad about making Gabon out to be something other than what it is? Maybe, but it's actually a pretty dull place, so if the country could talk, it would probably appreciate me spicing it up a little.

While we're talking about Gabon, we must mention the RHIB, rebreathers, and the lost-at-sea sequence. Believe it or not, all of the hardware I described in that scene is real. Having three commandos sneak aboard a one-hundred-foot, modified fireboat in the middle of the night may be a little farfetched, but it made for a pretty cool scene, if I do say so myself.

When I blew up the boat and left Hunter and Chase drifting hopelessly in the ocean, I didn't do it to be cruel. It was meant to demonstrate a bond between brothers-in-arms. I wanted to show Chase in a rare moment of helplessness and give Hunter an opportunity to show off his prowess in the water. The techniques Hunter used to ensure they didn't get separated—construct a raft, distract Chase from his delirium, and keep him alive long enough to be rescued—are all plausible and reasonable. I like the scene, and especially how it demonstrated the love between Hunter and Chase. If you're curious about the real Stone W. Hunter, please go back and read the dedication in the front of book #7, *The Devil's Chase*.

It's now time for satellite confessions. Although I went into some detail about how satellites were used for telephone transmissions and precise clocking to locate their signals, here's the truth: I made all of that up. None of it is real. In fact, I've never correctly spelled the word satellite without Spell Check correcting it for me. I know less than nothing about satellites. To me, they are magical robots circling the planet, miles above our heads, and doing mysterious things nobody understands, so I made it up. I hope I sounded at least a little convincing.

And now for the SEALs. I have enormous respect for Naval Special Warfare operators. They are some of the most elite special operations troops on the planet. They possess capabilities, mindset, and patriotism beyond measure. They are not only men of enormous individual fortitude and strength, but also some of this nation's finest and most patriotic citizens. The sacrifices they make in the name of preservation of freedom are second to none. Without men like them, freedom would likely wither and die. I'm sorry for the devastation I poured out onto the SEAL team in this story. It was done to highlight their fighting spirit and demonstrate the strength of the remaining team members. The realities of the defense of freedom are harsh and unfathomable to those who've never tread in the footprints of men who stare evil in the eye and refuse to flinch. Part of my responsibility as a writer of novels such as these is to pay homage and respect to the incredibly brave men and women who volunteer their bodies and minds to defend the way of life we've come to expect here in the greatest nation on Earth.

Master Chief DeAndre Lewis doesn't exist; however, the real-life person on whom he is based does. He is a friend, a father, and a patriot of our great nation. He's not a SEAL, nor did he serve in the Navy. His uniform was a different color, but he wore it with pride and distinction, just as he now lives his life after having hung up the uniform for the last time.

Here's the thing that bothers me most about what I made up in this story: It's Chase's loss of his right foot. My writing style is somewhat unique in that I never plan anything in my writing. I don't start with an outline, and I never have any idea how each story will end. Likewise, I never know what's going to happen along the way. It's all a huge surprise to me. Sometimes horrible things happen in the stories I write, and I don't understand why. Chase's foot is one of those things. I'll probably regret letting that happen to him as I continue writing the series. I don't know how badly a prosthetic foot will impact his work, but I suppose we'll find out together as the series unfolds.

Perhaps this wasn't a confession and plea for absolution after all. Perhaps it was just me having a conversation with some of my favorite people I'd love to meet, and sincerely thanking you for reading and enjoying my work.

—Cap

About the Author

Cap Daniels

Cap Daniels is a former sailing charter captain, scuba and sailing instructor, pilot, Air Force combat veteran, and civil servant of the U.S. Department of Defense. Raised far from the ocean in rural East Tennessee, his early infatuation with salt water was sparked by the fascinating, and sometimes true, sea stories told by his father, a retired Navy Chief Petty Officer. Those stories of adventure on the high seas sent Cap in search of adventure of his own, which eventually landed him on Florida's Gulf Coast where he spends as much time as possible on, in, and under the waters of the Emerald Coast.

With a headful of larger-than-life characters and their thrilling exploits, Cap pours his love of adventure and passion for the ocean onto the pages of the Chase Fulton Novels and the Avenging Angel - Seven Deadly Sins series.

Visit www.CapDaniels.com to join the mailing list to receive newsletter and release updates.

Connect with Cap Daniels:

Facebook: www.Facebook.com/WriterCapDaniels
Instagram: https://www.instagram.com/authorcapdaniels/
BookBub: https://www.bookbub.com/profile/cap-daniels

Also by Cap Daniels

The Chase Fulton Novels Series
Book One: *The Opening Chase*
Book Two: *The Broken Chase*
Book Three: *The Stronger Chase*
Book Four: *The Unending Chase*
Book Five: *The Distant Chase*
Book Six: *The Entangled Chase*
Book Seven: *The Devil's Chase*
Book Eight: *The Angel's Chase*
Book Nine: *The Forgotten Chase*
Book Ten: *The Emerald Chase*
Book Eleven: *The Polar Chase*
Book Twelve: *The Burning Chase*
Book Thirteen: *The Poison Chase*
Book Fourteen: *The Bitter Chase*
Book Fifteen: *The Blind Chase*
Book Sixteen: *The Smuggler's Chase*
Book Seventeen: *The Hollow Chase* (Spring 2022)

The Avenging Angel – Seven Deadly Sins Series
Book One: *The Russian's Pride*
Book Two: *The Russian's Greed*
Book Three: *The Russian's Gluttony*
Book Four: *The Russian's Lust* (Summer 2022)

Stand-alone Novels
We Were Brave

Novellas
The Chase Is On
I Am Gypsy

Made in the USA
Coppell, TX
22 March 2024

30437075R00189